My Senior Year

My Senior Year

The Memoirs of a Belmont Street Boy

Jim Towne

RESOURCE *Publications* · Eugene, Oregon

MY SENIOR YEAR
The Memoirs of a Belmont Street Boy

Resource Publications
An Imprint of Wipf and Stock Publishers
199 W. 8th Ave., Suite 3
Eugene, OR 97401

www.wipfandstock.com

PAPERBACK ISBN: 978-1-6667-3128-6
HARDCOVER ISBN: 978-1-6667-2362-5
EBOOK ISBN: 978-1-6667-2363-2

09/20/21

This book is dedicated to Becky and our kids—
Halee, Jimmy, Dylan, and Carly.
Thanks to Judy for being the first to read and
edit *My Senior Year*, and for your
encouraging words to "keep on telling stories."

Contents

1

The Belmont Street Boys

"YOUR LIFE IS OVER!"

Those weren't the words coming out of The Old Man's mouth, but that was the clear message rattling around in my brain. I had always held my dad in high esteem, but for a brief few minutes he had become The Old Man, my enemy, the opposition, the one person with enough power to ruin my life. And The Old Man was using that power to destroy me.

Just two weeks before the beginning of my senior year in high school, Dad announced that he had taken a job in another state. We were moving from exciting, huge, comfortable Chicago, Illinois, to dull, little, unknown Pueblo, Colorado. I begged Dad to let me stay in Chicago. There were plenty of friends and relatives I could live with for one lousy year so that I could graduate with the friends and teammates I'd had since kindergarten. I had a shot at being the starting third baseman on our high school baseball team. My senior year of tennis was shaping up to be a good one—maybe even a trip to state. I'd made All-State Choir as a junior. Mary Avery and I had started dating, and she was gorgeous!

"Please, Dad, don't make me go!"

I must have said that ten times. Begging wasn't working, so in desperation I tried to shame The Old Man by emotionally communicating the impact his choice would have on my life. All that approach got me was a stern look and a simple, "Guilt won't work on me, Sonny Boy."

The Old Man was emphatic.

"This move will benefit the whole family."

"We do things together as a family."

"This new city and the new schools will afford the whole family exciting opportunities."

"This will be character building for you, Nick."

Blah, blah, blah . . . justify . . . explain . . . rationalize . . . he went on for several minutes, but I tuned him out after seeing the look on his face. Well, I mostly tuned him out. Dad had a practice of saying absurd things or including made-up names or creating non-existent friends in his rants to see if I was actually listening to him. I privately called it garbage. After the rant he would ask me, "Do you understand and agree with me?" If I didn't respond to the garbage, he knew I wasn't listening to him, and he would start again with another rant.

The standard answer was supposed to be, "Yes sir," with some kind of acknowledgement of the garbage. My younger sister, Chrissie, and I were not allowed to argue with Dad. We listened, asked questions, said, "Yes, Sir," or "No, Sir," and then did what we were told. But in light of what he had just said, I felt free to say, "I understand but do not agree. This will be a terrible move for me, I am not looking for any new opportunities right now, I am not happy about this, I will leave to come back here the same day I graduate, Gerald Ford is a Republican and not a communist, you would look terrible wearing a mini-dress, and I don't believe that Yusef Begnar is a real person." I must have had a totally disengaged look on my face for Dad to have thrown a trifecta of garbage my way.

Mom was excited, and Chrissie seemed to be happy about the whole thing, but none of them were about to start their senior year of high school. This was the worst news ever.

My father, Dr. Jonathan Nicolas Bradford, had just been hired as the Superintendent of Schools for the Pueblo Public School system, which at that time consisted of twenty-five schools and more than 15,000 students. The previous superintendent had to retire suddenly for health reasons. Dad applied for the position, not telling Chrissy and me because he did not think there was a good chance that he would be hired. A friend of my father, Hal Yankovich, moved to Pueblo from Chicago six years earlier to take a job as a science teacher and assistant football coach at one of the Pueblo high schools. Hal and Dad played softball together and were on the same bowling team for years, and he and his wife, Lizzy, would come over to our house to play Rook or Euchre a couple of times each month. Dad and Hal had such a close friendship that when Hal moved to Pueblo, Dad decided to finish his PhD in Education since he was no longer interested in playing softball or bowling or playing cards without his good buddy, Hal. Dad figured that would be a good use of all the extra time he suddenly had, and in just a few short years he had become Dr. Jonathan Bradford. (My friends would ask me what kind of doctor Dad was and I always said not the kind who could help anyone. Dad heard me say that once and I was busted—no TV for a week.)

Along with Dad's experience as an administrator with the Schaumburg School District, a suburb of Chicago, Dad's PhD made him well-qualified for the superintendent position in Pueblo. So, when Hal heard about the superintendent vacancy, he immediately called Dad. Hal told my father that the winters in Pueblo were milder than those in Chicago, the dry air would be good for my mother's asthma, the pay would be about the same as what he was making as an assistant superintendent in his current school district, but the cost of living would be lower and that a population of 94,000 made Pueblo a nice-sized city in which to live. So, Dad put in his résumé, got the job, and my life ended.

My last two weeks in Chicago consisted of non-stop activity. Packing, hanging out with friends, spending time with Mary, and soaking in every ounce of what I knew and loved about Chicago filled my every waking minute. Geno's Pizza, the Gold Coast, Comiskey Park, Loyola Beach, Sears Tower, and Riverview Amusement Park were all on my agenda those final two weeks. Waking minutes is more accurate than waking hours because my mind raced at the end of each day. Certain words came to mind and pitched a tent there making sleep hard to come by. Words like "unreal," "impossible," "selfish," and every swear word I'd ever heard popped into my mind, followed by feelings of resentment towards my dad, self-pity, and fear over what the future held. What if I didn't fit in? What if the only people who would accept me were a group of kids I didn't really like? I could just see it—Nick and his weirdo friends. One question after another came to mind until I drifted off to sleep only to wake up in a panic with a new question, word, or feeling. To make everything worse, when my friends gave me a going away party, it soon became obvious that they were already starting to disconnect. My best friends were entirely focused on their final year of high school. I must have heard a dozen times, "It's going to be so cool"; "I can't wait"; "We are going to have so much fun"; "You are going to miss out"; "Too bad you won't be here to . . . ." They were going to be fine without me. It was way too sudden and way too surprising news for them to figure out what was going on in their seventeen- year-old brains and emotions, so they just moved on before I even left town.

The news had come out of nowhere for me. Mom, Lucille Bradford, knew it was a possibility that we would be moving, but she never talked about it to me because she thought it was unlikely that Dad would be hired. So, when Dad got the job, Mom was so excited about the move to a new city, proud of Dad for becoming a superintendent of schools, and happy about reconnecting with the Yankovich family that she kind of overlooked what I was feeling. When Mom was excited about something, Chrissie always followed her lead and got excited too. That made me the only one unhappy about the whole thing in the Bradford home. Even my girlfriend, Mary, was no help. Like my friends, Mary seemed ready to move on and find another boyfriend, which would not be a problem for her. It was all so surreal. One day I was as happy and content as any kid you could find in all of Chicagoland, and two weeks later that was all gone. I would now be the new kid starting over at the beginning of my senior year!! My life was over. At least that was how I saw it at the time, but that was before meeting The Belmont Street Boys.

Since our house in Chicago had just gone on the market and Dad's previous real estate ventures were still one to two years away from producing positive cash flow, we were forced to move into a modest, three-bedroom home on Belmont Street. Dad assured us that we would only live there for a few months before finding a home better suited for the Superintendent of Schools and his family. Three weeks after meeting the Belmont Street Boys, I informed Dad that I would not be moving again until after graduation. The rest of the family could move if they wanted to, but from August 19, 1975, to May 17, 1976, my place of residence would be in the 1800 block of Belmont Street on the south side of Pueblo.

While moving my bedframe, decorated with New York Yankee stickers, into the bedroom assigned to me by Mom (she was a distant cousin of former Yankee shortstop and 1962 Rookie of the Year, Tom Tresh, so I was a lifelong Yankee fan, which was pretty uncommon in Chicago), three neighborhood guys showed up to help us move in. After helping me set up the bedframe, they introduced themselves. Marco Tattalinni, also known as The Tatts, Frank Luna, who I later found out had a variety of nicknames because of his quirky personality but was usually called Q, and

Lenny Peeples, who had interchangeable nicknames of Peeps and Birdy. When all of my stuff was moved into the Yankee shrine, also known as Nick's room, Tatts smiled at me and said, "You moved onto our block, so you are now a Belmont Street Boy. I will pick you up at 7:45 tomorrow morning. You will be riding to school with us."

I wasn't sure what to say. What if I didn't want a ride with these guys? Dad had promised me a car soon after our move, and I was looking forward to driving myself to school.

As the guys were leaving our house, Lenny came back to me, put his hands on my shoulders, looked me in the eyes, and said with an air of total confidence, "Trust me. When you get out of Marco's car tomorrow morning on your first day of school and every day after that, life at South High will be a piece of cake. You will step out of his 1957 Chevy Nomad and onto Easy Street. You will thank God every day for the rest of your senior year that your parents moved into this house on this street." The Belmont Street Boys left my house, and I watched to see where each of them lived. Marco and Frankie lived across the street, and Lenny lived two houses down from me. The next day I discovered that Lenny, AKA Peeps or Birdy, must have had his hand on the Bible because he told me the truth, the whole truth, and nothing but the truth. Everyone at South High School knew that I was a Belmont Street Boy by the end of my first day of school. I was respected, protected, and never neglected. It was unclear to me all that it meant to be part of the exclusive club known as The Belmont Street Boys, but the benefits of being one were almost immediately apparent.

Between my first- and second-period classes, as I was walking the halls trying to get oriented, I bumped into a big guy named Carl Stepanovich. Just as I started to say, "Sorry," the lug shoved me against a locker and started yelling at me.

"What is wrong with you, new kid? I ought to split your ugly head open! Don't you ever run into me, look at me, touch me, talk about me, speak to me, or think about me ever again, you big-eared, pantywaist, goofy-hair, butt-chinned chump."

Apparently, Carl liked to string together as many putdowns as possible once he got started. He pointed his finger in my face, and, before he could start another run-on sentence of threats and put downs, this beautiful girl I'd never seen before said, "Carl, did you know that the new kid rode to school today in a 1957 Chevy?"

"Was it a Nomad?" he asked me with a stunned look on his face.

"Yes," I softly said.

"Well, you tell Tatts that I am sorry I messed with one of his guys," Carl said as he walked away. I later found out that the beautiful girl who spoke to Carl was Sheila—the prettiest girl in school and Marco's girlfriend.

She smiled at me as the crowd that had rushed to watch the pre-second-period entertainment of the day broke up and said, "Word will spread real fast, and you won't have any more trouble from now on." It was crazy! Carl roughed me up, but he apologized to Marco. Later that day during lunch period, I got more of The Belmont Street Boys story.

The four of us guys all had the same lunch period together, so we sat at a table in a corner of the lunchroom with Sheila and her best friend, Lana. When Frank spotted me walking towards the table he started laughing and yelled out, "I heard that Carl-the-Bull started to initiate you real good into life at South High until you cried for help and Sheila Do-right rode to your rescue and said, 'I'll save you, Nick.' Then she untied you from the railroad track and you went off together into the sunset, or to your second-period class." Frank got his nickname, Q, one of his many nicknames, because he was always quoting or paraphrasing TV shows, cartoons, commercials, and songs. In this case he was doing his best imitation, voice and all, of the Saturday morning cartoon "Dudley Do-right of the Mounties."

"I've got two questions for all of you. Is Carl-the-Bull short for Carl-the-Bully?" Heads nodded.

Q blurted out, "Carl's not too bright. He puts the more in moron," and got slugged real hard in the arm by Tatts, which I took to mean that talking bad about others was uncool in front of The Tatts. I was quickly figuring out that almost everyone at that school had a nickname, but, apparently, derogatory nicknames were not generally acceptable.

Sheila asked over the noise of Q moaning about how bad his arm hurt, "And your second question is?"

"Why did The Bull apologize to Marco instead of to me, since I'm the one who got roughed up?"

Peeps stood up and said, "I've got this. You see, here at South there are fifteen to twenty bullies—guys who would use their physical power to mistreat others and intimidate the students and some faculty—to get their way and basically run the show around here. But little of that crap actually goes on at South because of this fine, strong, agile (and handsome chimed in Sheila), and handsome," restated Peeps, "young man known as The Tatts." By now others were listening in, and Marco was getting a little uneasy.

Marco shook his head. "Keep this short or I will eat your dessert."

"Okay. The Tatts can beat the fool out of all the bullies at this school, so they don't act like the idiots that they are in fear of him, and they especially do not mess with the people at this table. Basically, he is Batman and St. Francis, keeping the order around this place while at the same time asking God to make him an instrument of his peace. Kind of ironic, isn't it?"

Q blurted out, "I called him St. Batman once, but he hit me in the arm so hard that it fell off. The reattachment surgery went well, though, so I am now able to put my arm around this beautiful young woman."

As he reached for Lana, she narrowed her eyes and said, "Touch me and you die!"

Marco had heard enough of all the talk about him, so he waved his hand in a way that everyone knew meant to knock it off. "What else is going on with you, Nick?"

"Well, I need to get a sports physical so I can go out for the tennis team."

Q yelled, "How about Dr. Lindy?" and everyone started laughing. Before Marco could tell me the Dr. Lindy story, the guys let me know how Marco earned a nickname he never let people use in his presence—KO.

2

Nicknames, Part One

ONE OF MARCO'S NICKNAMES was KO because, if he got in a fistfight, it almost always ended up in a knockout. He was 6'2" and, weighing in at 175 pounds, was inordinately strong for someone his age and size. If Marco hit you for fun, like guys in Pueblo often did while kidding around, it hurt. If he hit you and meant it, you only felt the pain after you woke up. Marco had knocked enough guys out to earn the KO nickname. Some say it was a dozen or more. Q said it was more KOs than Rocky Marciano had in the ring, which was forty-three, but everyone would just shake their heads when Q told his version of things. Probably his most famous knockout came one day during his junior year, when Sheila came up to Marco crying just after third period, while Marco, Q, and Peeps were on their way to lunch. According to Peeps, this is what happened,

"What's wrong, Sheila?" Marco asked.

"Mike Armijo grabbed my chest. Last week he brushed up against me with his elbow as we were leaving class and acted like it was an accident. A few minutes later, when I passed him and his friends in the hall, they were all laughing. I tried to give that creep the benefit of the doubt, but today he volunteered to pass out homework papers for Mrs. Hickman. He supposedly stumbled on accident in front of my desk and put his hand on my chest as he caught his balance. He said he was sorry, but I know better. He was *trying* to cop a feel!"

Marco knew where Armijo hung out between classes and started jogging in that direction. He hollered at Q and Peeps, "On me. You guys keep Bobby and Tony off my back. They're punks and probably won't try anything. I will take care of Mike and Nunez."

As soon as Armijo saw The Tatts, he squared up to fight while at the same time saying, "What?" pretending he didn't know why Tatts was coming at him. Mike got the first punch in—a glancing shot off the left side of Tatts's face. Marco hit Armijo with a combination right to the chin and left to the temple area, and Armijo was down—knocked out cold. Nunez tried grabbing Tatts from behind, but Marco was too strong for him, throwing Nunez against a locker, then punching him in the stomach followed by an uppercut to the chin. Two knockouts in under ten seconds.

Two of Marco's friends from the football team, Moses Sandoval and Levi Martinez, came running up to help him out, but, when they saw the two guys on the floor, they said, "If you ever need our help, which you probably won't, we got your back." Marco nodded at his friends just as Vice Principal Grant arrived.

Mr. Grant surveyed the scene, looked at Marco, and asked, "Are you alright?" As soon as Marco nodded that he was fine, Mr. Grant told Bobby and Tony and several others to help the two KO victims to his office, and then said, "Marco, I will need to see you after school." Mr. Grant knew from experience that those guys had it coming to them and that Marco was in the right, but he needed to hear Marco's version of things. Tatts never told anyone what Mr. Grant said to him, but The Belmont Street Boys were pretty sure it was words of thanks and something along the lines of "keep up the good work, we appreciate what you do around here, you make our job a whole lot easier, here's a medal, don't do that again but if you do need to beat the crap out of anyone else I will look the other way, etc." The Boys speculated all the way home that afternoon about what Mr. Grant had said, and Marco just smiled his little smile, shook his head, and, according to Peeps, he eventually just told them to knock it off. It would remain a secret between The Tatts and the Vice Principal.

That story was told over and over again for years by people who didn't see a thing. Even those who missed school that day would tell others about it as if they were eyewitnesses. By the time my sister, Chrissie, got to high school four years later, the story was that Marco knocked out five bullies and the Vice Principal held an assembly in his honor. Marco never once repeated the events of that day, but he did tell the story of knocking out Dr. Lindy whenever he had the chance.

"So, what is the Dr. Lindy story? Did you give some kid in school named Lindy the nickname of Dr. Lindy?" The Boys all cracked up.

"No!! He was a Real McCoy sturgeon! A DM," Q blurted out. At that the laughter went up a level.

Peeps finally controlled himself enough to say, "He's a doctor, not a fish! It's surgeon and MD, you goofball. And, Lindy is a physician, but not a surgeon. Although, he would probably love to assist in any kind of groin or hernia operation he could. Tell him the story about the perv doctor, Tatts."

"Gladly, because he is, or was, definitely a pervert who used his profession to get his jollies. I went to Dr. Lindy to get my sports physical just before school started for my sophomore year. The doc asked his nurse to leave the room, but my mom stayed in the office to answer medical history questions that I didn't know much about. Then Lindy asked me to pull down my pants. I was a little uncomfortable with that but figured he would ask Mom to leave soon, so I did what he asked since he was a doctor. Mom had seen me in my underwear before, but not in front of another adult, so that made the situation embarrassing to both me and Mom. Anyway, I was trying to ignore my feelings and be a patient patient when, all of a sudden, the doctor reached up and pulled my underwear down. Mom quickly looked the other way, and, as I turned my head to see the doctor, as clear as anything I have ever seen in my life, that twisted little punk of a doctor had a smirk on his lips which stayed there for another two tenths of a second. I hit him with an uppercut to the chin with my left hand as I was pulling up my underwear with my right. By the time he hit the floor, my pants were up, and Mom had turned to see what just happened."

"Marco!! Did you just knock the doctor out cold?"

"Absolutely I did!! Mom, he exposed me on purpose. He got some kind of twisted pleasure out of what he did. He deserved what he got. I should stick around until he wakes up and then knock him out again, but I won't. Let's go, Ma."

"As we left the office I told the nurse, 'You might want to go help your formerly smirking, creepy employer off the floor.' Then I told the receptionist, 'There will be no charge for my visit, and I want you to sign this form saying that I passed the physical.' She had a stamp she used for that purpose, and she quickly and nervously stamped my form. Then I stood in the middle of the waiting room and announced, 'You need to find another doctor. That little twerp of a doctor has a twisted mind. He uses his position as a doctor to satisfy some kind of weird, sexual fantasy.' Turning back to the nurse I firmly said, 'You tell Dr. Lindy that I will be back for round two if I ever hear of him doing that again.' I later heard that I was the last sports physical he ever gave. Well, almost gave."

It became clear to me as I got to know Tatts better that, when he told the Dr. Lindy story, he was not bragging or showing off. Tatts was getting the word out to everyone he knew to avoid a bad doctor who had some sort of emotional or psychological problems. He was also giving others an example to follow by encouraging them to stand up for themselves when someone, even one in a position of authority, tries to exploit them in any way.

By then, lunch period was almost over, and I asked the group to fill me in on some of the other nicknames I had heard or would be hearing. The general consensus was that I would learn them over time, but Lana volunteered a few.

"Well, Frankie used to want people to call him KC, which he thought stood for King of Cool. I called him that for a while because I thought it stood for Kind of Creepy. Once a dozen or so girls dropped the KC and just called him Creepy, he also dropped the KC moniker. There's a word for you, Frank. Moniker."

"I like it! Maybe that will be one of my nicknames. The Moniker! Once I find out what it means, maybe I will use it."

"Personally," said Sheila, "my favorite nickname of anyone at this school is Office Boy. Marco, tell Nick the story behind that moniker."

I was having trouble keeping up with all the nicknames being thrown at me, but if Sheila said 'Office Boy' was her favorite nickname, I knew this was a story I had to hear. A dozen or more kids had crowded around our lunch table to try to get in on all the fun we were having. They were welcomed by Marco and the others, but it was time to head off to our next class, so the story about Office Boy had to wait.

"I will tell you on the way home. But if people point at you and laugh the rest of the day, don't take it personally. They are just remembering the Office Boy event," Tatts said. Sure enough, several times that day a few kids saw me and spontaneously smiled or laughed. I was really looking forward to hearing about this particular nickname.

3

Nicknames, Part Two

IT SEEMED TO ME at first that everyone at my high school had a nickname. There was Crazy Ben Krezinski who would demonstrate various baseball slides in the hallways between classes. Baseball players told me that, one day last spring, Craze came to baseball practice sick and puked all over himself while chasing fly balls in the outfield. Not only did he refuse to take a break, he also refused to wash his sweatshirt for the rest of the season.

J. D. Weybright was one of the most interesting people at South High and was known as The Professor or Corry because he reminded people of the wild-haired comedian of the day named Professor Irwin Corry. J. D. was a unique fellow who did not seem to have a friend, other than The Tatts. He would sit with us at lunch or walk alongside us on the way to class regaling us with some story or theory none of us had ever heard or considered. Then there was Hatchet, Gumby, Goose, Slick, Grandma, Zeke, Freaky, Moose, Slim, Dinky, Zippy, and dozens of others. And if anyone wanted a nickname, Frankie would be glad to give them one, or even loan them one of his.

Early on, I had a hard time keeping up with all of Frank's nicknames. And, depending on who asked, he gave a wide variety of answers as to why his nicknames were given him. If a girl asked him what Q stood for, he would say that it was short for cute. He would say, "Just stare at me for thirty seconds and you will see how cute I really am." They wouldn't because he wasn't. Q insisted to others that it was short for IQ because his was so high. When he used that line, he usually raised the tone of his voice so that his statement was at least partly accurate. He was called TV, which was really just another version of Q because he quoted TV shows and commercials so often, but the Boys often shortened it to T or V. When asked about that, Frank would say that T was short for Tony, which he insisted was his real name; or it was short for Terrific; V stood for Victor or Vincenzo or whatever else popped into his mind at the time. Lots of students called him Outstanding or OS because of all the time he spent out standing in the hall after being kicked out of class in school, class at church, youth groups, clubs, Boy Scouts, and every other group in which he ever participated. Q seemed to be always in trouble for asking questions or making statements outside of what was acceptable in that particular setting.

Frankie didn't listen very well, but he always heard anything that had a remotely sexual overtone to the word or the context. Marco told me several stories about the trouble Q got in at the church he attended. In Sunday school when he was ten years old, he began to repeatedly ask his female teacher to tell him more about Adam and Eve being naked in the Garden of Eden. By the time he was twelve, he wanted to know all there was to know about Solomon's wives and especially his concubines. And, when the teacher gave a lesson about Abraham and the priest Melchizedek, Frank blurted out, "Was Mel his name and Chiseldick his nickname? What else do we know about this guy? Why don't we sing any Sunday school songs about Mel Chiseldick?"

His acting out wasn't restricted to things of a sexual nature. When his Sunday school class studied the life of Jesus, Frankie decided that he was possessed by a demon and asked two girls seated across from him to put their hands on his forehead and command the demon to come out of him. When they did so, Frankie passed gas and announced, "I guess I had a fart demon in me, but in the name of Jesus I am now free." Once he got on a roll, there was no stopping him. That poor Free Methodist Church could not keep teachers for any class Q was in until he finally stopped attending Sunday school and came only to the worship service. Since Tatts wasn't there to punch him and shut him up, this particular TV simply did not have an off switch.

In his sophomore history class, the teacher was talking about the juggernaut that was the Nazi war machine of 1942 when Q's hand shot up. "Yes, Frank," the teacher slowly said. Whenever his hand went up it was pretty certain that he would volunteer something that was off track or inappropriate as soon as he was called on. Q simply said, "Jugs."

Mr. Barnes said, "And what does that mean, Frank?"

"Well, Mr. Barnes, you were saying something about jugs or not and I wanted to inform you that I prefer jugs to . . ."

"That will be enough from you, Mr. Luna. Take your customary place out in the hall, and, from this day forward, you will not ask another question in my class. I will find a volunteer who is willing to sit next to you every day to field your questions and pass them on to me if they add to the class in any way. You will be allowed to ask said student three questions per day and that is all. Any violation of this rule and you will be permanently expelled from this class and be in danger of not graduating with the class of 1973. Furthermore, I am going to suggest to your other teachers that they enact this same policy with you in their classes. Now get out of my class this instant!!" Mr. Barnes had kicked Q out of class five times already that year and had no doubt been working on this plan since earlier in the year.

Mrs. Ward, the eighth-grade health teacher for Tatts and Q, was two years ahead of Mr. Barnes when she instituted a preemptive policy of her own for Q. The eighth-grade textbook gave one week of lessons dedicated to the topic of human anatomy and sexuality. Mrs. Ward was already well aware of how Frankie could disrupt class with his questions and outbursts, so she came up with a creative way to keep her class under control during that week.

Tatts's version of the oft-repeated story began something like this. "For all we knew, it was a normal day in our eighth-grade health class. I'd heard from others that Mrs. Ward would begin the section on human anatomy and sexuality by asking the question, 'Why do kids laugh and giggle when the topic of sex and anatomy is discussed?' Then several boys and at least half the girls would blurt out, 'Because they are immature.' 'Immaturity.' 'They're not grown up,' or some other variation on that theme. This question and that response usually had the effect of maintaining a calm atmosphere during classes filled with a high degree of embarrassing material. But a question like that would only put Frank Luna on alert, and he would then go into full Frankie mode. Mrs. Ward had figured out that she could avert a confrontation with Q by making him the honored Office Boy for the week. It was a plan she'd cooked up with Principal Spoelstra."

"When the bell rang to begin class that Monday, Mrs. Ward made an announcement that went something like this. 'Principal Spoelstra has asked me to pick out one student who he can depend on to run errands this week for him and his staff. The student has to be energetic, good-natured, and able to follow directions to a tee. The honored student that I have chosen is Frank Luna. You will be the Office Boy all this week during this class period.' She then started clapping for Frankie, and the class followed suit. I patted him on the back as he picked up his stuff and headed to the door. Just before exiting class, my little buddy said this, 'You mean I get to go to the principal's office without being in trouble?' Mrs. Ward nodded and said, 'That's right, Frank.' With a surprised look on his face Q replied, 'Cool!' It was about halfway through the sex ed movie Mrs. Ward had planned for that day that it dawned on me what was really going on."

"If Frankie had been in class that day, he would have pointed at the screen, laughed, offered other than clinical names for the body parts we were seeing, and been totally out of control. Every day in class he would have been begging Mrs. Ward to show the movie again. Since he would have been sent to the principal's office anyway, why not send him there for a made-up reason instead of a bad one? Mrs. Ward was not only looking out for her own sanity and the dignity of the class, she was also protecting Frankie, in a way."

"At the end of Monday's class, I went up to Mrs. Ward and started to say what I was thinking. But, before I could open my mouth, she said, 'You're right, Marco. I sent Frank to the office before I had to kick him out of class. But that will be our secret.' And it was a secret, until halfway through our ninth-grade year. Q wanted to go to the principal's office to see if he could be the Office Boy again before leaving Pitts Junior High, but I discouraged him every time he brought it up. Then, one day, I had to tell him the truth. I looked him in the eyes and told him that Frank Luna was the one and only Office Boy in the entire history of Pitts. Mrs. Ward didn't want him in class because she didn't think she could deal with all his comments about sex and anatomy. In true Frankie fashion, he listened, shrugged, and smiled as he said 'Office Boy,' then went on with his day."

I loved hearing the story and would call him Office Boy from time to time. Hearing that nickname always made Frank smile.

4

Initiation, Part One

I LEARNED A LOT about life at South High and The Belmont Street Boys that first week, but it was on the Sunday evening leading up to my second week of school that I learned about the initiation required of all of The Belmont Street Boys. The Boys told me they would come by my house at 5:00pm and that we would all go for a ride. They picked me up right on time and we drove to City Park, making small talk along the way. Marco parked the Nomad, and then we all walked to a nearby picnic table and sat down. As I looked around the table, it was easy to see the others smiling with expressions which clearly communicated that they could hardly wait to tell me what was up. Marco started the conversation.

"When The Belmont Street Boys formed during our eighth-grade year, we decided that there should be some sort of initiation into our group, but we couldn't decide what that initiation should look like. Since ours is not a formal club or gang, but more of a unique arrangement of friends, we decided that initiation into our group should reflect the unique nature of the group and its members. Then, during the summer leading up to our sophomore year, the three of us decided on two rules of initiation. Peeps, tell Nick the two rules."

"The rules are simple. First, no one can know that what you are doing is an initiation or that there even is an initiation into our group or that the Boys is an actual group, despite what Marco just said. The Belmont Street Boys are kind of a very small, secret society with only a few secrets to keep, and the most important secret is the initiation into our group.

People will suspect that something is going on, but you can never confirm or deny their suspicions. Under no circumstance can you reveal the existence of an initiation into The Belmont Street Boys. You have to deal with any questions that come up in your own way and keep your mouth shut about the initiation. Understand?" I nodded.

Q had to be involved, so he butted in to tell me the second rule. "The second rule is this: the other members of the group get to decide what the initiation is for the one being initiated." Well, that wasn't exactly what Q said. In fact, that wasn't even close to what he said. Q was so excited about the whole thing that he went on and on about the second rule, explaining and re-explaining and laughing until Peeps finally clarified what Q had been trying to say.

"Okay," I said. "I get it. But first tell me what each of you had to do for your initiation so that I know if what I have to do is fair."

Tatts responded, "Gladly. But first, for the record, I do agree with Lenny that we are, in fact, an actual group with some rules, although none of them are written down. Now, I will tell you what Frankie had to do so that we can get home at a decent hour."

"Come on, Marco, let me tell my own story. I never get to talk about the initiation, so this is my only shot at it. I will keep it short; promise." Tatts nodded okay, and Q was off and running his mouth.

"I don't get embarrassed very easily, but Marco and Peeps hit it out-of-the-park in humiliating me. It was Monday afternoon on the third week of school during our sophomore year. I only knew a few of the upperclassmen, and I didn't know any of the popular people. The Boys told me that, by Friday, I had to choose five of the seven senior cheerleaders and ask them out on a date. No telephone calls—each girl had to be in a group when I asked her out, but no more than one other cheerleader could be with her when I asked. I had to use a different line on each girl— no one could stand next to me when I asked, but one of the Boys had to be close enough to make sure I kept the rules, and I had to walk away from him once I was turned down. Oh, and I couldn't ask more than two girls out on any given day. It was a slow and incredibly painful process."

Peeps inserted, "Our first idea was to make him not talk for an entire day. It was the first day of school our sophomore year. Every time he spoke would cost him a queech—a quarter. By lunch period, he had become the Queech King and already owed us $10. We knew that he could not keep his mouth shut and would have to quit school to get a full-time job to pay us back, so we went to plan B and made him try out for the football team, knowing he would fail miserably. But he loved the attention. With coaches yelling at him and players laughing, he ate it up. The coaches would make him run laps, and Q would get exhausted and fall down, act like he was dying, and yell that he needed a cheerleader to give him mouth-to-mouth resuscitation. We made him quit the team after three days, but his cheerleader requests were what gave us the idea for plan C."

Frankie's eyes opened wide as he said, "I never knew that's where you got the idea! Anyway, this is how my week went. The first cheerleader I approached was Becky Papish. Every day, on my way to third-period English class, we would pass in the hall, and she always seemed kind of friendly to people. So, I stepped in front of her so that she had to make eye contact with me, and I told her that she was the prettiest girl in school, and that it would be my honor to have dinner with her on Saturday at the restaurant of her choice. She stared at me for about five seconds, then busted out laughing and announced to everyone in the hall that this sophomore weirdo that she had never seen before in her life had just asked her out on a date. Then everyone in the hall started laughing, and I knew I would be taking a new and longer route to my English class for the next week or so. So much for Becky being a friendly girl! Rejecting a cool guy like me like she did was nothing but harsh. I figured it was my opening line that had to be the problem, so I worked on it for Tuesday morning when I walked up to Marilyn Ellis at her locker just before first-period classes. A smooth line would do the trick!"

"Hey, good lookin'. How 'bout goin' out with me, and I'll show you who's who in America? Without so much as a blink, Marilyn snapped at me, 'Who's who! When I tell my boyfriend, he will show you what's what all over your face.' For the next few days, I tried to avoid her boyfriend, Rocco, but one day he caught me from behind when I wasn't looking, shoved me into an open locker, slammed the door shut, pounded on the door a couple of times, and ordered me to never look at his girl again or I was a dead man."

I asked him if it was loud when Rocco pounded on the door, and Frankie said, "My ears were ringing so loud that I couldn't hear anything my first-period teacher said that day. Of course, I never listened to him anyway, so it was no big deal."

"Thursday my plan was simple. Gina Oreskovich had the same lunch period as me, so I would get in the lunch line in front of her and do my thing, use my charm, and smooth talk her into a date. Of my five rejections, that one has both my clearest and fuzziest memories. The fuzzy memories are all about what I said, which I cannot remember. Obviously, I talked nonstop for the three to four minutes before we got our food, but the only thing I really remember is that Gina never looked at me and never responded in any way to me asking her out. She stared straight ahead, smiled at the lunch lady, paid up, and walked away as if I did not exist and was not standing in front of her yapping away. All my life people have tried to ignore me, but Gina actually pulled it off. My guess is that, if one of her friends saw what happened and asked her about it, she would squinch up her face and not have any idea what they were asking. She could say it never happened and pass a lie detector test. Dang, that was humiliating and by far the worst lunch period I ever had. But I got back in the saddle a few hours later when I asked Kay Thompson out as she was heading for cheerleader practice."

"Kay saw me down the hall walking towards her, and she picked up her pace, striding aggressively right up to me yelling, 'No, no, no, no, a thousand times no! Leave me alone, don't say a word, the answer is now and always will be no.' She was pointing her finger at me, waving her arms, yelling at me, and kind of going crazy. So, when I said that I would give her some time to think it over, she did one of those high cheerleader kicks aimed right at my head. It was wild! Gina never said a word, and Kay never shut up. I guess it takes all kinds to make a cheerleader squad."

"With only one more day and one more cheerleader to harass (and I use that word on purpose because, up until that day, I thought I had a chance with at least one of those girls), I chose the nicest of all the cheerleaders, Candy Cotton. She had to be sweet with a name like that, right?!? And she was sweet. Well, kind of. Candy saw me walking towards her after the pep rally South always had the Fridays of home football games. She had been on stage cheering, kicking, throwing stuff to the crowd, and getting everyone pumped up for the big game against our school rival— Central. Candy had a big smile on her face, until she saw me."

"Candy walked up to me and asked me my name. As I told her Frank Luna, my hopes were high. I was going to be initiated into The Belmont Street Boys and get a date with a cheerleader. Of course, she would have to drive and maybe have to go Dutch, but I would explain all that to her later. Then with that sweet voice of hers she gave me the lowdown.

"Frank, if I were to give you a sympathy date, I know what the rest of my senior year would look like. Every fat, skinny, homely, pimple-faced, bug-eyed, bucktoothed, obnoxious, immature, no-talent, goofy boy in this school would think they had a shot at dating me, and I can't let that happen. They would absolutely ruin my final year of high school, and, again, I just can't let that happen. Unless you are a millionaire, a genius, or have a Corvette in the school parking lot, I would like for YOU to leave ME alone. Please!"

"I nodded my head and walked away smiling and making plans on how to make a million bucks. It was pretty cool. I went from being embarrassed for four days to thinking I had a chance with a cheerleader if I became a millionaire. By the end of the month, I had saved $9.37 and went back to being embarrassed."

5

Initiation, Part Two

THEN IT WAS BIRDY's turn. By the time he was done, I knew that I was in for some kind of humiliation. Birdy was not initiated until the second semester of his sophomore year because it took that long for Tatts and Frankie to figure what would work best for him. Birdy smiled big, restrained a laugh, and told his story.

"The guys knew that both my mom and grandma played piano and that they forced me to sit down with them to learn how to play. When they died, I kept playing in order to honor the two of them. Well, these two losers used that information against me. When the spring school talent show, which, by the way no longer happens . . ."

"Peeps was the final and greatest performance in school history," Q inserted.

"As I was saying, when the Spring South High Talent Show was scheduled, these two lousy friends made me sing and play a song of their choice. Knowing that I love rock and roll, they chose "The Sound of Silence" for me to perform—a slow, reflective, Simon and Garfunkel pop song that I would never listen to—much less perform. And not only that, I had to introduce the song by saying, 'This is the greatest song ever written, which should be obvious to anyone who has ever listened to this artistic epic.'"

Tatts looked at me and said, "Wait 'til you hear this. It gets better."

Birdy continued, trying to act annoyed by the whole thing but obviously amused. "The night of the talent show, these bozos made me come dressed in a tuxedo that Tatts got from his uncle, which was two sizes too big for me, dramatically flip the tails behind the piano bench as I sat down, then sing and play as if I believed it was, in fact, the greatest song ever written. When I was done with the song, I had to stand and bow three times with one arm in front and the other in back before exiting the stage. As if that wasn't enough, when people would come up to me that night or any time later laughing because they thought it was all a joke or asking me if I was serious, I had to point at them and say, 'That song deserves all the respect I could ever give it! You should respect it, too!'"

"Every now and then people still hum that tune when they pass me in the hall. For months, my nickname was Garfunkel . . ."

I blurted out, "Yesterday I heard some guys talking about Garfunkel and had no idea they were talking about you."

Q added, "I gave him the nickname SOS. You know, Sounds of Silence, but it didn't stick for some reason."

"The reason is because it's a lousy nickname, you wierdo. If a nickname is initials, it has to be one or two letters, unless you sing Barbershop Quartet music and go by SPEBSQSA.[1] As I was saying, people would hum the tune and call me Garfunkel or Gar or Funky and all I could do was smile and nod. Girls actually asked me out on dates because they loved that song and wanted to talk to me about it. A few of them I would have loved to date, but I couldn't stand the thought of spending any time discussing that very average tune and its pseudo-intellectual lyrics, so I had to make up some weak excuse and say no. To this day, people who know me and my love of rock and roll ask me about that song, and I have to figure out what to say. My usual response is, 'If I have to explain it to you, you probably wouldn't understand.' Let me tell you, it isn't easy to justify performing that song to my friends who are big fans of bands like Emerson, Lake, and Palmer, Jethro Tull, The Moody Blues, Yes, or Spirit!"

Tatts laughed a little and then said, "Peeps, make up your mind? Are we losers, bozos, or weirdos?"

With no hesitation Peeps yelled, "All of the above and more."

Tatts laughed a little, and then casually replied, "And the best friends a guy could ever hope to have." Birdy gave a little smile and a slight nod, and I knew then that the four of us would be close for the rest of our lives.

---

1. Society for the Preservation and Encouragement of Barbershop Quartet Singing in America.

Before Marco gave the details of his initiation, I asked, "How long do we have to keep all this initiation stuff secret?"

Marco said, "We figured we should wait until our ten-year, high school reunion. People we haven't seen in a long time will definitely bring all this stuff up when we're together with people we haven't seen in ages, so that would be a good time to tell everyone what was really going on. Now let me tell you what these wonderful, thoughtful, and oh-so-creative friends chose for my initiation." Everyone laughed and then Marco got started.

"Since I was going out for the wrestling team and had a lot of success at the junior high level, there was a good chance of me wrestling varsity as a sophomore. After I won my spot at the 167-weight class, the boys figured my initiation would revolve around me on the mat during a wrestling meet. Since the football field was so big with lots of players on the field and sidelines and 1,000 or more fans at each game, any initiation in that setting would be too easy to miss. So, wrestling it would be."

Peeps interrupted, "Now it's my turn. Q and I thought that the best test of Marco's loyalty to our little group would be for him to throw a match. So, he would have to let a lesser opponent pin him in a home match. We knew it wouldn't be fair to the team if he got pinned and it cost the team a win, so we chose his victim carefully. Now, I know that it has been too long since Q has heard the sound of his voice, so I think he should tell Nick about the music and the wrestling."

"Hey, when is Nick going to get a nickname? Nick name. Maybe Nick is already short for nickname. What do you think?"

Marco shook his head and said, "Just get back to the story, Frankie. Nicknames don't get figured out; they just happen."

Q nodded and continued with his story. "We decided to try to embarrass Tatts before every match by serenading him onto the mat with Beatles songs. We sang a different song for each match, and when he heard us sing 'Roll Over Beethoven,' he had to roll over and get pinned sometime in the first period of that match. It was great! We started the season with 'Twist and Shout,' and all the upperclassmen stared at us like we were insane. We got Sheila and two of her girlfriends to join us, along with a couple of other sophomores that Marco had protected from bullies, so they felt obligated to join us when we asked them to be part of the serenade."

"Weren't you guys embarrassed to stand up and just start singing in front of the whole gym?" I asked.

Q got an incredulous look on his face and said, "No! You seem to forget that I am one trend-setting, style-defining, suave-talking, doctor-of-cool, motor scooter. For me, everything is everything (he said, quoting a Marvin Gaye tune). If I do it, it must be cool. I don't get embarrassed, because, after I say it or do it, everyone else starts saying or doing it."

Q was a legend in his own mind, and The Belmont Street Boys loved him for it. It was a lot of fun and often embarrassing being anywhere in public with him. Q continued, "The first few times we sang, Peeps and the others were less than enthusiastic vocalists. I was Gladys Knight, and they were the sore-throated Pipps. All of the other sophomores around us moved to other places in the stands, but we sang on. Well, I sang on, and the others moved their lips and sang like they had socks stuffed in their mouths. When Marco got to the bench after winning his match, me and Peeps enjoyed watching the treatment his teammates gave him. We knew then that we were on to something good."

"The next match we went with 'Get Back' and the upperclassmen started yelling at us to knock it off. There is no doubt that we would have been roughed up by the crowd if it weren't for Marco having already established himself as the baddest dude in the school. The third match we rolled out 'Penny Lane' and heard lots of abuse, but, by then, the Pipps were gaining in confidence and our volume was picking up. We had to stop singing once the whistle blew, so we only made through about thirty seconds or so of the song, but that was plenty of time to make everyone wonder about Tatts and his friends. The next match we did 'I Am the Walrus,' and Birdy stood up and waved his arms to get everyone to chime in on the chorus. After I sang, 'I am the egg man,' he probably had thirty kids singing 'woo' with him the first time and twice that the second time. We were on a roll. When he wrestled the #1 wrestler in his weight class in southern Colorado, we sang 'Don't Let Me Down,' and a bunch of juniors and a few seniors started singing with us. That was really cool. Marco got beat on a 7–5 decision, so even though he didn't win, he also didn't let us down. The following match, when I stood and broke into 'Come Together,' the crowd actually came together and started singing with us. It was a blast to have all those students, and even some parents getting into it, belting out, 'Here come old flat top, he come grooving up slowly; he got juju eyeballs, he's one holy roller.' Man, we were starting to rock the joint! Teachers and staff were into it, and even a few tough-guy seniors were singing. But the next song was the coop degras."

Birdy said, "Continue with the story and stay away from any improperly pronounced French terms."

"I said something in French? Cool. Anyway, later that same week, South wrestled Trinidad. Their wrestler in Marco's weight class had only won one match all year and that was against Aguilar High School, which barely had enough wrestlers to fill all the weight classes. Marco kind of knew it was coming, but when we broke into 'Well, gonna write a little letter, gonna mail it to my local DJ; it's a rockin' little record, I want my jockey to play; roll over Beethoven gotta hear it again today,' we saw his head and shoulders sink just a little bit. Sure enough, Marco managed to pull that guy over on top of him and get himself pinned. We wanted to storm the mat and carry him off on our shoulders, but that would have given the whole thing away."

"What did you say to everyone?" I asked Marco.

Marco smiled and laughed his little laugh. "Well, first I shook the guy's hand and told him 'Congratulations. I made a mistake and you made me pay.' I didn't tell him that my mistake was choosing to hang out with you two wonderful, thoughtful, and creative friends. Then when I got to the bench and coach was standing there with his hands on his hips, scowling at me, I said, 'Sorry, Coach' and took my seat. After the heavyweights wrestled, coach ordered everyone but me to the locker room. Coach DeVito was a little Italian with a lot of fire, and he fired every bullet in his gun right between my eyes. After swearing at me for three or four minutes he said something like this":

"Mr. Tattalinni, I do not know what happened on the mat this afternoon, but we are going to make sure it never happens again. Something was going on which I have never before witnessed in all my thirty years of wrestling and coaching, but we will be sure to put a stop to it over the next few days. If you felt sorry for that wrestler, then good for you, because his wrestling skills most assuredly deserved your pity. But now it is your turn to be pitied by every single teammate of yours as they think about you running the halls for hours on end, beginning with one hour tonight and one hour tomorrow before school begins. You will run tomorrow after school until I get tired of seeing you run past my office. You are going to run so much that you will probably qualify to wrestle at 152 next week. All your mama's pasta and pizza and pizzelles will not be able to get you back up to weight by the end of the season. Now, start running, and don't stop until I say so. You'd better pray that I don't fall asleep in my office, or you will still be running when your buddies, who I suspect put you up to this, show up for first period class tomorrow."

I was stunned and a little scared by what I had just heard. "Wow. That's terrible," I said.

Marco, ever the cool cucumber, just smiled and said, "It wasn't that bad. I even gave some thought after that about running track in the spring. Maybe being a two-miler. But Coach DeVito was also a track coach, and I didn't want to be in his line of fire again. Besides, I needed to do a lot of work on my car in the spring. Later I met that Trinidad wrestler, Buddy Otero, in the first round of districts and pinned him in nineteen seconds. He walked onto the mat full of confidence and off the mat in shock. When I shook his hand, I smiled and said, 'I just happened to put it all together this time. Good luck in the wrestle backs.' Coach DeVito had his hands on his hips with the same scowl on his face as I walked off the mat. I told him that I was ready to go and would score some more points for our team before the day was over. He patted me on the back but didn't say a word."

Peeps added, "The next year when wrestling season started, everyone showed up to the first match ready to sing, but we told them we were juniors now and had outgrown that stuff and had moved on, which I thought was pretty funny when you think about it. Once I explained to him what that meant, it was really hard on Q to tell people with a straight face that he had outgrown sophomoric behavior. Shoot, he still hasn't outgrown eighth-gradic behavior." Q just stood there and smiled, nodding his head ever so slightly.

By now I was really worried about what was in store for me. The guys were all laughing, but I wasn't sure if that was because they were remembering all the fun that they had watching each other get initiated or if it was diabolical laughter as they thought about what was ahead for me! I was about to find out.

6

My Initiation

"BOY, LOOK AT THE time. I really should be getting home," I said as I stood up and took a step towards the Nomad.

"Not so fast, New Kid," Marco announced, as he grabbed my shoulder and guided me back to my spot on the picnic table. Then the Boys proceeded to explain to me what my initiation was going to be so that I could spend some time practicing an accent that would be part of my initiation. The whole thing didn't really sound that bad. It was even possible that I could sail easily through the day without a hitch. The Boys even promised me that they would not give any hints or tip-off anyone to make my day harder, but they would also not lift a finger to get me off the hook if I got in trouble.

Peeps did most of the talking, explaining what was expected of me for the day of my initiation. "Tomorrow, from the time you get into the Nomad until you go to bed that night, if anyone asks you a question, you have to respond by saying these words with your best Scottish accent: I'm worried, there might be a squirrel in the garage. Worried isn't worried, it's more like waddied. Squirrel is more like squawdel, and garage sounds like guhradge with the emphasis coming on the first syllable. The word there has more of a d sound than an r sound. It is more like thahrd. Now, if someone in the hall says, 'What's up?' or 'Howzit goin'?' you can just give a head nod and that's copasetic. But any legitimate question that you are asked: What do you think? How are you doing? How is tennis going? Did you do your homework? or any other actual question must be answered with these words and these words alone with no explanation. I'm waddied. Thahrd might be a squawdel in the guhradge. Now, have a good night, practice your accent, and see you tomorrow."

As the Boys drove off, I could hear them laughing and saying things like, "This could be good; it's going to be hard to keep my mouth shut; Mr. Brown always calls on him; great idea Peeps." So I did what Peeps said. I practiced my accent and got a good night's sleep, hoping for the best the next day and being grateful that what I had to do wasn't nearly as involved as their initiations. Maybe I could even avoid total humiliation, but probably not.

When I got into the Nomad at 7:45 that Monday morning, Peeps looked at me and asked, "Where's your sack lunch? Are you eating school lunch today?" I calmly responded, "I'm waddied. Thahrd might be a squawdel in the guhradge." After the three of them laughed for thirty seconds or more, Tatts said, "Nice accent, Scotty." With that, I had just earned my nickname. Now I was an official member of The Belmont Street Boys, even before I had completed my initiation. That thought made me smile. I was one of the Boys after being in town for only two weeks. My very next thought was, *This is going to be a long day.* But at least I had a nick-name now—one that I thought was kind of cool.

Q leaned into the front seat and asked me, "Whatz up?" I looked at him and gave him a head nod. All three of the guys piped up with comments letting me know that I was ready to go, this will be great, you understand the rules, we will be watching, don't cheat, and other things that were simultaneously scary, yet also making me feel like I was part of a really unique club. When we pulled into the school parking lot and I got out of the Nomad, my knees were shaking a little, but the Boys were laughing and patting me on the back, giving me the feeling that I was beginning a day-long adventure. We walked into the school and the ad-venture began.

For the first two hours, I managed to keep my head low and avoid any and all social contact. In class my head was either buried in the textbook or regularly looking down taking notes. That strategy worked fine until third hour when, halfway through Trig class, Mr. Vinci stopped writing on the chalk board and said, "Mr. Bradford, you are unusually quiet this morning." I looked at him and smiled, praying that he would not follow up his statement with a question, but that prayer went unanswered. "So, Mr. Bradford, how would you answer this equation?" he asked.

"I'm waddied. Thahrd might be a squawdel in the guhradge."

"Well, Mr. Bradford, I am worried that there is a squirrel loose in this class and that the only place for squirrels is in the principal's office. Get your things together and head that direction without further comment on your real or imagined worries."

I tried to keep my head down and not pay attention to anyone, but it was unavoidable. There was some quiet laughter by the guys, stifled giggles by girls, surprised and funny looks on faces, and even a few hands slightly raised with 'What the heck was that?' body language. It was on. None of the Boys had my third-hour class, but I knew word would get to them in the halls seconds after class dismissed. My friends would all play dumb and act shocked by the news. Not even Q would egg kids on to ask me questions, so that was somewhat reassuring. At least now the Boys could be confident that I was keeping the initiation rules. They weren't cheating and neither was I.

Once in the principal's office, I reported to the secretary, Mrs. Bragazzi, that I had been kicked out of class for the day. There was no doubt in my mind that she would have to notify my father. Then I said two things to her. "You can ask Mr. Vinci later what happened, but please believe me that it was nothing serious and it will not happen again. And, please, do not ask me any questions. Just let me sit here and serve out my punishment." Mrs. Bragazzi saw the desperation on my face, smiled, pointed me to a bench, and then went about her business. Maybe my prayer was answered, just a little later than I'd hoped. When the bell rang, I beat it out of the office before the principal, Mr. Williams spotted me.

All of the Boys had early lunch, which began right after third hour. While on the way to lunch, Betsy Hooper, a cute girl I had talked to several times in our fifth-hour Political Economics class and was thinking about asking out sometime soon, walked up to me and started talking. "Hi, Nick. Since we have the same lunch period and are starting to get to know each other better, I was wondering if it would be okay to sit at your table today for lunch?"

Just as I started to respond to Betsy, I noticed that Q was right behind us, hearing Betsy's question, so I had to say, "I'm waddied. Thahrd might be a squawdel in the guhradge."

Betsy immediately shot back, "And I thought you were a nice guy, not some weirdo who doesn't have a clue about how to treat girls! Just tell me no thank you next time! If I wanted to date some clueless sideshow freak boy, I would go out with your friend Frank!"

Q stepped in between Betsy and me and with a huge smile on his face and piped in, "Hey, beautiful. Didn't I just hear you say something about going on a date with me? Yes, I will, and thanks for asking! This is your lucky day!"

Betsy narrowed her eyes, pointed at Q, and yelled, "Frank, you put the Luna in lunatic," then stomped off shaking her head and waving her arms, headed in the opposite direction of the lunchroom.

Q stood there for about five seconds then said, "Luna in lunatic." He repeated it several times. "Man, that hurts coming from such a pretty girl, but I kinda like it. I wish I'd come up with that one," he said with a smile.

I looked at him and said, "Peeps will wish that he'd said that," then lowered my head and walked as fast as I could to the lunch room hoping that I would get a break from all the negative attention. No such luck! When we told the guys about Betsy and the Luna in lunatic line, Peeps threw his head back and his hands in the air and semi-yelled, "Why didn't I come up with that one years ago!?" As I looked at Q and smiled, he gave me the patented Luna-look, his look of confidence. He lowered his head slightly, turned his chin a little to the right and raised his right eyebrow. I would see that look hundreds of times that year.

Word about Mr. Vinci booting me out of class had spread fast, along with me using a goofy accent to say something strange. I barely had time to eat my lunch because of all the kids coming to our table to find out what was going on. Six times someone asked me one version or another of questions about what I said or why I said it, and six times I had to respond with, "I'm waddied. Thahrd might be a squawdel in the gahradge." Tatts, Peeps, and Q were laughing, slapping the table, and choking on their lunch while the girls at our table were nervously giggling. The girls had no clue of what was going on.

Sheila tried to get Marco to tell her what was up, but he just waved his hand and kept laughing, eating, and saying, "Later, later." As the girls got up from the table, Sheila smiled at me and said, "Good luck." I just nodded at her and ate the last bite of my burrito. That evening Marco told Sheila that I was just a goofy guy who got a kick out of speaking with a foreign accent. My guess is that she didn't buy it, but she also knew that Marco kept some things secret from her and that she wouldn't get anything more out of him on this subject. As we were walking out of the lunchroom, Marco, Lenny, and I laughed about Betsy freaking out and her Luna-in-lunatic comment to Frankie. Man, it felt good to laugh for once rather than being laughed at. That post-lunchroom smile was my last smile of the day. Just three more hours and then I could go home. So, I lowered my head, again, gritted my teeth, again, and beat it to my fourth-hour class, Political Economics, which was the only class of the day I shared with both Marco and Lenny.

Mr. Miller taught PE, as he liked to call it, but the only dodgeball played in his PE class was trying to avoid all of his politically and socially charged statements. Peeps would take Mr. Miller on at least once a week, catching his political opinion ball and then throwing it back at him with some added mustard on it, often winning the debate in the opinion of the class. Mr. Miller would never acknowledge the superior argument Peeps was throwing at him, but when he would say, "It is time to move on," we all knew he'd just been knocked out of the game. But today my only goal was to sit behind Marco and Peeps, hide as best I could, and avoid eye contact with everyone in the class, especially Mr. Miller.

"Good afternoon, class. I trust that you have come to class having read your chapter for today. That is except for Mr. Peeples, who already knows more than this weary textbook can teach him," he said with a tone of superiority as he looked towards Birdy. My friend smiled and cheerfully said, "Thank you for your confidence in my knowledge of all things related to politics and economics." Mr. Miller nodded a friendlier nod than usual, then looked my direction and said, "I trust that there will be nothing squirrelly going on during class today." I did not respond, but there was light laughter from most of the class for five to ten seconds, and then class went on as usual. Everyone in the senior class and all of my teachers knew that I was acting and talking weird today and they all wanted in on the action. The thought that I just had two more classes before going home was a real relief. I was starting to think there was a squirrel loose in the school and that squirrel was me. I had become just as wary of human contact as the apple-stealing, furry creature living in the Ash tree in our backyard.

In the hallways, just before and after class, kids who had never talked to me came up within inches of my face to ask me questions. The questions intensified during the final two hours of school that day. Five hundred thirty-seven kids would graduate from South in May 1973, and it felt like every single one of them asked me a question on September 12, 1972. Shy kids, dopers, flunkies, stuck-up girls, even rich kids who never ventured out of their cliques walked right up to me and asked me some stupid question just to hear me say, "I'm waddied. Thahrd might be a squawdel in the guhradge." The look of concern on my face had to accompany the words, and I do believe I pulled it off. Those were the longest two hours of my life. Even as we were pulling out of the school parking lot, kids were coming up to the Nomad and hollering questions at me. I begged Tatts to drive off and he did, but two blocks away from school he pulled off on a side street so the Boys could laugh and brag about the great idea they had for my initiation. Once the laughter calmed down, I yelled, "At least it's finally over! I am skipping tennis practice today."

"Think again, Scotty," Q announced. "You can skip tennis, but you have to keep this up for the rest of the day. Parents, phone calls, visitors to your house—any questions that come your way, you have to turn it on again!"

"Really?" I asked.

"Take a deep breath, my friend," Marco said. His words sounded half sympathetic and half filled with anticipation of what might happen next. "You can do this! Just remember that we had to go through stuff just as bad as what you have had to endure today, and we had to hear about it from kids at school for two more years. I can't tell you how many times the three of us have laughed hard remembering our initiations, and you will too—tomorrow, or next week, or next month after the pain wears off. But we have been watching you, and there is no doubt that you have conducted yourself as only a Belmont Street Boy can. Stay strong, Scotty, and we will see you tomorrow morning. I have to get back for football and field all the questions about my strange new friend."

Once I got out of the Nomad, I quickly decided on my strategy for the evening. I opened the front door, walked up to my mother and said, "Mom, I have a big English assignment about the meaning of some Top Ten songs, so I am going straight to my room, turning on music, and will stay there until supper. If anyone calls for me, take a message, and I will call them back when I can but probably not until tomorrow. Thanks Mom, you're great, I am looking forward to supper," I said as I walked down the hall towards my room. Then I shut the door and immediately turned on the stereo so that I could not hear any question she might have been asking. I took a deep breath, let out a sigh of relief, and then began work on the very real English assignment I had described to Mom.

Around 6:00pm, Mom knocked on my door and said it was supper time. I hollered, "I'm coming right out," turned my music off, and whispered a quick prayer asking God for mercy. Once again, God was not listening, at least not to me anyway. The Boys were probably praying that I would be peppered with questions from my family, and, if so, their prayers were about to be answered. We were having one of my favorite meals: pork chops, green beans, squash casserole, mashed potatoes, and gravy, with peach cobbler made with the last picking of Palisade peaches. We had discovered Palisade peaches after moving to Colorado and all four Bradfords loved them. As nominal Methodists, we always said a prayer before a family meal, and it was always the same prayer: "God is great, God is good, let us thank him for our food, Amen." It seemed to me to be a weak prayer for a family that had a PhD school superintendent for a father, but it was the prayer we always said. But not this time if I had my way! Before any prayer or any questions could be uttered, I grabbed a pork chop and stuck it in my mouth as I was spooning up the side dishes. My tactic was simple. I would try to divert Mom and Dad's attention away from the usual questions they offered me at mealtime and have them lecture me about proper table etiquette. It didn't work. Mom slapped my hand as she said, "Shape up and fly right, buster," and then asked me how my English assignment was going. I shoveled as much mashed potatoes and squash casserole as my mouth could hold, then held up my hand hoping to stave off the timing of my answer. As soon as I swallowed the mouthful, I tried to do the same thing again, but Dad grabbed my arm.

"Okay, kiddo, knock it off. Your mother asked you a question and you need to slow down, look her in the eyes, and thoughtfully respond." And that is what I did!

"Mom, I'm waddied. Thahrd might be a squawdel in the guhradge."

Chrissie immediately hollered out. "It's true. Two of my friends came over an hour ago and said their high school sisters told them that my brother had gone crazy and was acting really weird at school today!"

I quickly shoveled more food into my mouth as Dad took charge. "Well, Son, as soon as you swallow what is already in your mouth, you can go back to your room and work on that English assignment because this family is not wasting anymore of this fine meal on a kid who thinks it is alright to disrupt an entire school and then bring that disruptive behavior into our home. That's right, Boy. I got a call from your principal, and he told me about your antics. Now, before you go to your room, do you have anything to say for yourself?"

"I'm waddied. Thahrd might be a squawdel in the guhradge." It almost made me laugh when I said it, but I turned away quickly, quietly shut my door, and turned my music on at a level that would not send any more attention my way. I was thinking about how hungry I was when the thought popped into my mind; there is something about worrying over a squirrel being in your garage that makes you work up quite an appetite. (I would have to tell the Boys about that thought later.)

Even though Dad wouldn't have approved of it, Mom snuck in a bowl of peach cobbler later that evening when he wasn't looking and asked me a question, "Nick, you're going to be alright, aren't you?"

It was the only time I had cheated all day, but I looked Mom in the eyes, then gave her a good hug and said, "Mom, I am going to be great. Now, no more questions today, okay?" She lovingly nodded yes and left my room, only to sneak in ten minutes later with another bowl of cobbler. I have a great mom!

At right around 9:00pm, Dad called me out of my room and sat me down on the couch in the family room. The TV was off, and Chrissie was in her room with the door closed, but I am sure she was trying to hear what was being said. She was a good little sister, but she seemed to be happy when I was in trouble, probably because it meant that she wasn't. Mom was sitting beside Dad with a somewhat stern look on her face, but also with an air of confidence and assurance. I had never seen that in her before. Dad began the lecture with these words: "There is no doubt in my mind that your new friends put you up to this, so don't even think about denying it. I called Hal Yankovic and asked him about Marco, since they both attend St. Mary's Catholic Church and Hal knows the family. Hal couldn't have spoken better about Marco. He laughed when I told everything I knew about your day and told me not to worry. Hal said that he wished his high school (Central) had a student of the caliber of Marco and that you are a fortunate young man to be a friend of The Tatts. I couldn't believe Hal used Marco's nickname, but he did several times. Anyway, you get a pass today on your behavior only because I believe this was a one-time event that really did no harm to anyone. Now, I am making a statement, not asking a question. Tomorrow will be a better, more normal day. Am I right?!!"

"Yes, Sir, you are 100% right," I said as I cheated for the second time. I smiled, shook his hand firmly, and thought, *My dad is a very wise man.* The next day I would tell the Boys that I had honored the initiation ritual in my home but had cheated twice. When they heard the whole story, I figured they would let me slide, and they did.

7

The Day After

I HAD A HARDER time sleeping the night after my initiation than the night before. This thought kept running through my mind: *I am now officially a Belmont Street Boy.* There would be a new pep in my step and confidence in my attitude knowing that I was now a full-fledged member of a very elite group comprised of myself and three other human beings. When Mom woke me with her usual words, "It's time to get up, Sunshine," her voice sounded sweeter than ever. Her homemade strawberry jelly spread onto toasted homemade bread tasted fantastic, and the two eggs with melted cheddar and two strips of bacon was a breakfast fit for a Belmont Street Boy, if not for a king. After getting ready for school, Mom said, "Why don't you let me make your bed and pick up your room this morning?" With those words, I felt so loved and valued by my mother that I gave her a big hug and a kiss. "Mom, you are the best! I love you Mom," I said as I walked out our front door towards the Nomad, which was already parked in front of my house. There must have been a huge smile on my face, because the boys wasted no time hammering me with questions and comments and laughter.

"Hey, Scotty!" "How's it going Squirrelly?" "I know your dad grounded you, but for how long?" "You have gone on your last date with any girl from South after the show you put on yesterday!" "Your accent was great!" and one after another slap on the back and aggressive guy hugs. When things calmed down a little, Marco looked at me and said,

"It must feel good to officially be a Belmont Street Boy!" My two-word answer surprised the Boys.

"No shit," I said, and the car immediately got quiet for about five seconds until Q started yelling, "Let me hit him, please. I get hit all the time, and it's my turn to pound on someone. Come on, Tatts, let me knock him around a little." I started to wonder if getting beat up was the final step of initiation.

"Nobody is going to do any hitting this time, so calm down Q. Lenny, please explain to Nick part of what it means to be a Belmont Street Boy."

"Gladly. Our fearless leader, one Marco Tattalinni chose to do a report in his ninth-grade world history class on William Wilberforce, an eighteenth- and nineteenth-century British politician and philanthropist. Willy Will, as Q likes to call him, was kind of an Abraham Lincoln in England, who worked tirelessly to abolish slavery in England and its colonies in the Caribbean. Tell us your Willy Will quote, Marco."

"So enormous, so dreadful, so irremediable did the trade's wickedness appear that my own mind was completely made up for abolition. Let the consequences be what they would: I from this time determined that I would never rest until I had effected its abolition."

I was impressed by the quote. Then Birdy continued.

"Not only did Wilberforce help bring an end to slavery in the British Empire, but he also did other things such as promote laws to outlaw child labor in the factories of England, work for the humane treatment of animals, and he also wanted to improve the speech of peasants and working people in England. Everywhere Wilberforce went, he heard people cussing up a storm and just being vulgar in their descriptions of normal life. He felt that language had the power to lift people up, but what he was hearing on the streets generally put people down and degraded the culture as a whole. So, Wilberforce decided that encouraging the use of good words and positive expressions should be part of his aim to bring reform to the country and people that he loved. How am I doing, Marco?"

"Just fine but wrap it up."

"Okay. Here goes. Marco was really impressed by Willy Will and wanted to be the same kind of person and have the same kind of influence at school as Willy Will had in England. So, Marco decided he could protect the kids in school who were being bullied, treat the overlooked and easy-to-ignore kids with respect and dignity, use his influence to create more of a kind and caring atmosphere at school, never use profanity, and discourage his closest friends from using cuss words by beating the crap out of them if they ever used a cuss word in front of him." That brought howls of laughter from all of us.

"Even though I overstated that a little, the Boys don't cuss or refer to girls with vulgar words or images or call obviously stupid kids what they are, goofballs. The idea is that we set a good example and raise the standard of speech in the school. So that is why you would normally get slugged for using the scatological word you chose earlier. It's not so much punishment for using the word as it is a reminder that you can do better. And Q, scatological is a more sophisticated way of saying potty mouth." Q nodded with no comment.

It was kind of funny to me that I chose those words that morning since I rarely cussed, but I was glad to hear Birdy's explanation behind one of the rules for The Boys. "I can do that, and thanks for not slugging me for my first mess-up. Now, I am ready to face all the questions I will hear today and give profanity-free answers."

As soon as I hit the halls in Wing 40, the hallway leading to my first-period class, I was being peppered with questions. By the time I got to my locker, no fewer than twenty kids had asked me questions, mostly some variety of how's it goin'? With a smile on my face and new joy in my voice I said, "I am doing great! This is going to be a good day! How 'bout you? You doin' alright?" Their responses were less enthusiastic than their questions, and by the time second period came around, the excitement was mostly over, and the insincere questions were rare. When I walked into Mr. Vinci's class, he looked at me and said, "No silliness today, Nick."

"None at all, Sir," I responded with a nod of my head and solid eye contact. "You have one serious student today, Sir."

"I hope I have more than one serious student," he said as he looked over the class and then began teaching us the finer points of trigonometry.

It was smooth sailing that day all the way up through lunch period. Some of the kids who knew me a little asked what the squirrel thing was all about the day before, and I gave them all one or another version of, "Later. We can talk about it later." Those who knew The Belmont Street Boys best just shook their head and figured later would never come. We ate lunch, laughed, talked about upcoming football games and tennis matches and cheerleading stuff with the girls, then headed off to fourth period.

It was a really normal day until about twenty minutes into class when Mr. Miller said something off the top of his head. He was talking about the different forms of political systems and the strengths and weaknesses of each when he said, "We all know that more people have been killed in the name of religion than for any other reason in the history of mankind." As some kids nodded their heads, Peeps raised his hand, and Mr. Miller somewhat reluctantly called on him. Man, was I proud of my fellow Belmont Street Boy as he proceeded to calmly and systematically dismantle the casual and dangerous comment made by the teacher.

"Mr. Miller, the statement you just made to the young and impressionable minds in this class needs to be backed up by actual numbers. I know for a fact that in the name of the godless political system known as communism, which our text will cover in chapter five, millions of people were killed in the most brutal ways. When Chairman Mao launched The Great Leap Forward, it resulted in massive famine all across China. Around eight million people were deliberately starved to death in the Henan Province alone. Stalin killed at least one million Ukrainians by starvation when they refused to allow their farms to become collectivized and around four million more in other provinces across the Soviet Union by the same means. Starvation is a horrible way to die! Then there were the prison and labor camps which Stalin used to kill millions of political dissidents. All told, Stalin was responsible for the deaths of tens of millions of his own people." Birdy was on a roll.

"Conservatively, over fifty million people died in World War II because one lunatic in Germany and another in Japan decided, for non-religious reasons that they wanted to rule the world. So far, my body count is well over one hundred million people dying because of godless and maniacal men in this century alone, and I am not done. WWI took the lives of over twenty million people because of a strange combination of political alliances and the crazy dreams of imperialism on the part of a few people. The Chinese and Mongols have killed each other in a variety of internal wars to the tune of over ninety million people over the past 1500 years. Earlier this year in Burundi, a small country in the heart of Africa, which only a few people in this school have heard of and fewer still could find on a map, over 100,000 Hutus were killed by the Tutsis in tribal warfare. Hutus make up over eighty percent of the population, but the Tutsis control the army, so the Tutsis played the game of see a Hutu, kill a Hutu. And how many people died for religious reasons during the crusades, which were on-again off-again for almost two hundred years? The research is highly speculative, and I think better research will bring the numbers down in years to come, but for now let's say that one million people died during the crusades. That is around five thousand people a year for the duration of the crusades. Shoot, it only took a few days for

Tutsis to kill five thousand of their fellow citizens and neighbors earlier this year in tribal warfare. So, I would be interested in the numbers you have to back up your statement that more people have been killed in the name of religion than for any other reason. But not tomorrow because I think I am coming down with something and won't be here tomorrow."

"It's time to move on," Mr. Miller said with a harsher than usual tone.

After class, I slammed Birdy against a locker and almost yelled, "You were unbelievable!! You are unbelievable!!! How do you know all that stuff? You are the intellectual Willy Will of South High. No teacher will ever bully a class when you are there. I am so impressed!!"

Birdy calmly said, "You are keeping this nice young lady from getting to her locker." A cute and shy red-headed sophomore girl looked at us both with a little grin as we apologized and headed for our classes. I looked back to see the girl's friends crowd around her and do their girly thing at having a brief interaction with two, well-known, senior boys. The next day I made it a point to look for her and learn her name. Jody. When I told the Boys her name, they would always greet her by name. It seemed the kind of thing Willy Will might do.

Fifth period Chemistry was a breeze, but Mr. Harr had a tough time getting our sixth-period, Carolaires, select vocal group to stop talking about the show Peeps put on in Mr. Miller's class. Four of the sixteen singers in our group had the same Political Economics class, and the others wanted the lowdown on what happened. Once we settled down, I was once again impressed with the sound of our singing group and the looks of the young ladies producing that sound. This class is no doubt going to be a prime location for scoping out some very nice dates for the new kid from Chicago.

8

Getting to Know Lenny

THE NEXT MORNING WHEN I climbed into the Nomad, Peeps wasn't in his normal spot. "Is Lenny sick today?" I asked.

"He sure is," Q said with a sound in his voice that should not go along with relaying bad news about a friend. All the way to school that morning, The Tatts helped me get to know our fellow Belmont Street Boy a whole lot better.

"Birdy is probably," he paused a moment then continued. "No, Birdy is easily the smartest kid in school. You saw some of that yesterday in Mr. Miller's class." As I nodded in agreement, Marco continued. "He has already read the entire textbook for that PE class, along with several other books on the subject. When he goes to study hall every day, along with once a day his sophomore and junior years, he reads the entire time. Birdy reads history books, magazine articles on cars and electronics, novels, and anything he can get his hands on that deal with medicine and science. He really doesn't need to attend school, but he also doesn't want to leave home quite yet, because his aunt and uncle need him around. Later I will fill you in more about that situation, but sometimes Lenny just needs to get away and do his thing. Did you hear that motorcycle go by your house at 6:30 this morning?"

"Yeah, I did." I heard the sound of what I later found out was a 1969 Yamaha 175 Enduro. Several times since moving in, I had heard that same sound going by my house, but I never knew who was riding the bike or what kind of bike it was.

"That was Lenny riding the motorcycle he repairs himself. He loves to fish, so he gets up a little early, packs a lunch and all his fishing gear, and spends the day on the Arkansas River, at Lake DeWeese, San Isabel, or on some stream or beaver pond he has discovered. His uncle has a 1970 BMW 750 touring bike, which Peeps is learning to repair by reading a manual Peeps asked his uncle to buy for him. He uses his uncle's bike when he wants to fish at Twin Lakes, Antero, Turquoise, or any body of water more than a ninety-minute ride from his back door."

"Or if he wants some cute girl to ride along behind him," Q added.

"That, too. Anyway, between his love of fishing, snow skiing, snow shoeing, and motorcycle riding, Birdy misses as many days each semester as he can to fish and hit the slopes and hike and ride mountain trails and hillsides. He knows how many absentees he can have and still pass all his classes, so he uses every one of his absences to get out and enjoy all that the mountains have to offer. I have seen him barf walking out the front door of his house on his way to my car, run to the bathroom in between classes, and sit in class totally miserable just so he can spend more days skipping school and heading to the hills. Teachers have tried to send him home or to the nurse's office, but he just shakes his head and tells the teacher that he will be alright. Since he really doesn't need to study, he also doesn't need to listen to what some teacher has to say in order to pass a class. And not only is he the smartest kid in school, he is probably one of the best athletes, too. At lunch we will fill you in about that. My guess is that there will be more to tell you, so why don't you plan on coming over to my house tonight after supper to get the full story?"

Of course, Q asked, "Can I come too?" but Marco said, "Not this time, my friend. You already know Peep's story. Besides, Nick and I haven't had any time with just the two of us." Q smiled and nodded, as Marco and I agreed on a time to meet.

We were in the parking lot by then, and it was time to head to class. When tennis and football practice ended at about the same time, I would get a ride home with Marco. When one of us was in practice longer than the other, I would catch a ride home with my doubles partner Corry Logan or with Sheila if she were still at school for cheerleading practice. Corry was a great guy, but dang, Sheila was gorgeous, so it was always an easy choice to catch a ride with her when I could. I was really looking forward to hearing the lunch crowd tell me more about Lenny and then hanging out at Marco's house for a while that evening to learn more. Marco was such a thoughtful guy that I knew he wouldn't tell me anything about Birdy without his permission. Lenny Peeples was quickly becoming a great friend, and I couldn't wait to learn more about my interesting and talented friend.

On my way to lunch, I saw Q coming out of the principal's office. "Kicked out again?" I asked.

"Yeah, again" he said, with a dejected look on his face. "In English, Mrs. Hatfield was reading us some poetry by some dead Roman guy who said something about *carpe diem*. Then I asked her what that meant."

"Seize the day, and the poet was Horace," I interrupted. Q must have been impressed because he stopped walking for a second, pointed at me, shook his finger, smiled, and then continued walking and telling me his story.

"'*Carpe diem*,' I said out loud to the whole class, and then continued my thought. I wasn't goofing off or trying to be funny. I just wanted to know what happens if you are having a lousy day and don't want to seize it? What happens if you just want that day to end as fast as possible? Is there a poem about a crappy diem? Well, I guess Mrs. Hatfield decided to seize the day and make my day a crappy diem. She sent me to the office and told me I had to write a one-page paper on a poem by a well-known poet. I'll show her! My paper is going to be on Ogden Nash's poem 'Fleas.' It is the only poem I have memorized. Here goes. 'Fleas' by Ogden Nash—'Adam had 'em.' That's it. Three words. But my paper will be about the time our dog brought fleas into our house. It took us two weeks to get rid of those things. We had fourteen crappy diems in a row in the Luna house, and my paper will give Mrs. Hatfield a crappy diem of her own. I am going to find a flea somewhere and tape it to the paper. Now, that part is a lie, but I am going to tell her that the name of the exterminator who came to our house was Horace. If she doesn't laugh at that, she has no sense of humor at all. And hey, how did you know about *carpe diem* and seize the day and Horace? How do you know all that stuff? Were you doing your best Birdy imitation today?" I didn't offer an answer to his question because he was doing his usual Q thing of being more interested in his questions than he was to any answer he might hear.

By then we were at our lunch table, and Q and I were opening up our sack lunches to see what we had that day. Marco got school lunch, so he saved me from standing in the lunch line by picking up two cartons of milk, one white and one chocolate, and I paid him back at the end of every week. By the time I took my first bite of a tuna fish sandwich, almost everyone was at the table, and the topic of conversation was already focused on Birdy. Lenny was right at 6'3," still seemed to be growing a little, and weighed around 170 lbs. He had good dexterity and carried himself in a way that good athletes do, so I figured he had some ability, but I was about to get the lowdown. Marco told Q to fill me in about his sophomore year in gym class with Lenny.

"Well, I don't know how you did gym class in Chicago, but, here at South, the coaches try to expose you to every sport they can think of during your sophomore year. You spend two weeks on volleyball, two weeks wrestling, two weeks on some stupid game I think they invented called speedball, and so on. When we played flag football, he was one of the three or four best players on the field, and there were fifteen guys in class who played on the JV football team. The same was true during our two weeks of basketball. His team won the class tournament when they beat a team with three guys who ended up on the JV basketball team. There were five guys in the class who made the basketball team, and they were all telling him that he should go out for the team when tryouts came. One day at the end of class, guys were seeing how close they could come to dunking a basketball, and one of the guys who ended up on the varsity his junior year, Danny Wilson, could dunk pretty easily with a good run at the basket. So, Peeps got a ball, stood under the basket flat-footed, bent his knees, jumped straight up, and dunked with two hands. Then he turned to all of us, and we were standing there with our mouths wide open in amazement, and with this shocked look on his face he says, 'That was fun. I'd never tried that before.' After that, the guys were begging him to go out for the team, and their coach, DiPietro, was pressuring him to do the same."

I was impressed with what I was hearing, but Q wasn't done.

"He was good at whatever sport we tried. In volleyball he decided to hit an overhead serve, and it worked. Everyone else had only been hitting underhand serves. In wrestling, the only guys who could beat him were the wrestlers on the JV or Varsity wrestling team, but only if they weighed more than him. When we did track and field, he spent extra time at the high jump pit. He had read somewhere that it was a good goal for an athlete to be able to jump his height, so Peeps worked at that for several days until he could do it. Since then, he got some tips from a varsity high jumper, and he has jumped 6'5"—better than anyone in the city. I know he could jump 6'7" or better if he worked at it during track season, but that would mean missing spring skiing at A-basin and fly fishing during the April and early May fly hatches. He told Mr. Vinci, the track coach, that he would be happy to jump for him if he only had to attend the meets and one practice each week, but, so far, the coach has said no. My guess is that there is no way that Peeps will agree to being at practice even one day a week this year because he will be hitting the slopes as many days as possible, and he will be on the water fishing every day after school that he can. Since the State of Colorado is putting in the Pueblo Reservoir, he will have many more opportunities to fish. He already uses the construction access to ride his bike up the river and fish in places he's never been able to before."

Marco piped in, "If he played football, he could have helped us at safety or wide receiver, but playing organized sports is just not something he cares about."

"I tried to get him to be a male cheerleader," Sheila added. "He's really strong and could easily hold us up and catch us, and he can even do back-flips and hand-springs and walk on his hands. But Lenny just laughs, makes some smart remark, and then says, 'no thanks.' The first time I asked about it he said, 'If I became a cheerleader, you would end up falling in love with me because of all the time we would be spending together. Then The Tatts would beat my face in out of jealousy, and I would lose my best friend. So, no thank you. It's not worth it.'"

"Peeps loves Mountain Dew, so every time someone asks if he wants a pop he says, 'Don't mind if I Dew.'"

"Frankie, what does that have to do with Lenny being athletic?" Lana asked.

"Well, nothing, I guess. But it popped into my mind, so I said it."

Everyone just smiled or shook their heads and moved on. We were all used to irrelevant things flowing out of Q's unfocused brain. A lot more was said by those at the table about Lenny and his athletic abilities. There was no doubt that my friend Birdy, was one of the most interesting and unique people I would ever know. That evening, I learned even more about him from Marco. And it occurred to me, as I thought about all I'd heard that day, that being Italian seemed to be a requirement to being a coach at South.

After Marco got home from football practice, I gave him time to eat supper. His family always waited on him to get home before they ate. When I rang the doorbell, Marco's mom, Carla, answered the door and greeted me with a big hug. She was such a warm and friendly lady, and, like so many of the Italians I was getting to know, she was also very pretty. "Nick, it is so good to have you in our home. Marco told me you were coming over." Marco's eighth-grade sister, Mary, shyly waved at me and then disappeared into their basement.

"Good evening, Mr. and Mrs. Tattalinni," I said. "It sure smells great in here."

"Carla is trying to fatten me up. I think she might be taking me to market soon to be butchered. And you can call us Joe and Carla."

I nodded and said thanks but knew I would never be that informal with them. Marco pointed me to the back door, and we sat in lawn chairs underneath what I learned was a Winesap apple tree. In early October when the apples ripened, I had a new favorite apple. Mrs. Tattalinni brought each of us a glass of lemonade, then went back into the house. After taking a long swig of lemonade, Marco started talking.

"You need to know that I have never done this before. I have never given background information on one of the Boys. But you only have around eight months with Lenny before everything changes. We will be moving on to different things, and it won't be then like it is now. TV is a character, but you will get to know him better and better on the fly, and I think you will love him like I do, even though the two of us have known each other since his family moved in next door twelve years ago. And me, I am not complicated at all. There are no layers to unpeel to get to the real me. You are looking at and listening to the real me. Now, there are some things I hold close to the vest, but there is nothing I am trying to hide. With Lenny, he isn't hiding anything, but he has lived a complicated life. I don't know anyone like him and doubt if I ever will." Marco paused for a moment, sipped his lemonade, and then continued.

"I told Lenny that the two of us would be having this talk, and he gave me the okay. He thought it was a good idea. Lenny was born in Austin, Texas, and his family moved to San Francisco when Lenny was barely six years old. His mom told him that his dad had been one of the first Americans killed in the Vietnam War. He was in Nam as a military advisor, got too close to the action, and was killed in an ambush. Lenny never met his dad, so he wasn't sure if his mom was telling him the truth, but, hey, he was just a little guy, so he said okay, shrugged his shoulders, and kept being a little guy. He and his mom and his eight-year-old brother, who also had no memories of a dad, started over again in San Francisco. Lenny's mom, Judy, smoked a lot of pot and did a lot of drugs, so she pretty much left Lenny and Billy to fend for themselves. They lived in a bad part of town and attended lousy schools and dealt with Judy's addiction until she overdosed on heroin and died when Lenny was nine. Judy's mom, Grandma Peeples, drove to San Francisco to move Lenny and Billy back to her home in a part of Houston, Texas, known as The Heights."

I noticed that while giving me all these details of our friend's life, The Tatts never referred to Peeps by anything other than Lenny. "Does Lenny talk much about his mother?" I asked.

"Not very often, but when he does, he always says that his mom loved him. I guess she told him and his brother that often." Hearing that bit of good news made me feel better about Lenny's situation. Marco continued.

"It didn't take long for Lenny to see where his mom got her habits. Grandma Peeples was an alcoholic. Their house in The Heights was shabby and close to several bars. Grandma Peeples spent two or three nights each week getting drunk in the bars and staggering home to Lenny and Billy. The neighborhood kids would walk behind her and mimic her walk then laugh at the boys the next morning. When she stayed home in the evening, she would watch television, listen to Country and Western music, and drink. Maybe that's why Lenny never watches TV and hates C&W music. He told me that he tried hiding the liquor from his grandma, but she would just go out and buy more. She would look for the stuff for two or three minutes then give up and drive to the closest liquor store. Mike's Good Times Liquor was closest, and she was on good terms with Mike. She loved the boys, and they loved her. She hugged them a lot, tickled them every chance she got, and told them how proud she was of them, but she was a drunk and didn't seem to try to be anything else."

"Lenny told me that sometimes it would rain in Houston like we have never seen it rain here in Pueblo. Well, one day when there was a tropical storm in the Gulf of Mexico, it poured rain for several days, but, at its worst, for eight hours straight, it averaged an inch of rain per hour. Grandma Peeples was at a friend's house drinking and doing her thing when she got concerned about the boys and tried to drive home about six hours into the deluge. She was drunk, of course, and everyone figured she couldn't see because of the combination of alcohol and rain. How this could happen I just don't know, but she drove her green 1959

Ford Country Sedan station wagon into a bayou and drowned. The road was covered with an inch or more of rainwater, and she went right over a curb, down an embankment, and into the bayou. They didn't discover the car or her body for two days. Lenny was thirteen years old when it happened. His mother's brother, Samuel Peeples, picked up Billy and moved him to Vermont, and Grandma Peeples' brother, William, brought Lenny here to live with him and his wife Martha. No one in the family felt that they could handle two teenaged boys, so Lenny and Billy have been split up and haven't seen each other for over four years."

What I was hearing was unbelievable. My friend, Lenny, had experienced more heartache and tragedy in his first seventeen years on earth than I could imagine. Hearing all this left me speechless.

"William and Martha have been very good to Lenny. William is a mechanical engineer who has a great-paying job at the Steel Mill. Martha is a certified public accountant who works as an administrator for Southern Colorado State College. They are really nice people with lots of money who never had kids of their own. They absolutely adore Lenny and try to give him whatever he asks for. Besides a weekly allowance of $30 they have given him concert tickets, albums, his Yamaha, a beautiful Guild D-50 guitar, a Fender Rhodes Electric Piano like the one Billy Preston plays, and a top-of-the-line stereo system. But, once again, his aunt and uncle are both hopeless alcoholics. That's why you have never been in his house and most likely will never make it past the entryway. Lenny calls them alcohol-induced-misanthropes, and one of these days I am going to remember to look that word up. Basically, they do not like to be around people, other than Lenny. Most nights Lenny has to help them to bed because they drink until they pass out. When the Boys are out late, you will notice Lenny often leaving the party or the group early on his bike, or, when we are all in the Nomad, he asks us to drop him off around 10:00 because he needs to help his aunt and uncle. Sometimes he will rejoin us later, but he has never told anyone other than the Boys why he has to go home early. Lenny just can't seem to escape his family's curse of addiction."

"Does he worry that he might become some kind of an addict?" It was hard for me to ask the question, but I was sure that Lenny and Marco had already talked about it.

"When he was fifteen, the summer after our ninth-grade year, TV and I went to his house to pick him up for a day at the City Park pool. We were going to pack a lunch, ride our bicycles to the pool, and do goofy dives off the high board until Lenny was burnt to a crisp, then ride home. Frankie does this great dive where he shakes his whole body like he is having some kind of a fit in midair. Everyone who sees it laughs because he is so good at visual humor. We knew that we'd have to leave around three because, although the Mexican and the Italian would just be getting darker and darker tans, the Peeples, whatever he is, would get sunburned and our day would come to an end. When Lenny rode up to us on his bicycle, it was obvious that something was wrong. Both Q and I had seen our dads and uncles drunk often enough to know that Lenny had been sneaking booze and was obviously hung over. He was ready for a day of fun but had to stop about a mile into our ride and throw up from the fun he'd had the night before. We did our thing at the pool and had a great time together, but, when we got home, Frankie and I had a little talk. It was then that The Belmont Street Boys formed. Q and I decided that if the three of us would become brothers, a gang with a code to follow, that we could help Lenny avoid the path that the rest of his family had taken. We never wrote the code down, but we talked about it often and would let each other know when any of us broke the code."

"Did your Willy Will report play a role in establishing your code?" I asked.

"It sure did. Our code has evolved a lot since the early days, but you are right to have noticed Willy Will's influence on us. That report helped us form the attitude and approach we brought to our three-man gang, but we also established some absolute rules. No law breaking was one of the rules and drinking before you are eighteen is breaking the law. Mischief is okay but stealing and vandalism is not. We didn't spell out what you could and couldn't do with a girl, but it was kind of assumed that The Boys would follow my lead on that. We didn't want to be a group of uptight rule watchers, but we didn't want to do things that would hurt our families or the gang in any way. There is a lot of talk about the Mafia here in Pueblo, and we didn't want to be that kind of a gang. We wanted to do good and be good, whatever that worked out to mean, and we wanted to limit the group to the three of us so that we could become as close as brothers. After Q and I talked that afternoon, the three of us got together the next morning and talked about forming this club. Lenny liked the idea and added some things about being there for each other, having each other's backs, and other positive-attitude kinds of things, and then added that we needed to be free to tell each other 'I love you' and not be embarrassed. For him that was an important part of being family.

We agreed, looked each other in the eyes, said 'I love you,' and instantly became The Belmont Street Boys. We make sure to say 'I love you' around special occasions like birthdays and celebrations, so you better get used to that. Since then, Lenny hasn't tried to sneak booze from the liquor cabinet, and the two of us talk about an alcohol-free life once we go off to different colleges."

Marco let all of that information sink in for a few moments then added, "Now you know why I needed to tell you about our friend. There are many layers to our fellow Belmont Street Boy, but at the core of our friend, Lenny, is a brilliant and talented stud. I thank God every day that Lenny lives on our block."

I drank the last of my lemonade, and we gave each other a brief hug as I walked past the Winesap tree, out the wrought iron gate, and down the street to my house. Once in the door, I found my mom in the kitchen and hugged her long and hard and kissed her cheek. She gave me a look of combined surprise and gratitude. Dad came into the kitchen, and I gave him a hug, told them both that I loved them, and thanked them again for choosing Belmont Street to buy a home. I opened Chrissie's door and told her that she wasn't annoying all the time, then went to my room and said the best prayer this nominal Presbyterian could come up with to express his heartfelt feelings to God. "Lord, please bless and protect my friend, Lenny Peeples. Amen."

9

A Typical Day

IT WAS AMAZING TO me how quickly life at South felt absolutely normal. In just one month's time, I went from being a scared new kid moving into a completely unknown situation to being a kid everyone recognized and respected. There was no doubt in my mind that if my dad had chosen a house one street over on Brown or Acero, that I would most likely still be a little scared and uneasy about my situation, but that was not the case. Dr. Jonathan Bradford had chosen a house on Belmont Street, and I was a fully initiated, 100 percent Belmont Street Boy. Everything and every situation that I was involved in now felt normal. Based on our first two matches, I thought it was normal for people to attend boy's tennis matches but found out that was not the case. For the first time in years, there were cheerleaders and a crowd rooting for the boys' tennis team, cheering every good shot and every point won, and it was because of me. Well, really it was because of Marco, but the guys on the team gave me the credit. Football games were a blast with Q acting like an idiot in the stands and Marco being a stud on the field. We laughed and cheered all game long. Whenever someone on South's defense would make a good play, Marco would point at him, and the fans would go crazy cheering while the cheerleaders led the pep squad in a short cheer of "way to go 54" or whatever his number was. Marco was an all-state linebacker, but he would always point at someone else, even when he made a solo tackle. The stands on our side of the stadium were almost always full, and the student section was loud and raucous. At my old high school in Illinois, it always seemed like the students in the stands were trying to be cool, but here it was all about having fun and supporting our team on the field. Being loud and crazy at a game now felt normal to me, and I loved it. What was also normal for me was the almost daily entertainment Q provided for the Boys.

I learned real soon to keep my mouth shut anytime Frankie said anything about anything first thing in the morning. *Just give Birdy a chance to respond* became my morning motto. One morning, Frankie got into the Nomad and was scratching his crotch. "Man, I can't get rid of this itch," he complained. Just as I started to ask a question, Peeps said, "I was reading in a medical journal the other day about this very subject, so tell me more about how it feels."

"I don't know! It just feels itchy, and the more I scratch the worse it gets. I put some lotion on it but that didn't seem to help much."

Peeps nodded slightly and said, "My guess is that it's not a skin issue as much as an irritation under the skin. When we get to school, you need to go straight to the nurse and tell her that you think that you have an inflamed labium. She just might have a pill that can take care of that."

"Thanks, Lenny," he said, and the three of us managed to hold it together until we got to school, and Q took off for the nurse's office.

"Man, this is going to be good," I said, and the others agreed.

"He really should have paid better attention in Mrs. Ward's eighth-grade health class the week when we studied human anatomy," Marco said, then quickly added. "Oh, yeah. That was the week when he was Office Boy," he said with a little laugh.

Lenny and I had the same first period English Literature class, and right after class began Q busted into the class, pointed at Lenny and yelled "You stink!" and then ran off to his class. When Mrs. Hatfield asked what that was about, Lenny just said, "I think he's off his medication." We laughed about that all day long, but we didn't tell others what was so funny. Q was our much-loved brother, and, although we gave him grief all the time, we tried not to make him the brunt of everyone else's jokes.

Another day, our gullible friend was complaining about a pain in the lower part of his stomach and said that he thought he might have some kind of a hernia. "For once you might be right," Peeps responded, "but don't rule out some other options. Maybe it's not that serious. Maybe you just strained a muscle or irritated your fallopian tubes. If you have been feeling a little fatigued, it could be that some prenatal vitamins could clear up the pain and give you more energy."

As uneducated as Frankie was about stuff the rest of us knew, the kid had great short-term memory. Q went to the school nurse after second period and then let us have it at lunch. "Alright! No more female anatomy humor at my expense. The nurse always makes time for me, because she knows she will get a good laugh when I tell her my problem. There can be three really sick kids in front of me, but, as soon as she sees me, she starts smiling and says, 'Mr. Luna, what is it this time?' Then she gets this excited look on her face as I begin to tell her what's going on. Someday I am going to be really sick, but she will just send me back to class because I didn't entertain her." Q was a bit of a hypochondriac, so it was normal for him to talk about some illness, normal for Peeps to give him a crazy diagnosis, and normal for the Boys to get a good laugh out of the whole thing.

When it was time for Q to meet with the guidance counselor to discuss what his plans were for when he graduated, he had no idea what to tell her. Lenny stepped up and said, "I think you ought to pursue a degree in flatulence. You are a natural, and I think that is something that could hold your interest for at least a two-year, junior college degree. Your guidance counselor will be able to show you the guidelines for the degree plan. Check it out, and, if it's not for you, the army is always an option." Q said thanks, and, after he walked away, we all looked at each other and said in unison "He's going into the army!" and laughed. Lenny always spaced out his off-the-wall advice to Frank so that he would be receptive to what Lenny was telling him and once again set up for some major embarrassment. Frankie was gullible, and exploiting his gullibility was normal, but not an everyday trick we played on our buddy.

Frankie was always quoting songs and TV shows to kids who had no idea what he was talking about, and it was up to us, mostly Birdy, to explain his behavior. There was a football player named Joe Sullivan who Q annoyed every time the two passed in the hall. Q would say, "Hey, Joe, where you goin' with that gun in your hand?" Joe didn't have a clue what Q was saying and being peppered almost daily with that question was starting to get on his nerves. Joe's parents both played in the Pueblo Symphony and Joe didn't listen to much popular music, and certainly not to rock n roll. One day, Joe came up to Marco and Lenny and said that he was going to pound Frankie to a pulp if he didn't stop saying that same stupid thing to him all the time. Lenny knew right away what was going on.

"He's quoting Hendrix to you. Just say, 'I'm goin' down to shoot my old lady; you know I caught her messin' 'round with another man,' and he will start laughing, most likely give you a high five, and probably never say it again." That's exactly what happened, and, later on, Joe and Frankie developed a decent friendship.

A kid named Brian Shaftner walked up to the four of us one day and yelled, "If you don't get that punk under control, I will take on all four of you at once. Every time that weasel sees me, he points and says, 'Shut your mouth' and I'm sick of it." Peeps peeled off from the group, put his arm around Brian's shoulder as they walked down the hall like best friends, even though Peeps didn't know Brian. Later he told me what was said.

Lenny asked, "Sorry I don't know you, but what is your name?"

"Brian," he said.

Lenny thought for a few seconds, then said, "I'm not making any connections there. What is your last name?"

Brian said, "Shaftner," and Lenny quickly said, "I got it. The next time Frankie says that to you, you just say, "Can you dig it?" to him, and he will leave you alone. Q is quoting a line from the song "Shaft," that's all. He isn't a mean guy, so, if you hear him say something that sounds mean, just think about it for a while and you will see that he is quoting some song or TV show or commercial. That's why we call him TV or Q, which stands for quote. So, it was nice to meet you, Brian, and thanks for not hitting any of us. Are we good?" Brian nodded yes and walked off. South was a big school, and I think I might have seen Brian only two or three more times the rest of the year. But that too was normal.

One day, I was called to the office to do my once-a-semester talk with the guidance counselor, which was something every senior had to do. In the distance I thought I saw Q standing outside a classroom with his back against the wall. At lunch, I asked him about it. "Yeah, that was my World History class. All I did was ask the teacher a question, and he pointed to the door."

We all sat there for a few seconds eating our lunch, looking at Frankie, and waiting for him to tell us his question. Birdy finally shrugged his shoulders and said, "Well are you going to tell us your question or what?"

Q shook his head and said, "Or what."

"Come on man, you've got to tell us. We won't laugh that hard, for that long, this time, today," Birdy said. By now we were ready. This was going to be good. Q reluctantly and slowly told us what happened.

"We were covering WWII in Europe and Mr. Maddox was talking about Hitler and Mussolini, and he said that Hitler was called *Der Fuhrer*, whatever that means, and Mussolini was called *El Duce*. I shot my hand up and asked him why a dictator, who could call himself any name he wanted and everyone would have to go along with that, happened to choose that nickname? He could have been the Great One, Mr. Big, Benito the Stud, Mussocoolo, or something like that. So, why would he want to be named after a feminine hygiene product? The class started laughing, he pointed at the door, and I spent the next twenty minutes in the hall wondering what I did wrong. I wasn't trying to be goofy or get a laugh or anything like that; I just didn't understand why Benito chose a nickname that was so stupido."

After we stopped laughing, Birdy enlightened our good friend. "Here is an answer, a suggestion, and an observation. *El Duce* is Italian for the Duke or the leader, not for the douche."

Q interrupted with, "So, Mussolini was calling himself The Duke. Maybe he was a John Wayne fan."

Birdy continued, "Maybe, but probably not. My suggestion is that the next time you have a question, you raise your hand and just ask the question without saying anything else. My observation is that if South were like Central, I know what award you would receive at the end of the year. At Central they give awards for stupid stuff like most likely to succeed, best smile, best sense of humor, and other adolescent kinds of things. I am really glad we don't do that here." Heads were nodding as he said that, but Marco slapped the table and almost shouted, "Amen, brother!!" We all knew that if South had those kinds of awards that Marco would win most of them. Birdy continued.

"But if we did have awards like that, there is no doubt that you my friend, Mr. Francisco Luna, would easily win the Most Outstanding Senior award, because you have, by far, without a close second, spent more time out standing in the hall than anyone else in our class." There were a lot of high fives, yeah buddy, that's right, and other such responses for the next twenty seconds or so. Then for the next month, Q had a new nickname, Outstanding, but it faded after a few weeks. Frankie Luna outstanding in the hall and new nicknames—that was just normal stuff.

Butt melons. That was a term I had never heard before moving to Pueblo or after leaving Belmont Street. After a mere six weeks on the block, it was a term I considered normal, having eaten several slices of butt melons in the Tattalinni back yard.

Four years prior to our move to Pueblo, so the story goes, Marco's dad was in the shower and felt something out of the ordinary as he was thoroughly cleaning his 5'10," two-hundred-pound body. At first, he was scared, wondering what it was he was feeling as he soaped up his rear end. When he moved his fingers more cautiously, carefully feeling what he feared might be some kind of growth in his crack, he realized that he had no pain and that the thing he was feeling was not attached to his body. So, he pinched it between his thumb and index finger, pulled at it, and was surprised at what he saw. It was a watermelon seed. Immediately after letting out a sigh of relief and several seconds of laughter, an idea popped into the mind of that son-of-an-immigrant, Italian farmer. Joe decided to save the seed, start it in a planter pot in the spring, along with tomatoes he put in the west windows of his home every April, and see what happened. Sure enough, the watermelon seed sprouted, so Joe cleared out extra garden space in the backyard and announced, "This year we are growing melons."

Joe immediately started several more watermelon seeds he got from an uncle who grew melons out on the St. Charles Mesa east of Pueblo, but, when the time came for planting the starts, he was very careful to mark and monitor one seedling in particular. The following August, Joe cut into the melons from the one special plant and insisted that family members save five to six seeds from every piece they ate. By the summer of 1970, every watermelon plant in his garden came from the seed Joe found in the shower. It was a Saturday in late August 1970 that Joe made the announcement.

"Today for supper we are having a cookout. I am going to grill some burgers and kobassi (the Pueblo version of kielbasa), your mom will make us some of her best-ever, potato salad and baked beans, and then we will cut into a butt melon."

"Joe, what are you talking about?" Carla asked with a combined look of wonder and disgust. "What in the world is a butt melon?" Joe then told the family his story.

Mary started crying and said, "I don't want to eat something that came out of daddy's butt." No amount of explaining could convince her otherwise. The girl was in her mid-twenties before she ever ate another slice of watermelon. In her young mind, every watermelon came from someone's butt.

Marco shook his head and said, "Dad, you are something else."

Carla said, "Joe, that is disgusting!" Joe just smiled and cut into a melon.

"It's just the thought of it that is disgusting. Carla, last year you were bragging to your friends about the watermelon I grew. Marco, you were happy to save the seeds because you wanted more tasty melons from our garden the next year. All three of you loved my butt melons before you knew what they were."

Carla reluctantly said after a few seconds of silence, "I guess you're right. But no one outside of the five of us can ever know about this."

Marco started to laugh and said, "It's too late for that. Almost every time we are in the backyard, Frankie is behind the lilac hedge listening to everything we say. He probably heard it all and wants to get invited to the cookout."

Right then, Q came around the corner and with a gigantic smile on his face asked, "Can I have a slice of butt melon? Please!?! That is the coolest thing I have ever heard in my life."

Once Frankie knew something, it was a sure thing that the rest of the block and beyond would hear about it within hours. By the middle of September, the term "butt melon" was a normal term used in the neighborhood. Half of the people laughed when they used the term, and the other half were mildly disgusted. By the time I moved to Belmont Street, almost everyone talked about butt melons with a matter-of-fact attitude, unless they were forced to tell the story to newcomers like me. Depending on who told the story, they thought the story was either really funny or really disgusting. It was pretty much a 50/50 split, and, once the story spread across the Italian population of Pueblo, it was only a few months before everyone in town and out on the St. Charles Mesa knew about butt melons.

Joe's uncle, Fat Tony, not to be confused with Uncle Tony or his other Uncle Tony known as Bumpy, farmed on the Mesa and had a fruit stand named, of course, "Fat Tony's." When watermelons were in season, people would ask him either with excitement or with caution, 'Is this a butt melon?' Fat Tony always said the same thing, "No, only my nephew, Joe, grows butt melons. My seeds all come from the other end of the body. I only plant Burpee seeds." Then he would laugh, people would be polite even though they had no idea what he was saying, pick out a melon, and come back a few days later for another.

I'd already eaten two large slices of a butt melon before I asked Marco why it was called that. After hearing the story, I was in the half who thought it was funny. My parents were offered an entire melon, but politely said, "No, thanks." That put them in the other fifty-percent group, but they were quick to acknowledge in private, *only in Pueblo,* with fond smiles and a little giggle from my mom. When Mom's cousin, Verla, and her husband, Dave, came to visit us for Thanksgiving that first year, they asked about life in Colorado, and my folks were talking over each other as they told the butt melon story. Mom started giggling and soon both Mom and Dad were laughing loudly and almost yelling, *only in Pueblo.* It wasn't a critical comment, but rather an expression by them of the unique quality of both Pueblo and the neighborhood here on Belmont. It was fun for me to hear them tell that and other stories about the Bradford family's first four months in Pueblo. They would shake their heads and say, *only in Pueblo,* then tell another story in such a way that I could see both Mom and Dad had quickly developed a strong affection for Pueblo and for our neighbors on Belmont.

Back in Chicago, the kids in my school would talk about stuff for weeks. Here in Pueblo those kinds of stories had a pretty short shelf life in the halls of South High and especially among The Belmont Street Boys. Butt melons, playing jokes on Q, goofy nicknames, even a once-in-a-lifetime activity like getting initiated into The Belmont Street Boys could happen on any given day. There was always something new and interesting going on. A typical day was a fun time with two or three crazy new stories or events. What Peeps told me the first time I met the Boys was true. Every day I thanked God that my family moved into our house on Belmont. I never knew a normal day could be so interesting and such a kick.

10

The Opposite Sex

IT USUALLY ONLY HAPPENED once or twice a day that all four Belmont Street Boys would be walking together through the halls of South High, and, when it did occur, something interesting often materialized. Usually, the four of us were together after lunch or following an all-school assembly of some kind, but one particular day I made a detour from my usual third-period route to trig class to ask Marco about a girl in that class who I was thinking about asking out on a date. The other three Boys always walked together between second- and third-period classes, and I knew where to find them. When I spotted them, I picked up my pace until the only people between me and the Boys were two senior girls walking and talking like almost all kids do between classes. All of a sudden, Q stopped, turned, and pointed at one of the girls and yelled, "Would you stop following me!"

She was shocked and apologetically said, "I'm just walking to my class. We have the same class, Frank." Her name was Cindy, and, as she and her friend Marla hurried around the Boys, Frankie smiled and said, "Tomorrow I am going to do the same thing, except that I will point at her and say, 'Are you free for a date on Friday?' See, I just got her attention, and she won't be able to get me off her mind all day. So, tomorrow, she will be ready to accept a date from the guy she hasn't been able to stop thinking about."

"Q, that is a fascinating and totally screwed up idea. If that is the best you can come up with on how to get a girl's attention for a date, then we are going to change your initial from Q to V for Virgin because you will never date, never get married, and never know a female in the biblical way," I said. "Marco, I am in a hurry, but I am thinking about asking April Jones out. She seems like a nice girl, and I was hoping we could double date Friday since your game is on Saturday. What do you think?"

"Yes, she's a nice girl, and, yes, we can do that. The two of us will talk later about the date, and the four of us will talk later about how to relate to the opposite sex." Marco then offered something I thought was a little strange. "Don't be surprised if the double date is less than what you'd hoped for." Peeps had a big smile on his face as I shook my head okay and hurried off to class. Trig that day was an especially boring review of things I already knew, but class ended in a very upbeat way when April said yes to a date on Friday. During lunch, Marco and I agreed on the time and the movie for Friday night.

The movie, "Joe Kidd," was enjoyable because I was and am a big fan of Clint Eastwood, but the date was a bit of a disappointment. It didn't take long for me to figure out why Peeps was smiling and why Marco said what he did about double dating with him and Sheila. Obviously, Marco and Peeps knew something I had not yet discovered, and we would talk about the date later on. Sunday afternoon, the Boys headed off to City Park where we sat around a picnic table drinking Pepsi Colas and talking about all things related to girls and dating.

"A couple of weeks ago I had a date with . . ." Q said and was quickly interrupted by Birdy with, "Give him the phone."

"I have heard that before and seen you guys and others hold their fingers up to their ears and mouth as they shake their heads. What is that?" I asked.

Marco pointed at Birdy, who then explained. "The phone is short for the bullaphone. When someone is exaggerating or flat-out lying, you give them the phone. We used to go, ring, it's for you, you're wanted on the bullaphone. Now we just say give him the phone or hold up our fingers like we are on the phone listening to a bunch of bull. So, anytime our friend, Frankie, talks about being on a date, we know what we are listening to. A bunch of bull. He probably plopped down uninvited next to some girl at church and called it a date."

"You guys might be the coolest guys in Pueblo, but you also stink!" Q halfway shouted.

Marco reached out and grabbed his neighbor's arm. "We can live with that, and you can, too, because you know we love you."

Q gave a little smile, nodded, and then said, "Tell us about your date with April. I'll bet it was a whole lot like the double dates I've been on with Marco and Sheila." Then our friend continued.

"If you felt like your date was more interested in being close to Marco than she was with being close to you, then, yeah, our dates were kind of alike. My dates were only interested in being close to Marco." Q's self-deprecating humor always made us laugh.

"That's what your big smile was all about when you heard us talking about the double date," I said to Lenny.

"You got it," he said and continued to explain his thinking on the subject.

"Double dates with Marco and Sheila are the easiest dates you will ever get and the most disappointing dates you will have while at South. No girl will ever tell you no. She might be engaged to be married, but she will still go out with you on a double date in order to spend time with Marco and Sheila. I dated a girl one time who was all over me in the backseat of the Nomad, and the whole time I knew that it was Marco that she wanted. It is pretty tough when it dawns on you that your appeal as a guy is mostly tied to your buddy known as The Tatts. He not only could KO every single guy in our school, he has KO'd the hearts of ninety percent of the girls at South. Your mission, Young Bradford, Nick, Scotty, should you decide to accept it, is to find the ten percent in our school or to venture outside of South to find girls who want to be with you because they like you for who you are instead of for the stud you hang out with."

The air over the picnic table was a little heavy until Frankie said, "Nice "Mission Impossible" quote."

Marco followed that with, "You know that it isn't easy being the coolest, toughest, and handsomest guy in town." From there we started laughing and adding, "What do you mean town? How about state, or country, or world? What a burden! We feel so sorry for you. If only you were rich and smart, you'd have it all." That went on for a couple of minutes before we got back on the subject of the opposite sex.

Peeps started the discussion after we'd settled down and opened up a second bottle of Pepsi for each of us. "My philosophy of high school dating
is that I want to date a lot of girls and see what kind of girls I enjoy being
with. So far, I have learned a lot about the female sex over the past sixty
or more dates with at least forty girls. And don't even try to give me the
phone, Q, because those are accurate numbers for the past twenty-six
months since I got my driver's license. Nick, there are few girls at South
who you will want to date that I haven't already asked out. Remember
Jody, that cute, redheaded sophomore we met when you slammed me
against the locker that day? Dang, that girl is attractive, but she is even
more immature than she is cute. We weren't twenty minutes into our date
before I knew it was a bad idea to ask her out. She was talking about terrible pop music, some guy she knows in another state she lived in, asking
me whether I'd rather be stranded on a desert island or eat cat food. It
was insane. But one month later after seeing her in the hall day after day
and thinking that she was so good looking that she had to be Jill St. John's
little sister, I just had to ask her out again. Then one hour into our date
she was driving me so crazy that I faked an appendix attack and drove
her home before we finished our burgers at The Red Barn. Now I know
that it doesn't matter how much I like a girl's face and body, her brain and
emotional development can quickly overshadow her appearance for me.
Looks are important, but mind and spirit are essential to my happiness
with the opposite sex."

"I also know that everyone is not like me, but that is one thing I
know for sure about myself. What I have also discovered is that I do not
enjoy being with needy girls or weak girls who want me to do everything
for them or girls who act dumb when I know they're not. Other guys
might think that stuff is funny or unique or appealing in some way, but it
drives me crazy! I am telling you guys, dating lots of girls is a great idea!
Then when the right girl comes along, you have a really good idea about
what it is that makes her the right one for you. The other option is to
somehow pry Sheila away from Marco, because she is as close to perfect
as I have ever been around."

Marco took a swig of Pepsi, smiled, and said, "Don't give them any
ideas," then he paused and added, "or false hope."

At that point I shook my finger and said, "I think you are on to
something, Lenny. My mom always says to be careful who you date because you just might fall in love with them. Mom has a cousin who fell in
love with a handsome, charming loser. She divorced him after he used his

looks and charm to cheat on her with lots of other women. At age twenty-six, her cousin, Betty, was left with a little boy and no money or job skills. It took her around four years before she could get some job training and was able to move on with her life. It seemed to me that Mom didn't like my girlfriend in Illinois, Mary Avery, because she often suggested that only dating one girl is not the best idea for someone in high school. Maybe Mom was just worried that Mary, or any other girlfriend I might have, could turn out to be a female version of her cousin's husband—all charm and looks and no substance. Mom hated Betsy's husband so much that I never knew his name. Mom always referred to him as that creep, that loser, or that no good bum married to my sweet cousin, Betty."

"Nick, since you brought up your mom, I'd like to hear how things go in your house when the subject of your mom's weight comes up," Marco piped in.

Q interrupted, as usual. "My dad would look at my mom and say, hey Tubby, why can't you look more like Lucille Bradford?"

Marco shook his head and said, "No, we are not all talking about Mrs. Bradford's weight! My question is this: does your dad, or Lenny's uncle, bring up the subject of his wife's weight or any other sensitive subjects in front of you guys, and, if so, what does that conversation sound like? Since we are talking about the opposite sex, I would like to hear how women other than my mom handle sensitive subjects."

Q said, "Yes, I have heard that subject discussed, and my answer is the same. My dad has said several times, 'Hey, Tubby, why can't you look more like Lucille Bradford or Carla Tattalinni?' and the fight is on. That is my cue to slip out of the house for an hour or two."

"It's funny you should ask that question because, around two weeks ago, I overheard Dad ask Mom if she'd put on a few pounds since we made the move to Pueblo. That night she made a pot roast for supper with potatoes and carrots, and, while we all chowed down, Mom sat there eating two celery stalks. When I asked her why she wasn't eating the great meal she'd fixed for supper, she just looked at Dad and with a halfhearted smile said, 'Oh, dear, this just sounded good to me tonight.' The rest of the week she fixed fabulous meals with cakes and ice cream for dessert while she ate simple salads with vinaigrette dressing served up with a silent treatment and an insincere smile directed at my dad. After a week of that treatment, Dad was bringing home chocolates for Mom and taking her out to eat and doing everything he could to get her back to acting and eating normal."

"What your mom did is known as passive-aggressive behavior," Birdy informed us. "In my house, my aunt and uncle fight about that sort of thing, aggressively drink, passively lose consciousness, and the next morning they don't remember a thing."

It was Marco's turn. "My mom is Italian, so there is no such thing as passive aggressive in our house. Once Dad said something about her weight, which I thought was out of line because my mom is beautiful, and Mom tore into him about his belly and balding head and the hair growing out of his ears. My dad hates meatloaf, so Mom made meatloaf for supper four nights in a row and, when he complained, she yelled, 'Well don't eat any then. I'll eat your share and put on some more weight! Maybe in a month or so I'll be as fat as you!!' Like with your parents, Nick, my folks worked it out a week or so later, and I doubt that the subject of Mom's weight will come up again any time soon."

We spent the next half hour talking about things we should and shouldn't say to girls or women and what makes women so unique. It was a great time together. The only conversations I had with guys at my old school about girls had to do with which girls would put out what and how to get them to do it. We talked about that, too, but it was so different with the Boys. Marco made a simple statement of awareness that we all thought about and finally agreed with—girls will sometimes give sex in order to get love, and guys will fake love in order to get sex. We talked about that statement for a few minutes and decided that using manipulative behavior with vulnerable girls was below the character of The Belmont Street Boys. Then, as we said 'I love you' to each other while giving hugs and back slaps, we drank the last of our Pepsis and headed home better enlightened about the opposite sex and who we wanted to be when with them.

11

Wrapping Up Fall, Part One

As THE WEATHER COOLED off and the colors changed in Southern Colorado, I was amazed at how my relationships continued to warm and intensify in their brilliance. By the time Halloween arrived, I felt like I had been living on Belmont Street my whole life. The Boys felt like the brothers I never had, the Tattalinni house felt like a second home to me, kids at school listened to me and respected my ideas, there was a warmth among the kids and faculty at school like I had never before experienced, and I laughed hard and often on an almost daily basis. South's sports teams had success, so there was a positive attitude surrounding all fall sporting events. Musically, our band, choir, and select singing group, known as the Carolaires, were all pretty good, which contributed to the positive and well-rounded student life at South. Even when games or events didn't go as well as we had hoped, there seemed to be something satisfying about those experiences as well.

When South played the best football team in Southern Colorado, Wasson High School from Colorado Springs, the Boys, without Marco's knowledge, decided we needed to do something special to prepare for that game. We got some girls from the Pep Squad to make us two ten-foot-long, roll-out posters, the kind used to decorate school hallways before a big game. One said GO SOUTH!! BEAT WASSON and the other was COLTS ALWAYS TROMP ON THUNDERGIRLS. Wasson was the Thunderbirds, so we thought that one was somewhat clever. Then on the Thursday night before the Friday game, Birdy, Q, and I hopped into

Birdy's Uncle's 64 Olds 442 and sped up to the Springs at around 8:00 to get into Wasson, hang our posters, and steal one of theirs. If we had to make a quick escape from their school parking lot, we knew we had the edge in that car. I told my parents that I had a few things to do to prepare for the big game on Friday and would be out a little late for a school night. They gave me their permission and didn't ask any specifics, so I didn't have to lie to them. Birdy's aunt and uncle were beginning their drunk for the night, and we would be back in time for Birdy to help them to bed. Q's parents were mostly non-parents so he could come and go as he wished. We were excited and a little scared, but our plan developed as we made the forty-five-minute drive to the Springs.

It was decided. We would walk around the school until we found a janitor to let us into the building. We would use the name of the tennis coach, which I learned when we played Wasson the week before, as the school sponsor who gave us permission to be in the school at that hour. Q would be our designated enthusiastic convincer to get the janitor on our side if there was any hesitation. Birdy told him to emote, then had to explain the word to him by saying, "Just get worked up and yell stuff like we're going to kill 'em; these are the best posters ever; are you going to be at the game; whoop it up and scream yah-yah-yah a bunch of times." Q was definitely up for that role.

When we got to the school, we found the locker room door open as a few football players were just then leaving school. As we wound our way through that room and into the gym and then the hallway, we ran into a janitor who asked us what we were doing. We started into our deal, and he quickly found a ladder and some masking tape to help us out. Once in the building we had our posters hung and one of theirs in hand in less than ten minutes. The janitor never looked at the posters and we never looked back once we were out the door. We didn't need to do it, but Birdy floored it as we were leaving the parking lot just in case someone noticed us as being the enemy. The next day in the school pep assembly leading up to the game, we unfurled the poster we stole and announced what we had done the night before. The auditorium went berserk. We had done our part to get the team and the student section fired up for the big game.

Marco had a great game that night with eighteen tackles, two pass deflections, and a blocked punt, but South still lost the game by a touchdown. It was the best performance by a defensive player I had ever seen in a high school football game. All game long, the public address announcer said "Tattalinni, Tattalinni, Tattalinni" over and over again as

Marco made one play after another. And every time his name was called, The Tatts would point at a teammate so the student section could root for the teammate, even as "Tattalinni" was still echoing around the stadium. When we lived in Illinois, Dad was a scout for Schaumberg High School's (SHS) football team. Every weekend from September through November, Dad took me to games all around Chicago as he scouted the next week's opponent of SHS. Along with looking for plays the team liked to run and schemes they commonly used, Dad told me what he saw about the best players on the field. By the time I was twelve, I was pretty good at noticing the talent and speed of the most athletic players on the field, and I was actually a help to Dad by being another set of eyes surveying the field. I saw a lot of good games and good players during those years, but that night in Pueblo, Marco played a game I would never forget. The next morning at breakfast, Dad completely agreed with me about Marco's great game and added that Marco was a sure bet to play major college football somewhere. But it was what happened immediately after the game that impressed me just as much as what I saw on the field that night.

As Wasson sprinted off the field to their bus, jumping and yelling and singing their school song, South players trudged to the locker room beat up and discouraged. South players knew that their shot at a conference championship and a state playoff game at that point was pretty much gone. As I watched the slow movement of the players towards the locker room, I noticed that one of our guys was jogging, but he wasn't headed to the locker room. It was #51, Marco, and he was headed right towards the Wasson team bus. As he came up unnoticed behind the Thunderbirds, he surprised the players, but they seemed to calm down a little as he patted some players on the back and made a beeline to the head coach. Marco touched him on the shoulder, they talked for a few seconds as the Wasson team finished filling up their two school busses, then the coach got on the first bus followed by Marco a few seconds later. I had to drag the details out of him later that night, but Marco finally gave me the scoop.

"I asked the coach for his permission to say a few words to his team, and he said, 'Sure thing.' He didn't even ask me what I was going to say, which really surprised me. The year before, when we played Wasson, he came up to me after the game and said that if I wanted to play for him next year that he would find me a nice family close to the school to live with. I laughed and told him thanks for the offer, so maybe he felt that he could trust me or something. Anyway, I started to talk to their team when some kid yelled, 'Off the bus you loser.' Their star tight end backhanded the kid in the mouth and said, 'Shut up, sophomore,' and I told them what I had to say."

"Well, what did you say, you loser?" We both laughed for a few seconds and Marco continued.

"I told them that they were the best team we had played this year and that I thought they had a good chance to do some real damage once the state playoffs began. South had played a really good game, maybe the best we could possibly play, but their talent, discipline, and size were too much for us. I was impressed with how hard and clean they played and that I would be cheering for them the rest of the season. My basic message was that me and my teammates had played our hearts out, that we couldn't have tried any harder, but Wasson was clearly just too good for South to handle. It's hard to remember exactly what I said, but that's about it. As I turned to get off the bus, the head coach said that he was sick and tired of hearing my name repeated so often by the public address announcer for the past three years and that next year it would be a relief not to have to deal with me. Everyone on the bus laughed at that and the coach patted me on the back as I left. Just as I started to jog to our locker room, the coach hollered, 'Tell whoever hung those signs in our hall that it took us until third period to figure out that we had been raided.' I just waved at him and thought, that was a pretty cool thing to hear about my Boys. You raided their school successfully but did no destruction. That's just what I would expect from The Belmont Street Boys."

The following Monday at supper, Dad told me that the head coach from Wasson called our head coach to tell him what Marco had said to his team and to brag on him for a while. Our coach called Dad to tell him how proud he was of Marco and that he had learned something about how to lose a game the right way from his star linebacker. Losing a hard-fought game stunk, but being an all-state person was even more inspiring than being an all-state linebacker. Coach also mentioned something else in their conversation.

"You wouldn't know anything about the raid on Wasson, would you?" I kept my head down, took a bite of salad, and said, "Maybe a little." With no pause or emotion, Dad coolly replied, "Well don't let it happen again." It was shocking to me how much slack Dad was giving me these days, but I loved it and wouldn't abuse it. "No, Sir, I won't." Dad was never this cool in Illinois, and I loved the change I'd seen in him.

∽∞∾

Cross Country in those days was a yearly fight for second place among the four Pueblo high schools. Centennial won the state championship six or seven years in a row, so South's runners knew they couldn't compete with the Bulldogs. Attendance was pretty sparse at the meets, so Birdy and Q decided they would make it to four of the cross country meets to root for South's long-distance runners and to try to help team morale. Just before the first dual meet of the season, it was announced on the school Public Address system that South's harriers would be competing against East High School that afternoon at the Southern Colorado State College Orman Avenue campus at 3:30. Apparently, Q had never heard that term before, and he blurted out, "Harriers; hairier than who?" From then on, his attendance at a cross-country meet wasn't just about a running competition, it was a chance for him to proclaim the winner of the meet based on who was the hairiest harrier. As the runners passed where Q was standing, he would announce who was hairier than the other runners in that particular group. "Number 13, you are the winner. Run, you hairy beast," or something like that throughout the entire meet. "You might be fast, but you are not a harrier in my book." As usual, once he got started you couldn't shut him up, but South's runners really enjoyed it. None of the guys on South's team shaved or cut their hair from the first meet until after the season. If they couldn't beat Centennial on the course, at least they could be hairier than them.

Attendance at meets and team enthusiasm was at an all-time high, and that was mostly due to Q and Birdy being at some of the meets and having a lot of fun with the team. As more and more students from South began to show up at meets, they would enthusiastically cheer the team on and follow Q's lead concerning all things hairy. At the end of the season, Q showed up at the team banquet and gave the two hairiest harriers bottles of shampoo as awards. Although their record indicated that South's harriers only had a mediocre season, it was their best year ever in terms of school support and overall fun. Their team morale translated into the runners stopping by the tennis locker room to encourage us before our matches to play hard and not to cut our hair. Once again, it was easy to see that good was coming out of even disappointing seasons. The atmosphere at South was just so positive. Marco had set the tone for all things related to school morale, and the Boys spread that positive tone everywhere they could.

My final high school tennis season was about as good as it could have been. Corry and I won all but two matches during the regular season and took second at districts, which meant we qualified for state. State that year was held at the Air Force Academy, and it was a lot of fun getting to use their first-class facilities for several days. Corry and I won our first-round match but ran into the tennis buzzsaw of Colorado—Cherry Creek—and lost our second-round match. We competed well, and I couldn't help but think that, if Corry and I had more time together as a doubles team, we might have done even better. And then I thought that if it weren't for our team captain and eventual school salutatorian, Marty Dickerson, I wouldn't have even made the team. Our coach, Mr. Walker, didn't know anything about tennis, so he lined up the team as best he knew, but, again, he knew nothing about tennis. Coach Walker was a tennis team sponsor, not a coach. One day after practice, Marty took Coach Walker aside and told him who should be playing where on the team. Coach had me on the JV until Marty did his thing. As it ended up, our whole team qualified for state. What had started out so badly ended up being pretty successful. Corry and I, as well as Marty's double team, were the only ones on our team to win a match at state, but it was a still a good season as we all won plenty of matches and had even more fun.

One evening after a match in Colorado Springs, we got back to South and were sitting in the van ready to get out and go home when Coach Walker decided to give us an inspirational speech. "I want you guys to remember that tennis is not the most important thing in your life. The most important thing is your studies. If you win at tennis and fail in the classroom you have failed at tennis. Don't forget that. The next most important thing is your health. Get your sleep, eat good food, and stay away from drugs and cigarettes and alcohol. And finally, the third most important thing in your life is your, your, your studies. Don't forget that boys!!" And we never did. I told my parents that night and have told the story at least a hundred times since that night outside the gym parking lot of Pueblo South High. Coach Walker rarely told jokes, but he kept us laughing all season long.

Other than the end of football, cross country, and tennis seasons, the homecoming dance was the informal wrap-up to fall. I had hardly given it a thought until the other members of Carolaires were talking about who they were going to homecoming with and asking me about my date. Homecoming was ten days away, and I needed to get after it if I was going to have a decent date to my first big dance. The Boys didn't talk about it because Marco knew that Sheila would be his date. Lenny knew he had his choice of most any other girl in the school (as I had learned earlier, a girl would likely break up with her boyfriend on the spot if Birdy asked her out). Q knew that he needed to ask some girl from another school if he wanted it to be a real date. So, who would I ask out? Jeannie, one of the girls in Carolaires was really interesting to me, but she was a strict Pentecostal girl who didn't believe in dancing, so I knew she was a no-go. I asked the guys in Carolaires if they'd heard whether Betsy Hooper had a date. Corry, my doubles partner and fellow bass in the Carolaires, said that he had Betsy in English and had heard her say that day that she still didn't have a date and was hoping she would get asked soon. So, Betsy it was; that is, if she had forgiven me for the squirrel in the garage incident a few months earlier. After Carolaires, I made a beeline towards Betsy's locker and caught her just as she was leaving the building. I asked her if she had a date to homecoming and, if not, would she think about going with me. With no hesitation, she said that she didn't have a date and that it would be fun to go to homecoming with me. Apparently, I had either been forgiven for being squirrely or she had formed a new opinion about me. She gave me her phone number, and we agreed to talk later about details. I caught up with the Boys in the parking lot and gave them the news about Betsy being my homecoming date.

Q started first. "So, Betsy felt sorry for the—what was it she called you—sideshow freak boy?"

"It was clueless, sideshow freak boy if I remember right," Marco said as he started up the Nomad.

"Good news, Scotty!" None of the boys had called me that in over a month. I guess the Betsy story brought it back to life, temporarily. "You have a date to homecoming. Now let me tell you how this date is going to go. We have it all worked out," Peeps informed me. "The Tatts told TV that if he could find a date that he would let him borrow the Nomad for the night, and believe it or not, our little buddy found some girl from the Colorado School for the Deaf and Blind to go out with him. She is both deaf and blind and her sense of smell isn't real good either, so she won't be the least bit annoyed by him. Her name is Helen Keller if I'm not mistaken. I don't do double dates, so Lana Jones and I will go to the dance in my Uncle's Olds, and you will need to borrow your dad's new car so you and Marco can take your lovely ladies out in style. A 1972 Gran Torino should be a suitable ride for the evening, don't you think?"

Frankie said, "My date is a girl from East that I met at my cousin's house one day." I smiled and nodded at Q. That guy could take a ribbing better than anyone I have ever known. "But her name does happen to be Helen." What a guy!

"Considering the circumstances, I think Dad will let me use the car. I haven't driven it yet, but this is a big occasion, and I think he will step up." Even in light of my earlier double date experience with Marco and Sheila, I thought Birdy's plan was a good one. At supper that evening, Dad said he was happy that I had a date and that he would be glad to let me use the car. (Dad was proud of his car, so I didn't tell him that Marco was a Chevy man and wasn't sure he wanted to be seen in a Ford). Homecoming was ten days away, but I was already starting to get excited about an event that I hadn't even given a thought to until earlier that very day.

12

Wrapping Up Fall, Part Two

THE BIG NIGHT HAD finally arrived, and I was way more excited than I had anticipated being. Maybe I was even a little nervous and somewhat scared. If I had known what was going to happen early in the evening, I would have been a lot more nervous and scared.

Homecoming started at 7:00, so I left the house to get Betsy at 4:45. We had dinner reservations at La Tronica's Italian Restaurant at 5:30, so that would leave time for the four of us to go back to my house for the pictures my mom insisted on taking. Betsy was ready on time, and her mom took a few pictures, then off we went to get Marco. Sheila's folks wanted to bring her to Marco's house so that everyone could be together for a few minutes, and, of course, to take pictures. This picture thing was new to me, but I just smiled and went along with it. Betsy looked really pretty in her dress, but, when I saw Sheila, I was momentarily speechless. It seemed impossible for her to be any prettier than she already was, but there she was, Miss Absolutely Gorgeous. I kept looking at Betsy and telling her how nice she looked and how much I liked her dress and how good her perfume smelled just to keep me from staring at Sheila. After a quick walk to my house for more pictures, we got into the Gran Torino and headed off to La Tronica's.

Although La Tronica's served really good food and was an institution in Pueblo, it probably wasn't the best idea to go to an Italian restaurant with the guys dressed up in our best suits and the girls in their brand-new dresses. We all worked hard at controlling the sauce and noodles, but I was worried that I had Italian sausage and garlic breath even with the breath mints that I kept in my mouth all evening long. We had preordered our menu, so we were out of the restaurant in record time and had a few minutes to kill before to going to the dance. Marco gave me directions on where to go so that I could see parts of Pueblo I had never been before, and that's when things got interesting.

We drove through Salt Creek, which was a rundown part of town on the backside of the Steel Mill. From there we drove past Walter's Brewery, and headed towards 4th Street. We hadn't noticed it at the time, but a car had been following us since we left Salt Creek. A couple of blocks before we got to the stop sign at 4th, that car passed us, and another pulled up kind of close behind us. At the stop sign, the car in front backed up and the car behind us boxed us in when it got just off our bumper. Marco saw what was happening and calmly began to tell us what to do.

"Nick, scoot over a little, and I will get out of the car first. Girls, lock the doors behind us. Once I am out of the car, Nick, you watch the guys in the car behind us and clear your throat if they have any weapons. Just keep an eye on them and let me do all the talking."

Marco slid past me from the backseat of the two-door hardtop, slowly stepped outside and began to take off his suit jacket and roll up his sleeves as he smiled at the three guys who were already out of the car in front. As my feet hit the pavement and I closed the door behind me, I saw two guys in their late teens, both slowly going around the back of their car in order to come up on the passenger side of the Gran Torino. I didn't see any weapons. Fortunately, there was a streetlight right over where we stopped, so we could see things pretty clearly.

"Hey, guys, how are you doin'? My buddy and I are headed to the South homecoming dance with our dates and thought we'd go for a little ride before the dance. What are your plans for the evening?"

Just as one of them started to speak, Marco pointed at the smallest of the three and said, "Hey, I know you. You are Ted Duran's little brother. I wrestled Ted my sophomore year when he was a senior. It was a really tough match, and I felt lucky to come out the winner. You wrestled at 126 for East the next year if I remember right." At that, the kid knew who they had trapped at the stop light, and he probably began to feel a little trapped himself.

With a half-smile the kid said, "Yah, my name is Billy. You're The Tatts," he said loudly so that the other four guys in their group could hear. Everyone except the driver of the lead car relaxed a little, knowing that whatever they had planned wasn't going to go down. That driver was bigger and a little older than the others and didn't seem to want to back off. When Billy whispered something in his ear, the big guy let out a string of profanities ending with, "I don't care who he is!" Billy gave a little signal to his friends and all but he and the big guy started back to their cars. Then as Billy started back to his car, he slowly turned to Marco and said, "We meant no harm. We were just messing with you. Enjoy your dance with those fine-looking women in the car. I would have recognized you right off if you were in the Nomad." The big guy went back to his car in protest, but I am sure Billy informed him what they were up against had they decided to tangle with The Tatts.

As Marco rolled down his sleeves, put his suit jacket over his shoulder and climbed into the back seat of the Gran Torino, he told Betsy to memorize the license plate number on the car in front and Sheila to do the same for the car in back. My dad always kept a pen and note pad in the glove compartment, and I wrote down the numbers when the girls gave them to me. "The car in front was a '62 Dodge Dart and the other car was a '64 Plymouth Fury." Marco knew his cars. He then said, "Four things as we head straight to the dance with no more detours. First, girls, are you okay?" They both shook their heads and said they were fine. "I agree with Billy that it is easy to see that you are fine, but I was asking about your emotional state," he said with a smile.

Sheila said, "Thanks for the compliment, and, yes, we are okay. I assured Betsy that everything would be okay and that we were safe because I know my man! And you too, Nick," she said as an afterthought. "I wasn't worried at all!" We all knew that it wasn't me who would keep us all safe, but it was nice of her to say that. Marco continued.

"Second, I think it is important that we don't talk about this tonight at the dance. It would be a huge distraction because we all know how things work at South or any other high school. The only thing anyone would want to talk about all night would be us almost getting jumped and all that could have happened. We would have to repeat the same thing a hundred times and the final homecoming dance of our high school lives would not be nearly as fun as it could have been. Agreed?"

"Good idea; I think you're right; agreed; that is a plan," and other short affirming comments made it clear that we were all on the same page.

"Third, my dad's cousin, Carlo, is on the police force, so I will make sure he gets the license plate numbers and the make and models of the cars so that he can have a talk with those idiots. I heard that some guys were boxing cars in, pulling people out of their cars, and beating them up for the fun of it, but I thought it was just a rumor. Now I know better. I have clocked quite a few people over the past six to seven years, but I never thought of it as being fun. It was all in self-defense or on a need-to-get-your-butt-beat basis," which made us all laugh. Marco smiled and said, "Hey, I like that. Butt-beat-basis—a triple B—this is a triple B situation. I might use that in the future. Anyway, and fourth, let's go dance up a storm, have some real fun, and watch Lenny tear up that dance floor." I couldn't believe what I was hearing. Our friend, Birdy, was also an outstanding dancer.

It was one of those beautiful evenings that I learned could happen in Southern Colorado any month of the year. The temperature was in the low 60s, and it was perfectly calm with a nearly full moon lighting up the night. The setting made our dates even prettier than when we were all posing for pictures an hour or so earlier. We walked in the door of our festively decorated and wonderfully transformed gymnasium, and the fun began. Everyone was so upbeat that evening—smiles everywhere you looked, good music filling the gym, and a room full of people who were genuinely happy to be together. None of the school dances in Illinois felt like this. Maybe I was just happy to be walking into the dance without a red face, black eye, and bruised ego from having just been jumped by a bunch of thugs. Maybe it was the pretty girl on my arm, who made me feel so good. Or maybe it was just me, but I don't think so. What I was coming to realize was this: all of the hard work that Marco and the Boys had been doing for the previous two and a half years at South, and even before that at Corwin Junior High, was coming together. There were definitely some bullies at the dance, but they weren't doing their thing. This was a safe place where kids could just relax and have fun and be themselves without fear of getting pushed around or laughed at. Marco and the Boys had consistently set the tone, a whole bunch of kids followed his lead, and I was the Johnny-come-lately who got to slide in and be on the team. Halfway through the night, I whispered into Marco's ear, "You have done a great job at this school, and I love you for it!" Marco stepped back, shrugged his shoulders, and genuinely didn't have a clue what I was talking about. That was okay. We would have time later to talk about it, but if and when that conversation took place, he would most likely do like he did on the football field. He would point to others and give them the credit.

I got a Pepsi for Betsy and me to share, not because I was cheap but in order to put my lips in contact with hers via the common straw, then found the table Q was saving for us. Because he wanted to make a good impression on his date, Q asked the Boys and our dates to call him Frank the whole evening, and we did. No one else got the message, so everyone outside of our group called him his wide variety of nicknames, and he spent the whole night explaining to Helen why he was known by so many names. It was really amusing to listen to his answers, some made up on the spot and others surprisingly accurate. I was listening to one of his explanations when I saw Birdy on the dance floor, and that held my attention for the next few minutes. We had a DJ that evening, and Lenny had brought a stack of 45s so that he could do a variety of dances. My eyes quickly moved from Frank to the dance floor when I heard "Surfin' Bird" by the Trashmen and saw Birdy just workin' it as the lyrics shouted *everyone knows that the bird is the word.* He must have danced with three girls other than Lana, his date, on that song alone. It looked like a scene from some Frankie Avalon and Anette Funicello movie. After a couple of songs, Birdy took a break and joined us at our table.

"I am sure everyone else knows the answer, but you've got to tell me how come you are twice the dancer of every girl in this place and ten times the dancer of every guy?"

Birdy smiled and told me and the others the story. "Really, I think it's only the Boys and a few others who know why I am an insanely good dancer. Sheila and Lana know because I told them, but you might be one of the few who have asked me how I developed my skills. When I moved in with my aunt and uncle, I soon discovered that they were not social people, borderline misanthropic actually, but they did love to dance. They never invited anyone to their house, and they never accepted invitations to other's homes, but, once a week, every week of the year, they would go to the Arthur Murray Dance Studio. Since I was now part of their family, it meant that, once a week, every week of the year, I found myself in a room with a bunch of weird old people dancing to music I hated. After a few months of that, I decided that, if I had to be there, I might as well learn how to dance. Once I got out on the floor, I started to enjoy myself. All the old ladies loved to dance with me, which was kind of fun for a young kid. The instructor saw that I was athletic, so he figured I might be able to do some really cool moves and offered to teach them to me. And that's it!"

"Come on Lenny, I know there is more to the story than that," I protested.

"Maybe a little more," he said, and then continued. "For three years I spent every Tuesday evening at the Arthur Murray Dance Studio from 7–8:30. That is ninety minutes a week for 150 weeks, maybe missing two weeks a year because of sickness or holidays. If Aunt Martha and Uncle William took a vacation, we left on a Wednesday morning and came back on Tuesday in time to dance. That is 13,000 minutes of learning new dance steps and just being on the dance floor while every normal kid in Pueblo was watching TV or goofing off. Once I realized it was kind of fun, I started asking the instructor to teach me how to do popular dances, ballroom, swing, and even lindy hop. Basically, whatever I saw someone do on TV or in a movie, I wanted to learn those steps and moves until I was good enough to be on the tube or the screen. After two years of instruction, the manager of the dance studio gave me a standing offer to be an instructor for him, which I did last summer, and I think I might do that again this summer before I head off to college. At some point, I started collecting records that were good for all the styles of dance I had learned. And here we are," he said with a flair.

At that, he asked Betsy if she wanted to dance, and, after I smiled my approval, Peeps was on the dance floor with my date. So, I asked Lana to dance with me, and we hit the floor, as far away as I could get from the professional dancer known as Birdy. And that's the way it went all night. We laughed a lot, had fun on the dance floor, danced with each other's dates, drank Pepsi, and told and listened to good stories. Q had a good time, but it was a little hard on him to watch his date pay more attention to the rest of us than to him. The Boys noticed what was happening between the two of them, so we each asked Frankie what he thought about something or to tell us some story we knew would be funny and interesting to Helen. Sheila asked him to dance with her, then Lana followed suit. We tried to make it obvious that Q was an important member of our group and not just some hanger on. That seemed to help Helen turn her attention back to Frankie.

As the dance came to an end, we all danced the last dance with our dates, said goodbye to our friends, and headed to our cars. When we stepped outside at 11:00, the temperature had dropped around twenty degrees, so that gave me the opportunity to hold Betsy close to me as we walked to the Gran Torino. Once in the car she scooted close and smiled. We dropped Sheila off, she gave Marco a little kiss, and then we dropped Marco off. He thanked me for driving and told Betsy how nice she looked. When we got to Betsy's house, I walked her to the door, and she squeezed me tight, gave me a big, long kiss, and said, "I had a great time. I sure hope you will ask me out again." That certainly was good motivation to have a second date, so I told her it would happen. The next week at school I had to tell her that we would go out again, but that I wasn't ready to have a steady girlfriend. Lenny's advice about dating had sunk in, and I was committed to his approach. But that night on her porch with that tight hug and the big, long kiss and the great night we'd had at homecoming, I was ready to marry that girl the next morning.

13

The Holidays and Winter Sports Scene

SEAMLESS. IT WAS ANOTHER of the unique experiences that I had during my senior year at South. We went from football and the other fall sports to basketball, wrestling, swimming, Thanksgiving, Christmas, and New Year's without blinking. There was no talk about anything being the last time we would do this or that together; no regrets about missed opportunities; no efforts to create memories or do something to make a name for ourselves during our final year of high school. One season blended into the next, just as one class mixed with the others to make up good and fun days, weeks, months, and seasons. The one word to best describe what I was experiencing was "seamless."

I wasn't able to be at all of Marco's wrestling matches, but I made a point to bring the Boys together when South wrestled a dual match with East. Billy Duran was wrestling at 132 for East, and I used the drive across town to tell Q and Peeps about Billy and our homecoming experience with him and his gang of tough guys. I drove to East, a fifteen-minute drive that I turned into twenty-five minutes as we traced the route taken on homecoming night. Marco and I had talked about it earlier and felt like it was a good time to tell the other Boys, since we tried not to keep secrets between us. It probably didn't need to be said, but I made sure they knew that this was a story that would stay in our group until it leaked out from some other sources, namely Betsy or the guys from East.

By now, I was so used to how things went with the Boys that I was not at all surprised at how they received the story. At my old school, the group of guys I spent the most time with would have been loud and animated at everything they heard, yelling and cussing and getting really worked up. Not the Boys. They listened, laughed a little, and said, "That sounds about right; no surprises there; Marco is an absolute stud; you were smart not to tell people at the dance," and other comments along that line.

Then Peeps said, "It will be interesting to see how Marco deals with Billy when they see each other." We were all looking forward to being in the gym when the two teams walked in, so we could see how things would go down between Marco and Billy.

Q nodded and said, "Now I understand why we had to leave so early to see this match." We got to East, paid for our tickets, found a good place to sit on the visitor's side of the gym, and waited to see the pre-match, match, and post-match excitement. Hopefully, it would not include us needing to fight our way out of the gym. If Billy and his guys felt a need to save face, they could have gathered a much larger gang for that night, so a big fight was a real possibility, and something that occurred in Pueblo from time to time. Within the first two minutes of the South wrestling team walking into the gym those concerns evaporated.

When we got to our seats and looked around, there were already a couple of East wrestlers on the mat loosening up and practicing moves. Over the next ten minutes, the rest of their team sauntered in. They were a cocky bunch for sure. When I spotted Billy, I pointed him out to the Boys, and when someone on East's side yelled, "Hey, Billy," I looked up and saw the tough guy in the lead car that boxed us in on homecoming night. The Boys figured out that's who he was just by how I reacted to seeing him across from us. I was still not nearly as cool about things like that as Q and Peeps were. We found out a few days later from a cousin of Billy's who attended South, that the tough guy was Billy's uncle Chacho, who was only four years older than Billy.

The day Q heard about the four-year difference in age between uncle and nephew he informed me, "That's the way it works with us Mexicans."

Marco laughed and added, "What about the Italians? I have uncles on both sides of my family that I would have attended high school with if they lived in Pueblo. Maybe it's more of a Catholic thing." I met some Irish Catholics later in life and realized Marco was right again.

Like I said, wrestlers tend to be cocky. Maybe in such an individual sport where you can find your face in the other guy's sweaty armpit or stinky crotch, you have to have a certain attitude to get through such disgusting situations. Plus, you want to try to intimidate your opponent, so you strut, flex, and glare to establish that you are one tough motor scooter ready to roll over the guy whose butt you are about to stick your nose into. (Wrestling was not the sport for me.) For whatever reason, The Tatts didn't act cocky at all, which was not really a surprise to me. He was intense on the mat, but friendly and himself before and after the match. When South entered the gym as a unit, Marco immediately left the team and walked over to East's squad. It was customary to turn your back on your opponents when they entered your gym, so when Marco came up behind the East wrestlers and tapped Billy on the shoulder, everyone was shocked, especially Billy. Marco smiled, stuck out his hand, and told us later that he wished Billy good luck and that Billy would have his hands full with South's wrestler. When Billy shook Marco's hand, someone yelled out from East's stands, "Billy, you take care of business tonight, bro." Marco glanced into the stands and saw that it was Billy's uncle who had yelled, and, from that moment on, Marco's friendly demeanor turned into a very intense approach to the rest of the evening. Right then I figured that whoever Marco was wrestling that night would have wished that Billy's uncle had been more low-key before the match.

It was a close match between the two teams, but everyone figured South would win because they were stronger in the heavier weights. Just as Marco predicted, Johnny DeCarlo beat Billy in a 5–3 decision, and, as Marco greeted Johnny when he walked off the mat, he also yelled out, "Nice match, Billy." Billy didn't acknowledge Marco, but then getting beat on a mat in front of about 150 people can be a pretty humbling experience. The match continued to be close and, by the time Marco shook hands with his opponent, South needed a five-point victory from Marco to guarantee a South victory. That meant that Marco needed to pin the East wrestler, and, boy, oh boy, did he pin that poor kid.

Marco's intensity was impressive. It was as if, in that moment, there were only three people in the whole world—Marco, his opponent, and the ref. He was always so confident that he didn't seem to need to be intense, but it was obvious to the Boys that something was going on with our buddy. When the referee blew his whistle, Marco moved in, grabbed the kid, slammed him to the mat, put a cradle on him, rolled him up on his shoulders, and the ref hammered his hand on the mat. Pinned in nine seconds! It was probably even a little faster than that, but the ref was caught off guard and was a little slow to react. Wrestlers have to shake hands at the end of a match, so Marco grabbed his hand, pulled him close and said, "Sorry to have to do that to you," then turned and stared at Billy's uncle for around five seconds. In that moment there were only two people in the world—Marco and Chacho.

Marco rejoined the world as he walked back to the South bench. He had sent a clear message with that stare of what would have happened to Uncle Chacho that night if Billy hadn't taken charge. The Boys tracked with Marco's stare and saw that Chacho looked away pretty quickly, but he got the message, and Marco got mobbed when he went to the bench. None of the guys had ever seen a pin in under ten seconds. Marco's final two teammates to wrestle that night were so motivated by what they'd just seen that they both pinned their opponents, giving South an easy win in their first, dual wrestling match of the season.

The East crowd was shocked and silent after what they'd witnessed, and the entire team was shaken by the experience. The team and coaches sat in their chairs with head in hands as South walked out, all except Henry Jones, the wrestler Marco had destroyed. Henry jogged to the locker room as soon as the final whistle blew after the heavyweight match. Jones won as many matches as he lost that year, so he was a decent wrestler. But not that night he wasn't. He looked like a guy who'd never wrestled before. As South's wrestlers jumped around and celebrated their victory, Marco walked across the mat and asked Billy to tell Henry that he was sorry to do that to him. Billy never looked up, but he nodded his head. South's team and fans left the gym with no problems. The next day at school there was a buzz about the match until just after lunch, then everything calmed down and went back to normal. Seamless.

It was a Thanksgiving Day tradition on Belmont to play a big game of street, flag football at 10:00am. Everyone on the block played, coached, or officiated from a lawn chair overseeing the field of play. I was told that some years the officials outnumbered the players because everyone on the block was so excited to participate. William and Martha—Lenny's uncle and aunt—were somehow able to push aside their anti-social behavior one day a year to behave like good neighbors and even act as the head officials for the game. By all accounts, they would make up a new rule or two every year and sometimes change the rules on the fly. All of the cars that normally parked on the street had to be moved to a driveway or the alley by 9:30 on Thanksgiving morning. If a new family moved onto the block, they had to provide a brand-new football for their first Thanksgiving Day game. Dad happily went to Herb's Sporting Goods on the Saturday before the game and bought the finest Spaulding football in Herb's store. The football was to be brought outdoors at 9:45 when teams would be chosen, and the head officials would direct everyone where to set up their lawn chairs in order to officiate the game properly, whatever that meant.

William and Martha would divide the teams with something random like, "Everyone with a middle name beginning with A-L is one team," then add, "Joe, make sure the teams are pretty equally matched." Everyone who was playing had to provide their own flag and a headband. The winners of the coin toss then decided if they wanted to wear the headband, which, according to tradition, they always did. The two teams were called HB and NHB—headbands and non-headbands. Only out-of-town visitors were allowed to play in the Belmont Grandiose Bowl, the name given the game by Peeps three years earlier. Otherwise, it was a Belmont Street, residents-only game. Mom's cousin, Verla, and her husband, Dave, were in town visiting for our first Thanksgiving away from Illinois, so they got to play, but it didn't change the talent level on the street since they were both very enthusiastic non-athletes. At exactly 10:00am, William blew the whistle for opening kick-off even though half of our team, the headband team, still did not have their flags in place and headbands on, but that didn't matter. When the whistle blew, one of our HB teammates ran up and kicked the ball because the exactly-one-hour game always began on time. What a hoot!

As soon as the ball was kicked, Martha called a six-yard penalty on us for not having our headbands on. The first play from scrimmage, she awarded the NHB a touchdown since we still didn't all have our headbands on and flags in place, and that's the way the whole game went. About ten minutes into the game, William called a timeout in the middle of an NHB play and ordered them to do a square dance for sixty seconds on threat of forfeiture of the game if they didn't. William would be the caller and the HB team would surround the NHB team and clap to the rhythm he "would clearly call out." Both teams protested and made it clear that, although William was commissioner of the Belmont Grandiose Bowl (BGB) and the head official, he was not the dictator. After a brief protest by William, he blew his whistle and the game continued. Eighty-year-old Mrs. Brown threatened the HBs with a penalty if her seven-year-old grandson didn't score a touchdown in the next two minutes, so we made sure he did. It was both the worst football game and the most fun I'd ever had playing football in my life. Someone on the street or on the lawns was laughing for the entire 3,600 seconds of the game. When William blew the game-ending whistle, I yelled out, "Who won?"

William looked at a notebook and said, "HB 625 and NHB 673." Peeps later explained to me that it was a running total of all the scores over the years. It was a never-ending and seamless football game even though the teams were totally random. It made no sense at all, but I loved it because the game was all about the community and not the competition. Football was simply a tool to bring the block together, and it could only happen on Belmont Street!

The Peeples family had their Thanksgiving meal catered the night before, so they had it warming in the oven while the game was being played, and they were eating by 11:30. The Luna and Tattalinni families had their own rituals and did their own things, but food was on the stoves and turkeys in the ovens while the game was playing. It was a beautiful sixty-three-degree day, and, with doors open to their homes, glorious smells filled the air around the playing field. Our family tradition was to eat promptly at 1:00pm, and the BGB would not change that tradition. Dad cooked the turkey, and Mom always prepared the same thing—mashed potatoes and gravy, cornbread stuffing, homemade rolls, green bean casserole, corn casserole, sweet potatoes, and pumpkin pie. I knew what we would eat, and I knew everything would taste great—that is, everything except the sweet potatoes. Mom was the only one in our family who liked them, so she made them for herself.

The Tatts and I had a talk the Sunday before T-Giving about what to do after the big meal. He explained to me that Lenny's aunt and uncle would start drinking early in the afternoon and be wasted by about 4:00. Q's folks would be tired and a little drunk about the same time, so it would be a good idea for our two buddies to have someplace to go late that afternoon to get away from their families. Since Q usually showed up at the Tattalinni home every T-Giving afternoon looking for seconds, it would be a good idea for me to invite Birdy to our home for the same. My folks agreed. Birdy showed up, gorged himself on Mom's warmed up feast, and forever endeared himself to my mother with repeated compliments on her cooking. At 6:50, Tatts pulled up in front of the house and the four of us headed over to Sheila's house for another round of dessert.

On the way to Sheila's house, Marco told Q to inform the rest of us about what he said at the Tattalinni meal table an hour earlier. "Well, Mrs. Tattalinni, who is a marvelous cook and a wonderful lady, offered me some sweet potatoes, and I just told her the truth. These were my exact words. 'My brain says tells me to be polite and eat some sweet potatoes, but my mouth says that, if you put that stuff in here, I will spit it right out! I just can't get my brain and my mouth to work together on this. It must be my taste buds that are the troublemakers. They are very sensitive fellows.' Then Mrs. Tattalinni kind of giggled and said, 'Thanks for the explanation Frankie!'" We all shook our heads and laughed at our friend.

"I hope Sheila's mom made sweet potato pie for dessert," Birdy chimed in. "There is no way in the world you will be able to turn down anything Sheila offers you."

We all nodded in agreement and laughed at the thought, but no such luck. Sheila's mom had pumpkin, apple, and pecan pies for us to choose from, and we all had a small slice of each, except for Marco who had a large slice of each. (The way Sheila's parents looked at Marco, it was obvious that they loved their daughter's boyfriend.) We ate, talked about the BGB, told stories, and left about 8:30. It was a great day. One good time and good meal flowed into the next that day. Seamless.

14

Practical Christmas

IT WAS A SURPRISING thing to hear on several different levels. On our way to school, The Tatts announced, "Our Christmas event this year will be at my house, but, Nick, since you're the new guy, you decide what we will be doing that evening." How could Christmas be just ten days away? It seemed like it was just a few days ago that we were playing the Belmont Grandiose Bowl. I had been so busy with the Carolaires singing at a variety of events around town, attending wrestling matches and basketball games, and going on a few dates that Christmas just appeared out of nowhere. Once the news sunk in, I asked the Boys what it meant to be in charge of the Christmas event, and by the way, what is the Christmas event? Birdy explained.

"Every year, the Boys get together on December 23 for our Christmas event. We don't exchange presents at the event or anytime during the Christmas season. Since we are a pretty unique gang, we try to celebrate Christmas in a unique way. We each take our turn at deciding what we will do together that evening and the others happily go along. One year, Frankie decided that we would all go see a movie together. At our first Christmas event, Marco had us all watch 'Mr. Magoo's Christmas Carol,' and last year we all brought our favorite record albums to my room, drank Pepsi, ate pizza, and listened and talked about music for two hours."

"That was the only time I have ever been in Birdy's house," Q blurted out.

"Zip it," Lenny said with a stare. "So, you get to decide the agenda, but I guess The Tatts has decided it will be at his house."

Immediately, I knew what we would do for the event this year. "Having it at Marco's house is fine, but we might need a little bit of privacy because of the subject matter. December 23 will be practical joke night. Come ready to tell the best practical joke you have ever pulled on someone or had pulled on you. If you have more than one story that is fine, but you can't tell someone else's story. This has to be something that you have personally experienced. And I like the pizza and Pepsi idea, so I will steal that from Birdy."

"Sounds good. Just make sure there are no practical jokes involving the Pepsi and pizza," Marco said with a smile. I knew it would be a fun night because I could see the other boys already thinking about what they might tell us that night. My guess was that all four of the Boys would be telling their story for the first time. I knew I would!

I blinked my eyes a few times, and the next thing I knew it was December 23. At least, that's the way it seemed. Christmas was on a Wednesday that year, so our last day of school was Friday the 20th. The week leading up to Christmas, I attended four parties and an afternoon shopping marathon with my mom before the Boys met at the Tattalinni home for our event. My dad picked up three large pizzas from Ianne's Pizzeria—a Pueblo institution. He kept one for the Bradford family and sent two with me for The Belmont Street Boys. The Boys met me at the door, grinning in anticipation of our time together. Marco had a card table set up in his room with a six-pack of cold Pepsi, four plates, and plenty of napkins just waiting for me and the pizza to arrive. I opened the pizza boxes, we each found a place on the floor or the bed to sit, and I announced, "Marco, you go first. And remember, these stories stay with the Boys." They each nodded in agreement and Marco began.

"It was the summer of 1969. My dad had just bought a 1965 Chevy C/K Truck from his cousin, Joe—the Joe everyone calls Fat Joe, who lives in Trinidad. Fat Joe had bragged to my dad that it was be the best truck he ever had, the most reliable, with great gas mileage for a truck, and that my folks would drive that truck to his funeral someday thirty to forty years later. Dad had never had a truck, so he bought it from Fat Joe, and I could see right away that he was proud of his new/used truck. It was a perfect setup for a practical joke."

"Dad always kept track of the gas mileage of his cars, so I let him run through three fill-ups before I started the joke. Dad bragged that because of the standard transmission he was getting a little over twenty miles per gallon with the truck, and I convinced him to try Texaco gasoline to see if his mileage improved. He always used Conoco up to that time, but when the Texaco commercial came on TV promising better mileage, I bugged him to stop at Dalton's Texaco, less than a mile from our house, and he finally agreed to give it a try. I had a two-gallon gas can in our shed, and every few nights for the next six weeks, I would slip out after he went to bed and put a quart or so of gas in his truck. It was just enough that he wouldn't notice it on his gas gauge, but it amounted to about an extra gallon per fill up. When his gas mileage went up to twenty-two to twenty-four miles per gallon, he started singing the praises of Texaco gas, and Mr. Dalton was his new best friend. Everyone at work, on his softball team, all our neighbors, people at church, and especially all of our relatives knew what a great truck he had and that everyone should buy Texaco gasoline."

"The following four weeks, after the bragging had time to settle into most of Dad's regular conversations, I slipped out every few nights and siphoned a quart or so out his tank. When his gas mileage dropped below nineteen miles per gallon, he cleaned the spark plugs after the first tank, changed the oil after the second tank, then put in a new air filter and a little extra air in the tires, but nothing worked. He asked Mr. Dalton if he was watering down his gas, which almost caused a fight right next to pump #3. By the end of the fourth week of my practical joke, everyone at work, softball, etc. had heard that Texaco gas was unreliable and that Fat Joe might have sold him a lemon. When Dad switched back to the Conoco brand, my joke was over, and he decided that maybe his truck just ran better on Conoco."

"I can't believe I am hearing about this for the first time; that is so cool; what a great idea; how did you come up with that; way to keep a secret." It took us about five minutes to wind down from our comments and congratulations for Marco's ingenious practical joke. As I grabbed another piece of pizza, I pointed to Q and said, "Now it's your turn, my friend."

"Well, I have two jokes to tell you about. The first is that, for the past five years, I have managed to make Lenny and Marco believe that I actually like them and that they are my closest friends." Without missing a beat, Q was jumped on and pummeled by his two best friends, with all three of them laughing the whole time.

"Hey, that beating was no joke," Q said as he was rubbing his arms and legs. "You guys hit hard—way too hard when you're having fun! If the two of you ever got really mad at me and beat me up for real, which you never will because you don't want to risk losing the coolest guy in the gang, I think you'd leave me in a pain-induced coma! So, don't ever beat me up for real," he said, as he pointed and scowled at his buddies.

"Okay, here goes. This isn't really a practical joke, but it's the best I could come up with. As the three of you know, my dad isn't exactly a peach of a guy. He yells a lot, hits way too often, never compliments or encourages me, and is super quick to criticize and tell me how stupid I am. When I have a cold and need to blow my nose, he likes to say, 'If it wasn't so much, I'd have thought it was your brain.' His other favorite saying to me is, 'If you had a brain, you'd be dangerous.' If he wasn't my dad, I would avoid him every chance I got." As the three of us nodded in agreement, Q continued with, "And it's a good thing I was born with such good looks and natural self-confidence!" As usual the three of us smiled at Frankie, shook our heads, and encouraged him to continue with his story, which he did after pointing to his supposedly handsome face and saying, "You wish you had my good looks."

"Well, when I was in the eighth grade, I decided it was time to try to get even with my old man, so I made a three-part plan which would last for two weeks. If it was any longer than that, I was afraid that I might be discovered. When Dad came home from work, he would walk in the back door and take a deep breath through his nose to try and figure out what was for supper that night. Mom would usually just heat some shredded onion in a little oil and the smell of the frying onion made the old man think supper would be something tasty. It always put him in a good mood, until he started eating and compared Mom's cooking to the great meals Grandma Luna used to make. Then the fighting would begin and . . ."

"Back to the practical joke, Frankie," Marco interrupted.

"Sorry. Anyway, part one of my plan was to go to the back door two or three times a week and let a fart just before Dad walked in the door and be out of sight when he took his deep breath. Man did I enjoy hearing him say, 'Smells like chili' or whatever he guessed that night. It cracked me up every time, but I had to be sure to go to my room and laugh into my pillow." The Boys all looked at each other and nodded approval. So far so good with phase one of Q's three-part plan to get some revenge on his mean-spirited dad. Along with thinking it was pretty funny, we could all appreciate the joke he was pulling on his old man.

"Part two of the plan was to swish Dad's toothbrush in the toilet on two of the days I didn't fart at the back door. I thought about peeing on his toothbrush but decided that was too much."

"If you had told us that you did that, all three of us would have piled on you, beat the fool out of you, and put you into that pain-induced coma," Marco warned, as Birdy and I nodded in agreement.

"Q, you wanted to get even with your dad, not debase or degrade him," Birdy added.

Q pointed at Birdy and looked at us and said, "What he said. I don't know what debase means, but I know I shouldn't do it. Now, if you don't mind, stop interrupting and beating on me so I can continue with my story." He paused, looked for agreement, and continued. "Dad asked Mom if she'd switched toothpaste brands after the second toilet treatment, so I had pretty much pushed the limits on part two of my plan."

"Part three of my get-even plan was to clean out Dad's electric razor and wait for just the right time to sprinkle his own whiskers on his plate at suppertime. Dad loved pepper, and his whiskers looked like pepper, so, as I passed him the bowl or plate of whatever Mom made that night, I sprinkled a little extra seasoning as my hand passed over his food. That's when I started working on some magic tricks because my sleight-of-hand and creating a distraction while I did the deed needed to be pretty dang good!" Frankie was real good at sleight-of-hand tricks like pulling coins out of people's ears and doing card tricks, so it was easy to believe that he could pull off the pepper trick. Plus, it was also real clever.

Birdy could hardly wait to holler out, "That's why he didn't like your mom's cooking. The food tasted like Aqua Velva!"

Marco and I added our comments and laughs, concluding with me saying, "Gross, but, under the circumstances, that was a pretty good practical joke. So far, we are two for two. Our best practical jokes were played on our dads. What do you have for us, Lenny?"

"Obviously, I am going to break that streak." I felt a little bad about my observation, but Lenny took it in stride and started on his practical joke story.

"I had kind of a hard time coming up with one joke, so like Q, my practical joke is a series of little jokes played on my family. But unlike our little buddy, there is nothing disgusting in my story."

"Little buddy. I like it. Maybe you have a new nickname, Frankie,"
I said.

"Yah, add it to the list," Q popped off.

Birdy continued. "A few times, I hid my grandma's liquor bottle
from her so she wouldn't get more drunk than she already was, but that
made her so mad that she would hit me. She tried to hit my older brother,
too, but I always intercepted the slaps headed his way. It was just so funny
to watch her try to figure out where the bottle was. She would get frus-
trated and cuss, stagger around, and look in the same place five times,
then head our way swinging and yelling, 'Where's my booze?' The next
morning she'd cry and hug me and apologize, and I would wink at my
brother as I was being smothered with hugs and kisses. Billy would ask
me if the laughs were worth getting hit, and I would always say, 'Ten
times worth it.' After three or four times of that, we stopped hiding her
bottle because it just seemed too mean. She was a drunk, but she was also
our grandma, who loved us and gave us a home to live in, so the laughs
just weren't worth it, but it did give me an appreciation for the humor of
a good practical joke."

"When I moved in with my uncle and aunt, I saw in the first year or
so that he was a prime target for the same kind of practical joke. Uncle
William is so smart that I knew I had to be very subtle with my jokes and
space them out over weeks at a time. But I couldn't just pick on him. Aunt
Martha was afraid of spiders so I would do the same thing over and over
and she knew it was me every time. It was simple with her. I would sit in
the front room and shoot the rubber band from the evening Denver Post
on top of the cereal boxes which sit on the kitchen shelf with no door
on it. The next morning, when she would pull the boxes off the shelf, a
rubber band would fall in her hair or on her neck and she would start
squealing, thinking she was being attacked by a spider. When she saw it
was a rubber band, she would come at me ready to flick me in the head
with her cocked and ready-to-fire index finger, but I would dodge her fire
as Uncle William roared with laughter. I would wait a few weeks and do
it again. A couple of years into this, she made it my permanent job to get
the cereal boxes down for breakfast first thing in the morning. Tricking
Uncle William wouldn't be that easy."

"Like I said, my uncle is very intelligent, but what anyone who
works with him or is related to him knows is that he is also a creature of
habit. Really, he is obsessive compulsive, but for Q's sake I will stick with

him being a creature of habit." Frankie shrugged his shoulders and Birdy continued.

"This is probably going to sound really anti-climactic, but I would do little things like move his reading glasses two inches from their normal spot. Every evening, Uncle William sits down to read the newspaper and a magazine at 9:00 sharp. He has his glass of Highland Park Single Malt Scotch Whiskey, usually his third of the night by then, sits in his chair, puts the scotch on a coaster, then without looking reaches out and gets his reading glasses. Just watching him fumble for his glasses was kind of a big deal. Aunt Martha noticed the second or third time this happened, looked at me, and winked. From then on it was our joke. Uncle Will refused to look for his glasses before he reached because he was always very precise in placing them in the exact same spot every night. It always amazed me that he could pull that one off considering how drunk he usually was by the time I helped him to bed. I could only do that trick once a month or so, but every time it was worth a laugh and a half-drunken wink from my aunt."

"Once I had some success with the glasses trick, I expanded my repertoire, being very careful with what I did and how often I did it. Sometimes I would get the newspaper and remove a page that finished an article begun on page one. He would yell at the newspaper, threaten to stop his subscription, and Aunt Martha would look at me and wink. Every so often I would move the bookmark forward or backward from where he had been reading in his novel or slightly change the position of where he kept his house slippers every night. He would holler every time, 'Something's out of whack' and continue on with his business. Uncle William always put his wristwatch on the kitchen countertop immediately following supper and picked it up the next morning as he walked out the door for work. Every six to eight weeks, I would advance the time on his watch by two minutes. He never looked at the watch until he pulled up to work exactly five minutes early, where he would then sit in the car two minutes and calmly walk into his office right on time. On the mornings that I moved his watch forward, he would rush to his office thinking he was later than usual, readjust the watch, once he figured out that he was arriving at work early, and ask for a new watch for Christmas or his birthday or as an anniversary gift. I was never there to witness his early arrival at work, but he always gave us a play-by-play recap that night at supper, and my aunt would give me a wink. And every week for a year, I switched the two stations on the second and third preset buttons of his car radio until he was convinced that he simply couldn't keep those two stations straight. It was just a bunch of little ornery things, which made me smile. It is crazy how much enjoyment I got out of those winks from Aunt Martha. Those goofy little practical jokes were a whole lot of fun, and they surprisingly bonded me and my aunt together. That's it for me, boys. Not real exciting, but no one got hurt," Birdy concluded. High fives were spread around the room, and the last of the pizza was snarfed down, as I got ready to take my turn.

"Like the rest of you, my story involves my family. But unlike the rest of you, it was my dad and me pulling a practical joke on an obnoxious neighbor of ours in Schaumberg, a guy named Mr. Rogerson, or Roger to everyone on the block. Roger was the king of one-upmanship. If we went on a vacation, he went on one that was better. When he found out our cousin was Tom Tresh, he all of a sudden was a cousin to Ted Williams. He had a better TV than anyone in the neighborhood even if you had the exact same brand. That's the way he was about everything, but especially about his lawn. Roger kept his lawn spectacularly green, perfectly manicured, and the lawn ornaments around the edges looked like what you would see around a mansion. Roger was proud that, while the neighbors all had gas-powered lawnmowers, he used a manual push mower and also felt superior about that for some reason. No one in the neighborhood tried to keep up with Roger and, every year, the yard sign for the best lawn in our part of Schaumberg was always on proud display at the Rogerson home."

"So, let me guess. You sprayed poison on his lawn?" Q hollered out.

"Just the opposite, my devious Little Buddy. Dad came to me one night in mid-May right after Roger had fertilized his lawn and told me his plan. Dad had talked with a friend of his who knew a guy on the grounds crew at Comiskey Park. Since major league infields are spectacular, Dad talked with that friend of a friend to find out what his crew did to make the infield so green. You guys know how great the grass looks in big league parks, and you never see burnt grass from too many chemicals? Right?" The guys looked at me and nodded, and I continued.

"Dad got the inside scoop on how to get Roger's lawn to grow greener and faster than ever before. Then, Dad bought the chemicals and, starting the second week of June, I snuck into Roger's yard between around 2am and carefully spread chemicals on his lawn. I did that twice a month for two months. So, this is how it went: in the heat of the summer, Roger had to mow his lawn at least twice a week; everyone in the neighborhood congratulated Roger on his best-ever lawn, and, early on, he was proud and smug just like you'd expect him to be. As the summer wore on though, when the neighbors saw him out in the yard and stopped to tell him about their vacations or weekend getaways, Roger didn't have any stories to tell them because he had to stay home all summer to take care of his lawn. Roger went from mowing and doing his yard work with a smile on his face and an air of superiority in that grin, to being completely exhausted and beaten down by the heat and begging God for an early winter so he could get a break from yardwork. By the end of the summer, Roger had lost ten pounds, but he wasn't bragging about his weight loss or anything else. Roger had been humbled by his lawn! He bought himself a gas-powered lawn mower for Christmas, and, the following Spring, he didn't fertilize his lawn. Dad and I were the only people who knew about this until one month ago. Since we are long gone from Schaumberg, Dad told Mom about the joke, and she cornered the two of us and said, 'You boys ought to be ashamed of yourselves! But Roger deserved it!' And that is what gave me the idea for what we would do this evening."

"Great stuff; I didn't know your dad had it in him; funny; the two of you teamed up for one really cool joke." Comments like that went on for around thirty seconds, then Marco took charge.

"One last thing. It is a tradition of the Boys to finish up our annual Christmas event with one of us singing a Christmas carol for the rest of the Boys, and, since you are the new guy, it is obviously your turn. Here is a drum, two sticks, and a hat. Now, sing 'The Little Drummer Boy' for us to wrap up this fine evening." The Boys nodded in agreement, so I put the hat on and the drum harness around my neck and sang the song. When I was done, I asked Birdy what he sang when it was his turn.

"Well, the real question is what I will sing next year since this is a new tradition Marco initiated three minutes ago." Now everyone was laughing at me and mimicking my performance. On practical joke night, Marco came prepared to make sure that the last joke of the night was on me. Unlike the other practical jokes, this was one prank the Boys could and would repeat to others every chance they got.

The next day, Christmas Eve, Marco let the Boys know that we were all invited to Sheila's house again for dessert after our family activities were done on Christmas Day. All four families gave the okay, so it was set. Sheila's house at 7:00. I was looking forward to it because Mrs. Grassley was a great cook. If she made her incredible strawberry rhubarb and her best-ever coconut cream pies like she did at Thanksgiving, I could hardly wait. "It's gonna be a great day start to finish," I said to my dad. That seemed to spark something in Dad because he smiled and told me that he wanted me to have another great day over our Christmas break. Dad insisted on us hosting a New Year's Eve party at our house for the Boys and their dates. Our family would provide the food, and Dad would plan the games for the night. My dad loved games and was pretty creative in making up some of his own. When I told the Boys, they were all excited to have plans for that night already taken care of. So far, it was already a great first-Christmas season in Pueblo, and, by the sound of things, it was only going to get better.

Christmas Eve was the same every year, whether we were in Illinois or Colorado. We ate London broil steak with baked potatoes and corn casserole, attended Christmas Eve service at the First Methodist Church, came home, and Chrissie and I each opened one present of Mom's choosing (usually socks or underwear), then did a Christmas-themed jigsaw puzzle together. It was so predictable, and I absolutely loved it. I would tease Mom about it while secretly hoping that she wouldn't change a thing. Christmas Eve was completely up to her, and I totally enjoyed every moment of the tradition she had created.

Christmas Day was much more fluid. We would get up somewhere around 7:30, mostly because Chrissie couldn't stay in bed longer than that, eat the cinnamon rolls that Mom had prepared the day before, then take turns opening presents. Mom thought it was important for each of us to experience the opening of every present. That sure was hard when I was younger, but in my later teen years it made sense. It was great to see the look on Dad's face when he opened the envelope that I gave him and saw two tickets to the Colorado College vs. Denver University hockey match at the Broadmoor World Arena. He was completely surprised and really excited at the idea of the two of us taking in that event together. I had an envelope to open, and it had two one day passes to Monarch Ski Resort with permission to skip school those days to go skiing with Birdy, who had a season pass to Monarch. How cool is that? I thought. The superintendent of my school district is telling me to ditch school and go have fun! I could hardly wait to tell Birdy. The other presents were the usual sweaters, shirts, pants, along with albums by Jethro Tull and The Moody Blues. Everyone was happy with what they got for Christmas, and, as Mom was cleaning up and Chrissie was going to her room to play with her toys, Dad asked me if I wanted to go to see the early showing of the new James Bond movie "Diamonds are Forever" that afternoon. He said it started at noon at the Cooper Theater, and I quickly said, "You bet." We ate an early lunch, since, as I said, our Christmas traditions were more fluid, and Dad and I headed off to the movie.

On the way home, Dad and I talked pretty much non-stop about the movie. We both got a kick out of the stunts and the humor and agreed that Jill St. John was gorgeous. Of all of the Bond movies, this was our favorite. Maybe part of the reason was that this was the first Bond movie we'd ever seen together. I hadn't been home more than ten minutes when Q called to see if I wanted to join the Boys for the 4:30 showing of "Diamonds are Forever" at the Cooper, and I said, "You bet." We had time to see the movie and still get to Sheila's house at 7:00 for dessert. So, I ate an early supper, piled into the Nomad, enjoyed the movie, got a kick out of the stunts and humor, and agreed with the Boys that Jill St. John is a gorgeous woman. All four of us said almost simultaneously that of all the Bond movies, this was our favorite. Part of the reason for that might have been that it was the only Bond movie the four of us had seen together. As Yogi Berra would have said, "It was déjà vu all over again.." As we were speaking in glowing terms about Jill St. John, Q tried to make a case that Lana Wood was better looking than Jill St. John, but he got outvoted three to one. We finished our analysis of the movie and Jill St. John's looks just as we rang the bell to Sheila's house. It wasn't until we were telling Mr. and Mrs. Grassley about our day that I told the Boys that I had seen the movie with my dad a few hours earlier. While the Grassley's were all surprised by that news, the Boys all smiled knowing that they would have done the same thing.

Just after walking in the Grassley's front door and exchanging greetings I announced, "My dad has invited our gang of guys and their dates to our house for New Year's Eve. He loves to plan games, and Mom will have some great food, so what do you think?"

Q immediately said, "Sounds great, and, Sheila, will you be my date?" Everyone laughed, the Boys looked at each other, and nodded in agreement.

Birdy said, "Sounds like fun as long as I get to bring the notes," as we all headed for the table with the pies. (Birdy always controlled the music anytime the Boys got together).

The dessert was every bit as good as we expected it to be. I was glad I had eaten an early supper so that I had room to eat a piece of three of the four pies being offered. The strawberry-rhubarb was the best with the coconut cream barely edging out the apple for second. Birdy said the banana cream pie was the best he'd ever tasted, and Q agreed. Marco ate a piece of all four but insisted he couldn't pick a favorite. We hung around about ninety minutes eating pie, laughing, and telling the Grassleys about the great stunts in the movie, but never mentioning the gorgeous women or suggestive humor in the movie. Since we were sitting in a home with Sheila and her very pretty mom, even Q knew that it would be in poor taste to bring up that stuff. In those ninety minutes, it was again easy for me to see how much Sheila's folks had fallen in love with Marco. After that night, I noticed that they attended all of Marco's in-town wrestling matches and even showed up in Denver when Marco went to the state wrestling tourney in February. I didn't know it at the time, but five months later there would be three hearts broken by my new best friend, Marco Tattalinni.

15

New Year's Eve

ON THE WAY HOME from Sheila's house on Christmas Day, Marco informed me that the time between Christmas Day and New Year's Eve was always a free time for the Boys. That week was dedicated to being with family, other friends, girlfriends, and whatever else we wanted to do. I shrugged and thought that sounded cool, then started to make plans the next morning for what I thought would be a good use of my time. It felt a little strange to be making plans that didn't include the Boys, but, hey, maybe it would be a good thing to branch out a little.

With all of those free days and no homework or music rehearsals or school responsibilities of any kind, I decided to pack in all of the fun activity that I could. There were movies, an ice-skating date in Colorado Springs, a snow-tubing trip to the mountains with several Carolaires, a party with kids from church, and I even took my little sister and two of her friends to a concert at the city auditorium. It was kind of fun not having to think about what the Boys would be doing as a group, but, as New Year's Eve got closer, I started to get more and more excited about being with the best friends I'd ever had. Dad was getting excited, too, and he kept telling me not to worry when I asked him about the games for the night. "This has to be a fun night," I said a couple of times, and Dad calmly replied every time I brought it up, "Don't worry, Sonny Boy, it will be memorable." Every time he used the word "memorable," he said it slowly, accompanied with a smile and a little laugh.

"Just as long as it's not memorably bad," I said once, and Dad saw how nervous I was about the big party I was hosting.

"Trust me, Nick," Dad confidently stated as he patted me on the back. I trusted my dad, but doggone it, this is the Boys and their dates in my home! We can't mess this up! My date was going to be Cindy Reynolds, a girl from East that I'd met at a District 60 choral event. Hanging around the Boys had given me confidence like I'd never had before, so when I saw Cindy again, downtown with some of her friends on Dec. 28, I walked right up and asked her to come to the party with me. But I knew that one lousy party at my house could badly shake my newfound confidence in just one night. Mom's food would be great, Birdy's music would be the coolest, and the Boys would be fun like usual, so the only unknown was my dad and his games. But after the party that night, I would never doubt my dad again.

Naturally, Marco would be bringing Sheila to the party. Cindy would be coming with me, but I didn't find out until the afternoon of the party who Peeps and Q would have with them. It was an absolute surprise to hear that Sheila's best friend, Lana Jones, would be Q's date, although she made it clear that she would be the fourth girl at the party to keep the numbers even, but she in no way could be called Q's date. She would come to the party and leave the party with Marco and Sheila but would pair up with Frankie when a game required couples, and that was it! She threatened to slug Q if he ever called her Lana Luna, which was his pet name for her. Q would look at her with the Luna-look and say, "Admit it, someday you want to be Lana Luna." That look and statement usually earned him a punch in the arm and a Lana-scowl. Lana had broken up with her boyfriend a few weeks earlier and jumped at the chance to come to a party with us, even though "us" included the guy who had a bad crush on her and zero chance of ever winning her favor. Peeps would be bringing a college girl named Gina Martinez, who he had met at the University of Southern Colorado library one day. They'd talked a little from time to time when they were both at the library, and when he ran into her waitressing at Sam and Ray's Pizza and asked her to go to a New Year's Eve party with him, she said yes. It was crazy. Birdy was at the restaurant on a date with another girl, but, when she went to the ladies' room, he took the opportunity to ask Gina out. That guy never ceased to amaze me. Gina was from La Junta and was a sophomore in college. She had no idea, when she said yes to Peeps, that she would be going to a party with high school kids. She thought Peeps was a college student since she met him at the library. On the way to my house, Peeps told her who would be at the party, so she walked in the front door with a too-cool-for-school attitude. But it didn't take long for Sheila and Lana to make both Cindy and Gina feel at home. Everyone started snacking, mingling, listening to music, catching up on the week's activities, and, by the time Dad began the first game all eight of us were on board and fully involved in the evening.

Lenny brought more music than we could listen to in our eight-to-midnight party, but he wanted to see how the evening went and have the right tunes to match the mood of the evening. He always had music from bands we'd never heard of, and that night was no exception. Along with familiar stuff like The Beatles' "Revolver" album, "Pet Sounds" by The Beach Boys, and "What's Going On," by Marvin Gaye, he also had albums by The Jeff Beck Group, Larry Norman, The Stooges, Savoy Brown, The Moody Blues, Spirit, and Mountain. Birdy was always way ahead of the rest of us when it came to cool music, so when we weren't making too much noise playing one of Dad's games, I always had my ear tuned to the background music. Before heading back to school a few days later, I bought "Only Visiting this Planet" by Larry Norman, "The Family that Plays Together" by Spirit, and "The Jeff Beck Group." It took me trips to four record stores before I found the Larry Norman album, but it was worth the effort. Thank you, Lenny Peeples!

"Let the games begin," rang out at exactly 9:00pm. Dad's announcement began what turned out to be a really fun, three-hour binge on a wide variety of games. When Dad made the announcement, I saw Gina look at Birdy and roll her eyes.

After the first game she clapped her hands and made her own announcement: "Alright, so what's next?"

Dad got everyone's interest when he said, "Our first game will be a kissing contest." Lana shot back, "I lose. The rest of you can kiss up a storm, but I am sitting this one out."

Dad laughed and continued, "It's not what you think. My lovely assistant, Lucille, will be bringing out cardboard cutouts of movie stars and assigning each of you one of those stars. Each cardboard cutout is a life-sized movie star, just like the ones you see at a movie theater. You will each take a turn kissing your star for no more than ten seconds while the rest of you judge the quality of kisses given by your friends. Everyone will be given seven small pieces of paper on which you will score each contestant with the pencil you will also receive, and each score will be handed in to my lovely assistant, Lucille, before the next kiss begins. After each kiss, you will score the quality of that kiss on a scale of one to ten, with ten being great and one being pathetic. (It was funny for me to hear Dad giving such precise instructions. He was playing the role of a game show host to a Tee.) My lovely assistant, Lucille, will collect the scores, tabulate the results, and the male and female winners will each receive . . . A NEW CAR!!" Mom held up two little matchbox cars and paraded them around the room. All of the Boys and their dates laughed at Dad's excitement and Mom playing the role of one of those game show girls on "The Price is Right."

"Or you can choose a bag of Peanut M&M's, a Big Hunk, Payday, or Snickers if you prefer," Dad added. "Pass out the Hollywood stars if you would please, lovely assistant, Lucille." For the rest of the night, if Mom helped with anything, Dad and all of the party attenders referred to Mom as 'lovely assistant, Lucille.' She really got a kick out of that.

Here's how the Hollywood stars lined up with the real people at the party: Q had Marilyn Monroe; Marco had Sophia Loren; Birdy had Gina Lollobrigida, which made us all laugh since his date was also Gina; I had Ann Margret; Lana had Tony Curtis; Sheila had Sean Connery, AKA James Bond; Gina had Cary Grant; and Cindy had Paul Newman. We went in male/female order, with a guy kissing first followed by his date. I was up first and thought I did a decent job, but really had no clue of what to do. I put my hand behind Ann's head and laid a big one on her, which had everyone cheering. That kind of set the stage so that everyone knew how to improve on what I'd done. Going first pretty much insured that I would not be a winner, but it was fun to start the ball rolling. Every kiss got whoops and hollers, but when it was Gina's turn, she started off with a little peck on Cary's lips, went back for a little longer kiss, than finished with an aggressive attack. The girl who started off the night being too-cool-for-school ended up being more into the games than anyone else at the party. When the winners were announced, everyone knew Gina would be the girl, but when Dad said, "Frankie Luna" for the boys' winner, Q insisted on givingan acceptance speech.

"I would like to thank all the peaches and plums that helped me practice up for this moment." When he said peaches and plums, he made kissing motions with his lips. "But truly, it was the alfalfa that put me over the top," he said, making a point to stick out his tongue as he said alfalfa. "And, I have to say that Marilyn Monroe is the worst kisser ever. I got nothing from her."

"Get your car and sit down, Romeo," Lana shouted. Gina had to show everyone her cool car and share an M&M with whoever wanted one. She took a car and the M&M's, but she deserved it. It was then that she looked at Dad and said, "Alright, what's next?" I think she was ready to win the next contest. Next, we played a couple of games Dad made up that involved moving around in circles and putting body parts together, elbows on knees and that sort of thing, along with jumping on someone's back while music played. From there it was Twister, and then a calmer contest of getting to know each other by telling two true things and one false thing about yourself, with everyone trying to guess the lie. Next, the lovely assistant, Lucille, taught us all how to make a dart out of a straight pin and some thread. Once we'd each made one dart apiece, we tried to shoot the darts through a straw at balloons pinned to cardboard. We each had our own straw, but we got four shots at balloons, and the one who popped the most balloons won a prize. Cars and candy were the prizes all night long. What we didn't know at the time was that the balloon-popping contest was really just a lead into what Dad was about to announce. "And now for the grand finale of the evening, drum roll please, lovely assistant, Lucille . . . Pin the Tail on the Jackass!" The Boys looked at each other with a level of concern because of the way Dad looked at us when he said jackass. And we were right to be concerned!

Mom brought out every pillow in the house as Dad was giving instructions. He had the Boys get on the floor side by side, pressed closely up against each other, and Mom placed pillows on our backs and necks as Dad gave our dates instructions. "Each girl will be given two darts to go with her straw; each girl will stand behind this line and will be given two, and only two, opportunities to shoot the dart into the rear end of her date, from the distance of twelve feet. For every dart that hits its mark in one of those jackasses, the shooter will get to keep their dart and the jackass will receive one or two band aids, depending on how accurate and powerful the shooter is. Lana, you are up first."

Lana's first dart missed low and into the carpet, according to the commentary the Boys were hearing from our stationary and vulnerable positions on the floor. When Dad said, "Okay, dart number two," Frankie tensed up and then relaxed when the girls were yelling with excitement. "Didn't that hurt?" Lana yelled. "No," Q matter-of-factly replied. Q wore corduroys to the party, and we guessed that the dart had penetrated one of the fabric folds but hadn't reached his butt. We told him to hold still to be sure that the needle didn't wiggle to one side or the other and make contact with his skinny rear end.

"It's not easy to hit The Unbutt," I said. When Cindy asked what that meant, Sheila explained. "Since the 7-Up commercial came out calling it the uncola, the Boys have called him The Unbutt since he lacks what the rest of them have. An actual rear end."

The Boys were talking among themselves the whole time. Just as I was saying that it couldn't hurt that much to get stuck, Cindy shot her first dart and scored a direct hit. "Owwwww, owww, owww, oweee that stings! Man alive, that hurts." What was more startling than the pain I felt was how hard our dates, the Boys, and my parents were laughing at my pain. "Wait till you get shot. You won't be laughing then," I said to Marco and Lenny. Cindy's second shot went high and into a pillow, probably because she was laughing too hard to be accurate with her second dart. Gina was next.

"More arch," we could hear the girls advise Gina after her first dart fell short. Just as Birdy was saying that he wished he had worn blue jeans instead of slacks to the party, his sentence was cut short with howls of surprised agony as the second dart penetrated his hiney. Even with all his pain, Birdy started laughing when The Tatts asked, "Do you have bleed?" When Marco's little sister, Mary, was two years old, she would cry and say, 'I have bleed' whenever she scraped a knee or had some sort of cut. Marco thought that was super funny, so he began to say that whenever he was bleeding, and it stuck.

"I have bleed," Lenny hollered over and over again, acting like he was crying from the pain. The Boys couldn't stop laughing, but we held our places on the firing line.

"Will someone please bring us a box of Kleenex over here. Our heads are down, and we are getting a little snotty with all this crying and laughing going on." The lovely assistant, Lucille, responded quickly to my request, just before Sheila completed the grand finale game in royal fashion.

Marco had just told us that there is no way that Sheila would be willing to shoot him in the rear. "She is just too kind of a person to . . . yowza that hurts!! I was determined not to make a noise if she shot me, but I couldn't help . . . dad gum that is painful!! Twice. You shot me twice!!! You are walking home tonight, Grassley!!" No one had ever heard Marco call Sheila by her last name and that just added to the laughter. The Boys jumped up to see our dates and my parents lying on the couch, the floor, or bent over a chair laughing their heads off. Three of us hurried to the bathroom to see if we needed band aids. I didn't, but Marco and Birdy did. The Tatts and Peeps were laughing so hard, that it was almost impossible for them to have a steady enough hand to peel the band aid wrappers and stick them to their bleeding butts. I volunteered to peel a band aid wrapper, but that was all I was willing to do.

In the midst of that crazy scene in the bathroom, Birdy looked at me and said, "Man that was funny, but I don't ever want to play that game again."

When we came out of the bathroom and things had finally calmed down, my dad announced, "As much fun as that was, I believe that is the one and only time we will play that game. I don't think it is possible to top what we just experienced. What are the chances that I would ever find four, good-natured, good-sport jackasses like The Belmont Street Boys who would be willing to make darts that would be later used against them?" (I couldn't believe Dad knew about that name for our gang or that he used it that evening). Everyone agreed with how funny the game was and that it should be retired, laughed a little more, and then prepared for our Pepsi toast to welcome in the New Year.

We counted down the clock, yelled Happy New Year, drank a toast to 1973, and then kissed our dates. Even Lana let Q give her a little peck on the cheek. He commented that she was just a little bit better that Marilyn Monroe, got slugged in the arm, naturally, and then we all headed home. Everyone thanked my parents for such a great night. Gina had so much fun that she kissed my mom on the cheek and hugged my dad. The college girl had come to the conclusion that it could be cool, once in a while, to hang out with certain high school kids. When I drove Cindy home and walked her to her door, she gave me a very nice kiss. She had such a good time that it felt like a she-wanted-to-spend-more-time-with-me kind of kiss. I made note of that and dated her two more times before leaving for college.

16

District and State Wrestling

THE DAY BEFORE OUR second semester courses started, Birdy and I hit the slopes at Monarch Mountain. He was a whole lot better than I was on skis—well, really, Birdy was a lot better than me at most everything, but it was a great day of cutting through a couple of inches of fresh powder. We skied fast, caught some air, I crashed hard a few times, but, by the end of the day, I was much better on skis after learning from someone who was an eager teacher on the finer art of bombing down the slopes. It was a great day together.

Once school was going strong, Q was singing the praises of his Biology 1 teacher, Mr. Price. Q was the only senior in the class, so Mr. Price gave Q lots of freedom to mouth off and add to his joke repertoire. Mr. Price was known for making lots of corny jokes, like pointing at a certain part of a flower and asking for the anther; warning the class to be careful when dissecting an egg or the yoke will be on you, and lots of other really bad jokes. Q added a few new ones to Mr. Price's repertoire of jokes and goofy questions that he would then repeat to every class, every year, probably for the rest of his career. "I know I can trust you because The Price is Right; when Darwin found all the finches in the Galapagos Islands, did he discover any chain link finches; if blowing gigantic snot bubbles is part of the mating ritual for male harp seals, why aren't they extinct," were three of his comments that lived on after Q's days in Bio 1 were over.

Mr. Price did a great job keeping Frankie's attention by making a statement, pointing at Q, and expecting him to start singing a pop or rock song that made his point for him. When Mr. Price covered evolution, he asked the class what they thought, then pointed at Q, and Q tore off into The Monkeys, "I'm a believer yah, yah, yah, yah." When the class started losing focus and grades started to slide it was The Jeff Beck Group song, "Goin' down. Down, down, down, down." And when the class wasn't listening, it was Q belting out the Led Zeppelin lyrics "Communication breakdown," which he had to sing at least once a week. Even though Q informed Mr. Price on the first day of class that "listening is not my strong suit," Mr. Price got Q's attention and held it all semester long. School was easy, and learning was fun for the other Boys, but Biology 1 was the only A that Frank Luna got during his three years at Pueblo South High. The Price Was Definitely Right!

The District 60 Wrestling Tournament took place in early February, and we figured that Marco would take first and receive a number three seed for the state tourney—that's exactly what happened. There was one wrestler from the Denver area and one from the Western Slope who had wrestled tougher competition that year, so they got the higher seeds. Marco wasn't concerned about his seed. He just loved to get on the mat and compete against whoever his opponent was at the time. Before getting on the mat for the first time at districts, Marco found Henry Jones—the wrestler from East that he had manhandled earlier in the season—and encouraged him as best he could. When Henry won his first-round match, Marco congratulated him, but that was as far as Henry would go, getting beat by a guy, who then got beat in the following round, so there would be no wrestle back for Henry. Marco, on the other hand, cruised until the semi-finals where he won a five-to-three decision against a very solid technical wrestler. His moves were better than Marco's, but his strength was no match for The Tatts. Marco pinned his opponent for the district championship, and Sheila's parents, who were at all of Marco's matches that weekend, looked every bit as proud as the people that surrounded them—the Tattalinni clan. Marco made the crowd of thirty-to-forty family members very proud of him that day, but not nearly as proud as they were a week later when he went to state as the Number Three seed in his weight class.

The Monday after districts, a huge storm blew in, and Dad cancelled school district-wide. With eighteen inches of wet, heavy snow on the ground, it seemed to him that cancelling school was his only option. When Mom didn't wake me up with her usual, "It's time to get up, Sunshine," I figured there was no school that day, and I was right! According to the Boys, it was the only snow day they'd ever had. It took a new superintendent to do it, but they were glad it finally happened. Marco called me at around 9:00 and shouted, "It's party time! Mrs. Grassley invited us to their house to play in the snow, eat lots of food, and generally goof off for the day. But how do we get there?"

I told him that I had that one covered and to be ready at 11:30. As soon as we hung up, I called my fellow Carolaire, John Stjernholm, who had a four-wheel-drive Jeep Wagoneer, and he gladly agreed to pick us up to join the party. Q was already out shoveling snow from sidewalks and driveways in the neighborhood. When the snowfall was two to four inches, Q would make around six bucks by clearing the sidewalks of the elderly in the neighborhood. Q bragged to us later that he'd made $47.50, since no one on Belmont, Brown, or Acero wanted to shovel all that snow without at least some help. As our good buddy was seizing the opportunity to make a killing in the snow removal business, the rest of us were seizing the opportunity to kill the day with pretty girls, good food, and all fun all the time.

Years later someone asked me what my favorite day in high school was, and with no hesitation I said, "The snow day my senior year." We made snow men, built an igloo, and had several spontaneous snowball fights. At the end of the final snowball fight of the day, the guys turned on the girls who were on their side, picked them up, and dumped them into the deepest snow drifts we could find in the neighbor's yard since most all the snow in Sheila's yard had been turned into snowmen and our super-cool igloo. I picked Lana up, and she feigned helplessness as I carried her to the chain link fence and dumped her in the drift that had collected there. Lana was a cheerleader and a pretty good gymnast, who was probably strong enough to fight me off, but, in that moment, she was a damsel in distress. I almost fell in love with her on the spot. Lana and I had dated a few times, but when her older brother, Dan, brought a friend home from college over Spring Break and he got a good look at Lana, my chance at romance with her quickly evaporated. Sixteen months later, Lana would become Mrs. Shawn Trousdale. I often said, "Her loss," when friends asked me about her, but I never really believed what I said. Even though she broke my heart by falling for a 21-year-old, college senior, that snow day was still my favorite day of high school.

We all seemed to get cold about the same time, so the party moved inside where we warmed up with hot chocolate, ate sandwiches, and played some games. Mrs. Grassley insisted that we sing two songs before we left, so John played "A Song for You," by Leon Russell, which the guys had to sing to the girls, and the girls serenaded us with "Big Yellow Taxi," by Joni Mitchell. When Mrs. Grassley waved the sheet music to both songs in our faces and told us what we had to do, most of us protested because it just sounded corny. But since she hosted the party and had a piano in the front room, we honored her request, and it ended up being a lot of fun. Marco was the only non-singer in the bunch, but, by the end of our song, he grabbed Sheila and belted out *but we're alone now and I'm singing this song for you.* Well, they weren't really alone, but the look in her eyes communicated that Marco and Sheila were the only people in her front room right then. Since Sheila was already in love with Marco, that little bit of tenderness didn't change a thing, but it also didn't hurt a thing either. On our way home, Birdy looked at me and said, "There will be around a foot of fresh powder at Monarch, so how about two days in a row of missing school and having fun in the snow?" I gave him a thumbs up, told my folks the plan, and they gave me the okay. "Dang, life is good," I repeated several times before nodding off to sleep that night.

It was just two days before the state wrestling tourney began when Birdy and I headed back to Monarch. It was the second of the two one-day passes that Dad gave me for Christmas, and the second day that Dad would allow me to skip school that year. Birdy and I would be hitting the slopes while all of our friends were hitting the books. I was so excited I could hardly contain myself. When we got to Monarch, it was a perfect day. There were eight-to-ten inches of fresh powder with no wait in the lift lines. We skied from the time we got there at 9:00 until early afternoon when I decided it was break time, literally!

Birdy had built up a little jump on a blue slope that we'd been going down together. He would hit it full speed and catch some serious air, and I would hit it at less than half speed and catch some decent air, for me anyway. As my confidence got better and better, my airtime increased. I was probably trying to impress my buddy, but I tried the jump going too fast and made an impressive crash landing. Birdy skied up to me laughing and spraying me with a face full of snow as he stopped, asking, "Are you okay?" expecting to hear me laugh and say, "Man that was fun."

I smiled, laughed a little, and said, "I can't lift my left arm." Birdy helped me down the mountain and got our lunches out so we could eat them as we drove home. All in all, it was a nice trip down the mountain and along the Arkansas River. We ate our sandwiches and fruit pies, drank a couple of bottles of Pepsi, listened to and talked about the eclectic cassette tapes Birdy had recorded. Once home, my parents took me to the Corwin Hospital emergency room where we found out what Birdy and I had already expected would be true. It was a broken collar bone. There went my baseball season!

With my arm in a sling, I headed out the door Wednesday morning at the usual time, but instead of the Canyon Coral Nomad sitting in front of my house, it was Birdy's 1969 Chevelle SS. Marco had some kind of a stomach virus and was going to come late to school. The district rules were that if you weren't in school the day before competition, you would not be allowed to compete the following day. So, Marco showed up just before third period, went to class for one minute and then headed to the nurse's office. He did that for the rest of the school day, and, when I saw him, he looked terrible. "I'll be fine," he would say to everyone, but the Boys doubted it. Marco was one sick cookie, or one nasty slice of pizza as he would occasionally say, the day before he would need to be at his best for the Colorado State Wrestling Championships. Seeing Marco like that made me forget all about my broken collar bone and lost baseball season. The Tatts was a much better athlete than I was, and what he had been working forward to all season long and what most all of South High was hoping for could easily end up in one big, fat, ugly forfeit. Speaking of big, fat, and ugly, with my head hanging low at the thought of Marco having to forfeit, I walked right into Carl the Bull and remembered right away that my collar bone was broken. Wowie zowie did that hurt! Carl must have been sad for Marco, too, because he just looked at me, pointed at my sling, shrugged, and said, "Sorry," then walked off. That was a first—the Bull felt bad about causing someone else pain.

Thursday at noon, Marco and his parents left for Denver and went straight to the motel where the team was staying. The rest of the team, the four wrestlers, who qualified for state, and the coaches headed out for the Denver Coliseum and then to their motel. Marco stayed in his own room, but there was an adjoining door so that Mrs. Tattalinni could help her son if he got sick during the night, which he did. When Marco stepped onto the mat Friday morning for his first match, his singlet was looser than normal. The Tatts would easily be the lightest wrestler at state in the 185-pound class.

Just before his match began, I sat next to Mr. Tattalinni and asked him about how Marco was doing. He shook his head a little and said, "He is pretty sick. We would have kept him home today if it were a normal school day, but, dad gum, that kid is tough. He ate a little something, threw it up fifteen minutes later, smiled, looked at his mom and said, 'I will be okay.' Last night, we talked a strategy for the day, and Marco felt that his best bet was to be really aggressive and go for early pins so that he could get off the mat as soon as possible to conserve energy. That sounded really smart to me, so I told him that was the way to go. We called in the coaches, and they agreed with us. It was really risky since he would be exposing himself to counter moves from the kind of good wrestlers you run into at state! It could end up getting him pinned, but that was really his only chance to advance. "Man, I am proud of that kid," he said as he turned away to keep me from seeing that he was getting choked up.

Marco's first-round opponent was a wrestler from Cherry Creek High School in the Denver area. The two of them danced around the mat for the first thirty seconds or so, which is pretty customary stuff. By then, Mrs. Tattalinni was out of her seat, leaning in between the rails, which separated the stands from the Coliseum floor, slapping the wall, and yelling at the top of her lungs, "You wrestle, Marco; Marco, you wrestle; wrestle, boy, wrestle!" She was so emotional over her son being on the mat when he should have been home in bed that she was kind of going a little crazy. Just then Marco shot for the other kid's legs, pulled them to his chest, slammed him to the mat, and had a pin in 1:23. Mrs. T was screaming, "Good job, Son," as Marco shook hands with the defeated wrestler and his coach, then ran off the mat where Coach DeVito had a bucket waiting for him in case he needed to throw up, which he did. Marco threw up and dry heaved for almost as long as the match lasted. All of his family and friends just hung their heads. Sheila and her mom cried. And then an interesting thing happened.

A lady walked up to Mrs. T and asked, "Are you Marco's mom?"

Mrs. T nodded and said, "Yes," barely making eye contact.

The lady continued speaking. "I am the mother of the boy your son just beat. My name is Elizabeth." Mrs. T sat up and apologized for being so loud during the match. "It's just that my son is so sick, and I just didn't know what to do with all that I was feeling, so I yelled and waved my arms in order to keep from crying my eyes out the whole time."

"You don't need to apologize at all," Elizabeth said. "I am a nurse, and, when I saw Marco throw up after the match, I got as close as I could to your son to see his skin color and overall physical condition. He was staggering after he vomited, and he is obviously dehydrated and terribly weakened by whatever his illness is. I think he needs to get hydrated with IV fluids and meds to calm his stomach. If it is okay with you, I will call my doctor, and he will get word to the ambulance sitting outside the Coliseum to get your son in there ASAP and get him some help. That should give Marco a little more strength for his next-round match, and then, when he is done for the day, get him some spaghetti for a carb-load, which should help him a little tomorrow. Make sure he goes easy on the meatballs. Even though he needs the protein, his stomach still won't be able to handle too much. Good luck."

Mrs. Tattalinni gave the woman a long, hard, absolutely Italian hug, which means two rounds of hugging and a little kissing, then took off to find her son and get him to the ambulance. The treatment worked well enough to get Marco through the next two rounds that day, but he had to be carried off the mat following his third-round, 4:40 pin of a wrestler from Centennial he had pinned twice before that year in under two minutes both times. Three matches on the day and three pins. So far so good, but Marco was weak, thin, and the coaches from his next round opponent had seen the risky moves Marco had been taking and would no doubt have their guy ready to counterattack. The only thing he could do now was to eat some pasta, drink lots of lemonade, and go to bed from seven to seven to try to gain strength for three more rounds of wrestling on Saturday. For the first time all season, no one mentioned what had been our regular topic of conversation—Marco winning a state championship. Now, we just hoped he could survive one more round and not get pinned. The Tatts getting pinned. That thought had never crossed our minds before, but now we were all thinking it even though no one would say anything out loud.

The Boys were waiting for Marco and his family when they showed up at the Coliseum Saturday morning. Lenny asked Marco how he was feeling and in typical Marco fashion he said, "Ready to wrestle." I thought, yeah, maybe in the 167-pound weight class. He looked thin and tired and weak, kind of like Q looked normally, but he had his normal Marco smile.

Everyone who knew Marco knew that he would wrestle hard and accept his results with no excuses, but we all probably wanted a state championship for him even more than he wanted it for himself. Marco would be more satisfied with how things turned out this day than the rest of us would be, and that was one of the things we loved so much about the guy.

Up first was a wrestler from Lamar, which is in Eastern Colorado. Although it was one of the smaller 3A schools in the state, they almost always had strong programs in all the sports. Marco took some risks, almost got pinned once, but summoned all the energy he could muster, and, although he gave up two points for a near pin, he won the match on a six-to-four decision. While it was obvious that the IV treatment and the sleep had helped, our good buddy and the leader of our gang was not back to normal as he staggered a little walking off the mat. Next up was the Number Two seed in his weight class—a wrestler from Greeley West.

Once the match began, it was obvious to those who had seen Marco wrestle before that he was stalling. Marco circled his opponent, changed directions, acted like he was shooting for his legs, but stopped, pushed him around the mat a little, let him try to grab a leg and before pushing him to the mat, and so on. He managed to eat up the first period without giving up a point, but the ref warned him against stalling. One period and two minutes down with four minutes to go. The GW wrestler won the draw and chose to take the top position for the second period. As soon as the whistle blew, Marco laid flat on the mat and scooted around as the GW wrestler tried to turn him. The move worked great until the ref blew his whistle, warned Marco again, and started them again with Marco in the down position. By then, three minutes were gone, and the period and the match were both half-over with neither wrestler putting up any points. Marco made a few moves in the final minute of the period, but also managed to scoot off the mat twice. Even with his efforts to conserve energy, Marco's tank was empty, and his stomach was about to be too. As soon as the whistle blew to end the second period, Marco waved to Mr. DeVito, who came running with a bucket, and his oatmeal, toast, and orange juice breakfast was history. Now the entire audience in the Coliseum knew the situation of our guy, and all but the GW fans started cheering for the South Colt. It also helped them understand why the crazy lady was hanging through the rails screaming at the boy on the mat, "You wrestle, Marco, wrestle, boy, go, go, wrestle." Mr. DeVito wiped Marco's face and neck with a cool wet towel, slapped him on the back, and pushed him onto the mat. Two more minutes to go.

Marco was in the up position, and he just let go of his opponent. GW 1 and Marco 0. As soon as they were both upright, Marco shot for his legs and got a take down. Now it was Marco 2 and GW 1. Marco let him go, and the score was even at two apiece. As soon as they were both on their feet, Marco shot again for his legs, pulled them to his chest, slammed him on his back, and held on for dear life with a four-to-two advantage. With just one minute to go, if Marco could just hang on, he would win the match. The Coliseum was going berserk, and we thought he was going to pull it off. It was a great strategy to save everything for the third period, but, unfortunately, he was just too weak. The GW wrestler escaped and controlled Marco with two quick moves just before time expired. GW 5 and Pueblo South 4. We were sad it was over, but relieved that Marco could finally rest and recover. Mrs. Tattalinni was crying, all the cheer leaders were crying, but the Boys were at the rail screaming, "Marco, you are the best; The Tatts is king; Marco is the Man!" and whatever else popped into our minds. When we turned around, we saw the entire Coliseum crowd giving our friend a standing ovation. Giving a standing ovation for someone who would end up being the fourth-place finisher in the state wrestling championships had to be a first. Marco chose to forfeit his final match to wrestle for a third-place finish.

A few minutes after his match, Marco was interviewed by a reporter from our local newspaper, the Pueblo Chieftain. He was asked about his disappointing fourth-place finish at the state tourney. His reply was classic Marco. "I finished fourth because there were three better wrestlers in this state in my weight class." When the reporter clarified his question, adding that Marco's illness was a factor in his finish, Marco just shook his head. "Wrestling is an individual sport, and I do not want to take anything away from the talent and dedication of the individuals who finished ahead of me. I am happy and proud to be the fourth-best wrestler in the state of Colorado in my weight class." After saying those words, he threw up again.

Marco's folks drove him straight home and put him to bed. By Monday morning, he was getting his strength back, and there he was in front of my house Tuesday morning, ready for school. All day at school, people were slapping him five, giving him skin, and congratulating him for how hard he fought to place at state. Even the guys who hated him, Mike and his gang, gave Marco head nods when they saw him in the halls. On the way home that night, Marco announced, "Since wrestling is over and Scotty won't be playing baseball, I think we should get together and talk about what is looming ahead for all of us. How about we get together on Thursday at my place for another pizza and Pepsi night and we talk about our future." Everyone nodded in agreement, we decided who would bring what, and I began thinking about what I wanted to be when I grew up.

17

What Do You Want to Be
When You Grow Up?

"I THINK WE SHOULD all get jobs at the Steel Mill, and Marco could pick us up every morning so that things pretty much stay like they are right now," Frankie said to lead off the conversation.

Lenny chimed in, "That would be a blast," which made Marco lean his head back and laugh a little while Q dropped his head and said, "Oh yeah." I didn't get it at the time, but later Lenny explained to me that it was pretty common for Colorado Fuel and Iron (CF&I) to put their new employees to work at the blast furnace, which was a miserably hot job. Lenny then continued with his thoughts about Q's idea.

"So, you are telling me that you want to slowly have your intestines and internal organs baked to well-done; and you are telling me that you will continue living with your parents? If that's true you will be dishonorably discharged from The Belmont Street Boys." Q lowered his head again and shook it in a dejected sort of sad acceptance to what Birdy was saying. After a few moments of silence, Birdy continued. "CF&I is a fine place to work. It provides lots of honorable work and a good wage for thousands of men in Pueblo and a few women, too. The mill produces a variety of steel products needed across the country, which is great, but I want to say this very clearly, it is not for me! Working with the Boys would be great; it would be so much fun to work you guys no matter when or where it was, but the idea that things wouldn't change is crazy. People change, culture changes, life changes. Our relationships will always be strong, but they will change and, hopefully, for the better. Trying to keep things as they are right now is impossible. It is not realistic. What we have now is really good, but, if it doesn't grow, it will get stale, spoil, and turn into something none of us want to be part of."

"Preach it, brother! Amen!" I couldn't believe I just hollered out those words. That was the first time in my life I had said that. The night before, I had attended a Wednesday night service at an Assembly of God church with a girl I was interested in, and there was a lot of that going on there, so I guess those words kind of stuck in my brain. A slightly embarrassed smile slowly inched onto my face right after I blurted out the words, and the Boys looks turned from surprise to nodding agreement. It was something that I had grown accustomed to in Pueblo. Nodding agreement often eliminated the need for words.

The Tatts took charge of the meeting. "Now that we have that out of our systems, where do think you want to go in life? What grabs your interest? What do you want to pursue as an occupation? We all know Frankie is going to join the Army, but what about the rest of us?"

"Hey, I might not join the Army," Q shot back. "I was committed to working at the Steel Mill until my supposed friends shot that idea out of the air. Who knows? Maybe I will join the Navy or the Air Force or go crazy and try the Coast Guard."

Lenny offered this to Q. "We all know that you don't like school, but if there is something you enjoy doing, you could always consider going to the community college and learning a trade. Give it some thought, talk to people who are in the trades, do some tests to find out what you are good at, and then join the Army." We all laughed at that, even Q. "But seriously, my friend, when you go into the Army, don't just be in the infantry; get some training that you can use once you are dishonorably discharged." Marco choked on his pizza at that line, but it went right over Q's head, which was also where a small, half-chewed bite of pizza landed when it exited my mouth. I didn't take another bite until Birdy was done talking to the good-hearted and often oblivious Frankie Luna.

"If you don't learn some kind of trade, at least try to become a helicopter pilot or something exciting like that. Just because all of the other men in your family for three generations served in the military for one term and then got out doesn't mean that you have to do the same. Make the most of your time in the military; find some girl in another state who thinks you are interesting and will let you kiss her, marry her, and make some little Lunas that our kids can make fun of."

"That's not funny, but thanks for the advice," Q said as he pointed at Lenny. At that we jumped on top of Q, wrestled him around for a few seconds, and confirmed our love for the little guy. He tried to act mad, but we knew he enjoyed it. We were his brothers.

"What are you two thinking about studying in college?" Marco asked as he looked first at Lenny and then me.

Frankie said, "Birdy should be a doctor since he spends so much time in the library reading about medicine and stuff. You know," he said slowly, "doctors get to see chicks naked."

Birdy shook his head and said, "Yeah, chicks like your grandma and your Aunt Stella and your aunt . . ."

"Stop!" Q yelled as he interrupted Birdy. "I get it, I get it!"

"Don't worry, I will clean it up," I said. That time, I'd lost my entire mouth full of pizza.

"Break time," Marco announced, and, after I cleaned up my mess and we all quickly ate the rest of the pizza, our discussion resumed. Marco pointed at Birdy, who seemed kind of eager to tell us his plans.

"I am thinking about majoring in Political Science or International Relations. I've given some thought to Russian studies or some other country or region of the world that grabs my attention. Becoming part of the US diplomatic corps is something that fascinates me. I have been reading a lot about that lately and think that is something that could hold my interest and keep me in class for four years. That probably means I will be at the University of Colorado or Denver University for that kind of a degree. Botany and aquatic biology are also possibilities, but the political stuff has grabbed my attention for now."

"Wow. You sure hold your cards close to the vest. This is the first I have heard about any of this. Plus, a political education could also put you on a path to be an elected official someday. Who knows, Birdy for governor has a nice ring to it," I offered.

Q jumped up and said, "Birdy for governor is okay, but, if I were your campaign manager, you would have a catchy campaign slogan. Picture this." Q spread out his hands and said, "Lenny Peeples: guaranteed to put the goober back into gubernatorial." Once again, our friend, Frankie, had us all laughing. Q rarely laughed at his own humor. Usually, he just stood there with a look of confidence that he had just spoken the truth and, if others found his words funny, so be it. And that style of dead pan humor made the rest of us laugh even harder and longer. I know he got a kick out of his own humor, but he didn't show it.

As Marco slapped high five with Q, he pointed at me and said, "That sounds great, Lenny. Now it's your turn, Scotty." The Boys used that nickname so seldom with me that it always made me smile just to hear them say it.

"Just for the record, I have slapped high fives more in my seven months in Pueblo than I did in the almost eighteen years I spent in Illinois. Now, to answer your question, right now I am looking at an engineering degree."

Q blurted out, "You need a college degree to learn to drive a train?"

The three of us briefly lowered our heads, appreciating the unique, interesting, and sometimes naïve characteristics that Frankie brought to our group, but I continued talking, knowing that he was a smart guy who would figure it out once I gave more information. "The idea of building things and designing machines or structures excites me. Dad and I have talked about this quite a bit lately, and civil, mechanical, or architectural engineering seem like the best way to put my skills and interests to use in a career that would be fun and challenging for me. Colorado School of Mines has all the engineering degrees I would want, so I have been looking at Mines to see if it would be a good fit for me." The Boys all were excited after hearing my thoughts and poured on the encouragement the way they consistently did. "Sounds great; you will be good at that; you will be an engineering stud," and so on.

Q always had to mouth off, so he shook my hand and said, "And if that doesn't work out you can always drive a train." I laughed and said, "Frankie, you are FAU, funny as usual." That new nickname lasted as long as it took me to say it.

"What about you Marco? What does The Tatts want to do when he grows up?" Birdy asked. "I know that so far CSU, New Mexico, and Kansas State have made you offers and see you as a potential strong safety on their football teams. And, according to reliable sources, Sheila wants to be a lawyer so she can get her degree from the same school you decide on. So, tell us what you are thinking, O Fearless Leader."

Marco lowered his head a little, paused for about ten seconds, and then slowly tried to let us in on his plans. The three of us were looking at each other, a little concerned about his slow response. Then Marco raised his head and began to be really vague and very guarded about his future plans. He hemmed and hawed, starting a sentence and not finishing it, pausing, shaking his head, contradicting what he'd just said, and generally speaking in a way none of us had ever heard from him before that night. After about two minutes of that, I interrupted him by saying, "Marco, it sounds like you have no idea about what you are going to do." Again, Marco lowered his head a little, paused for a few seconds, but this time, when he spoke, he really did let us know what was going on in his head and heart.

"Thanks for interrupting me, Nick. I needed to start all over again, so here goes. The problem isn't that I have no idea about what I want to do. The problem is deciding on what few things I am going to do out of the hundred things that I want to do. Right now, I don't think that playing college football makes that top one hundred list. Sure, it would be fun to do that, and it would pay for my education, but I think I am ready to move on to new activities and new challenges. I am not sure what I want to do when I grow up, but I am certain who I want to be. William Wilberforce. How that will look vocationally and what to pursue educationally is a mystery to me right now, but that is where I am headed."

"Nick, a few months ago you said something to me that I didn't understand at the time. You thanked me for the tone I had set on the campus of South High and the influence I had on the student body there. A few days after that, I met with Father John, and we talked about what you'd said to me. Father John told me that, over the past two years, he'd been hearing from parishioners at St. Mary's things that confirm what you'd said. So, we began to have regular conversations about the best way for me to continue to be a force for good in the future. Do I focus on repeating what I've done in a school setting and become a teacher, coach, or maybe even a principal? Would it be better to go into politics and try to set public policy that would encourage the kind of behavior I have been able to pull off at South? What about being a social worker or a policeman or getting a degree in business in order to shape the culture of a particular industry or community? The possibilities seem to be endless."

"And when should all that start for me? The Peace Corps really appeals to me, as does serving with the Franciscans someplace for a couple of years and living among the poor in some South American country. Father John has connections with a parish in Kansas where a custom wheat cutter attends. Custom cutters travel with their combines and a crew and spend the summer traveling to Texas, up through Oklahoma, Kansas, Nebraska, and South Dakota following the wheat harvest. I have been guaranteed a job on a crew if I decide to take it. The crew doesn't make a great hourly wage, but they work six days a week for fourteen hours a day and have no time left to spend the money they are making.

I could easily earn enough money to pay for two years of college from just one summer of work. Or he has another connection with a parish in Alaska, where workers earn big bucks in the salmon fishing industry. The point of both of those jobs is that I wouldn't have to work while I was attending school and that would free me up to get involved somewhere doing something that would make a positive difference in people's lives. Plus, it would free me up to be a senate page or to volunteer somewhere the summer after my freshman year. Guys, I am just getting started on what has been running through my mind these past few months, but I am going to stop there. Father John is the only person I have talked to about these things, so let's keep this between him and the Boys for now."

We all looked around, nodded, and knew that Marco's thoughts and feelings about his future were safe with us. As mouthy as Frankie was, the guy was a vault when it came to keeping secrets, but he was also very bold when it came to asking questions. "Where does Sheila fit into all this?" he asked.

After a very long time of silence, Marco, without making eye contact with any of us said, "I don't know, and that tears me up inside."

Marco then stood up, hugged each of us, said, "I love you guys and am so glad that the three of you are the best friends a guy could ever hope to have." We stood and followed suit by sharing words of affection for each other as we left Marco's room. Birdy hit the nail on the head when he referred to Marco as "O Fearless Leader." Marco was our fearless leader, our William Wilberforce, the head of The Belmont Street Boys, our friend and protector, and our example to follow. Simply put, he was The Tatts. I wasn't certain what he was going to do when he grew up, but I knew for sure who he would be. My friend would always be The Tatts.

18

Springtime In the Rockies

FOR THE FIRST TIME as far back as I could remember, I would not be playing baseball in the spring. I had memories that went back to when I was five years old of my dad playing catch with me, hitting me grounders, pitching to me, and teaching me how to get under a fly ball. Every year, I could hardly wait until the Illinois weather consistently warmed up enough to get outside and play ball with my dad. Once I hit ten years old, there were community-based baseball leagues I could join, and those teams became the highlight of my spring and summer. Every year, from ages ten to fifteen, I made the city-wide, all-star team that competed against all-star teams from surrounding cities at the end of the regular season. Man, I loved everything about baseball. If it hadn't been for the Boys, this would have been the worst spring of my life. But there was no room for feeling sorry for myself with those guys around. It would take about six weeks for my collar bone to heal enough for me to get out and start doing physical activity, but the Boys let me know that they would only give me four weeks, and then the fun would begin. "Drink lots of milk, take calcium pills, stretch as much as possible, and ice it every day because there is too much fun to be had for you to be a sissy and wimp out on all that we have planned." Almost every day the Boys said stuff like that to me, and I slowly was able to say goodbye to baseball and hello to springtime in the Rocky Mountains of Colorado. When I thought about the fact that Coach Walker, my tennis coach, was also the head baseball coach, I knew that baseball that year would probably be pretty disappointing, while spending time with the Boys would be anything but that.

"What's on the agenda?" I asked.

"What isn't on the agenda?" Lenny hollered. "Where do I start? There is night skiing at The Broadmoor and spring skiing at A-Basin in April, but no jumps for you, Jean Claude Crashy. There is a World Championship Tennis event in Denver in April, Led Zepplin is at the Coliseum in May, the caddis fly hatch on the Arkansas River is always the first week in May, and, of course, being one of the first guys to throw a lure or fly into the water of a mountain lake when the ice has melted is super exciting. And that is just what popped into my mind without any serious thought. We will keep you busy, my young, crippled up, little buddy!" With his size, Lenny could call most of his friends and two of the Boys his little buddies.

Marco nodded and gave me his signature look while Q pumped his fist and yelled, "The best spring ever!" No one could have made the disappointment of not being able to play baseball dissolve as quickly as the Boys did that afternoon. In a matter of minutes, I went from being bummed out to getting excited about all of the good times I would be having with my three best friends. And, once again, that night when I went to bed, I thanked God that, in August 1972, my dad found a simple little house in the 1700-block of Belmont Street for our family to live.

It took me several days to work up the courage to ask my folks if I could go skiing again. When I assured them that I would wait until I had hit the four-week mark of recovery from the break and that I would play it very safe, I was pretty sure they would go for it. Dad listened, looked at Mom, then paused for about ten seconds after I'd made my spiel and said, "Yes, on one condition. We make this a family outing. I had no idea that The Broadmoor Resort had night skiing until you just mentioned it. That would be a good opportunity for the rest of us to get up on skis for the first time, and we could invite the Tattalinni family, too. Judging from past experience, I don't imagine that Lenny or Frankie's family will be interested, but you could invite the Grassleys to join us. It should be easy for me to reserve one of the district's fifteen-passenger vans for the evening, and I will get off work a little early so we can hit the slopes for as long as possible. That is thirteen people total, so we could all go together.

So, yes, you can go if it is a family affair." That sounded great to me and to the Boys, so we scheduled it for two days after the four-week mark of my healing, which fell on a Friday night. The resort would be a little more crowded on a Friday, but none of us cared about that. It would be a first-ever experience for all of us but Lenny, and the idea of skiing under the lights with family and friends and finally doing something physical sounded great to me.

The whole crowd made it into the van by 4:30 that Friday afternoon, and it seemed to me that the adults were as excited as the kids. Dad was driving, Joe was shotgun, Melvin Grassley was in the front bench seat with the two younger girls, the ladies were in the second bench seat, Marco and Sheila had the next row to themselves, and the back row was occupied by the Fungis—a nickname we gave ourselves for the day. "We are the fungis, that's plural for fungus; we are the fungis, not a dull guy among us." That was a little rhyme I made up for the ride to the Springs. My dad was a huge Ogden Nash fan, so I knew at least he would get a kick out of our three-man-motto. What he wouldn't like was what happened shortly after the boys in the back row had chanted our poem several times.

We had barely gotten out of Pueblo city limits when Q pulled a cigar out of his jacket pocket. As he pushed the cigarette lighter in to get it hot, I asked him, "What are you doing? Are you crazy?"

Without batting an eye, he said, "I am starting a tradition. Whenever I go skiing, I am going to smoke a cigar," and promptly lit it up. Marco and Sheila turned around immediately but didn't say anything. The moms smelled it a few seconds later but said nothing. My guess was that they knew my dad would smell it and take charge in a few seconds.

Q got one good drag on the cigar when Dad hollered out, "Lucille, you know I told you to leave that cigar at home. You need to put it out now." Dad had looked in his rearview mirror and knew who the culprit was but had decided to try and keep the whole evening fun. Frankie panicked a little, looked at us, and asked, "What should I do?"

With no hesitation, Peeps said, "Spit in your hand and put it out," which Q did without thinking.

As he was crying out in pain and hollering at Peeps, "I will never believe anything you tell me again!" the Boys and Sheila were once again having a laugh at our good friend, Frankie's, expense. Lenny bought him some hot chocolate later that night to try and make up for it, and it worked. Frank Luna is probably the most forgiving person I have ever known in my life, and, later on that night, he would impress us once again with how he could be the brunt of a joke and never hold a grudge.

Once we got to The Broadmoor, we all got fitted with equipment except for Peeps and Joe. Peeps brought his own gear, and Joe said he was just along to laugh at the rest of us when we fell. Peeps gave our group ski lessons before everyone made their way to the lift; then he continued all the way down to the bottom of the hill for the first two runs of the night.

I was his helper since I had been on the slopes several times, but Q ignored me and hollered, "I don't need lessons on how to break my collar bone!" Everyone in the group had some athletic ability, so they all picked up the basics pretty well. After the first two runs, we pretty much skied in the same groupings as we were in the van with Lenny on his own going at a pace that we couldn't keep up with. Skiing with Q kept me on the easiest slopes at a safe speed since I couldn't afford to fall. But there was plenty of falling with all of the beginners and lots of good times for everyone. It was on our fifth run of the evening, though, that some unexpected fireworks lit up the evening.

Q got a little over-confident in his abilities and couldn't stop when he hit the icy conditions at the bottom of the hill. When he laid on his side, wrongly thinking that would slow him down, Q started yelling, "fore, heads-up, here I come, watch out," and slid into the legs of a guy who was casually standing around talking to a couple of high-school-aged girls. The guy popped up and started yelling and cussing at Q, threatening to kick his ass. Just as Q got to his feet, apologizing repeatedly, Marco, Peeps, and I skied up.

"Are you guys his back up or something? I'll take you all on." Then he looked a little more carefully at Marco and calmed down a little.

"Aren't you that guy from South they call The Tatts?" Marco nodded and said, "That's me."

Then the guy really calmed down. "I am Richie, #81 on Wasson's football team. When we ran an end around and you tackled the guy for a ten-yard loss, that guy was me. You hit me so hard that my head was spinning, and I could barely find my way to the sideline. That was in the first quarter. In the third quarter, the coach sent me in with the same play call, and I changed it in the huddle. When I got to the sideline, I told coach that I got the numbers mixed up, but the truth was that there was no way I was going to run your direction again. What's up with your friend here, crashing into people like that?"

"This is his first time on skis, and he just got a little wild. He didn't mean to clip you like that, Richie. You did tell him you were sorry, didn't you, Frankie?" Marco knew that he had, but he wanted to give Richie another chance to save face in front of the girls Richie was talking to.

"Probably ten times, but I will say it again," Q said. "That was totally accidental, and I am really sorry that I knocked you down, especially since it happened in front of these really cute girls." Q was always trying to impress the ladies, and he did so even as he apologized for being so lousy on skis. The girls smiled, Richie accepted the apology, and the three of them moved away just as Sheila skied up and asked what all the excitement was about.

After Q told her what had happened, I asked him, "Are you trying to add getting your butt kicked to this new skiing tradition of yours?" Sheila laughed at that, and then went on a roll that sounded like it was coming from one of the Boys instead of Sweet Sheila.

"Why would he threaten to kick your butt? You don't even have one! Every time he tried to kick it, he would most likely miss. You are the un-butt; your rump has no ump; most people have a gluteus maximus, but you have a gluteus minimus; your derriere is a derriaint; your caboose never made it onto the track; your hiney ain't so finey; your buns didn't get enough yeast; your padunkadunk can't dunk; your arse is a farce."

Q interrupted her and said, "Thanks, Marco, for saving my hide, again. And thank you, Sheila, for being Miss Perfect in Every Way, so that I don't have a REBUTTAL to your attack. Now, I am going to make one more run down this mountain, and all of you will be staring at my un-butt as you eat my snow dust or whatever they call it," and he skied off. What a guy. And he did, in fact, beat us all down the hill on our last run of the evening. Peeps let Frankie have his moment of glory and skied along behind with the rest of us.

When we got back to the van, Mrs. T asked Marco what had happened when Q knocked the boy down, since all the adults were done skiing for the night and saw the whole thing from a distance. Marco gave her the scoop, even telling her about Sheila's impromptu butt-monologue, and Marco's mom promptly thumped him in the forehead. Marco rubbed it off, laughed, and asked, "What was that for, Ma?"

"Frankie is a sweet boy and the rest of you give him such a hard time. I should thump you every day, just figuring that you have abused him somehow. Now get in the van and treat him right the rest of the night," she said with authority.

As I got in the van, my mom thumped me in the head and said, "That goes for you too." She had never thumped me before.

"Looks like Pueblo is starting to rub off on you, Mother dear," I said, covering my head in case she tried to land another thump. When Q got in the van, Mrs. T and the other moms gave him big hugs and kissed his forehead, then looked at the rest of us and nodded.

"Did your mother ever thump you in the head?" Mrs. T asked Lenny.

"No ma'am, I had a good mother," he said with a smile as he moved past her quickly.

"Marco and Frankie, thump him good for that," she said through her laughter. And we did thump him good. Even Shelia's mom gave her a thump in the noggin.

"I had it coming" Sheila said.

Once we were all in the van, my dad hollered out, "I thought it would be good to finish our trip to the Springs by going to Michelle's. I am buying, and everyone who didn't get thumped gets to order whatever they want. The rest of you only get a cone with one scoop." The little girls started squealing, and Frankie rubbed it in. We all enjoyed our ice cream, laughed a lot on the way home, and thanked my dad over and over again for his great idea and generosity. By the time we opened the front door to our house at 12:30am Saturday morning, Springtime in the Rockies was off to a great start. The fungis and everyone else had an outstanding evening that stretched into the next morning.

Peeps was right. Night skiing at The Broadmoor was just the first in the line of new and exciting events he had planned for me. If my dad would have let me skip school, we would have done even more. Lenny taught me how to fly fish on some beaver ponds on Marshall Pass, where I caught my first Brook Trout and Cutthroats. Then later, I used some of those skills the first week of May when the caddis fly hatch was happening on the Arkansas River. We camped out one Friday night at Smith Reservoir and caught some big fish the next morning. In mid-May, we hiked into Rosemont Reservoir right after the ice melt and tore it up on some very hungry Rainbows and German Browns. Peeps taught me how to tie line, clean fish, spy out good water, set hooks, and, somewhere along the line, I got hooked for life on trout fishing.

The Led Zepplin concert was really loud and really cool. I wore the most stylish pants I had to the concert because, of course, I wanted to look my best. Peeps and I were going to a rock concert in Denver, for crying out loud, so I wore my orange and blue plaid bell bottoms. With those pants and the silk shirt I had on, when I looked in the mirror, I thought *you are one classy looking dude, Nick Bradford*. When Peeps saw me, he asked, "Are you sure that's what you want to wear?"

"Absolutely," I said, wondering why he could even ask that question considering how sharp I looked. He was wearing a Jethro Tull T-shirt and a beat-up pair of jeans. That should have been my clue. When we drove up to the Denver Coliseum and I saw the crowd milling around, it was obvious that I had made a major fashion *faux pas*. As we walked to the entrance and then inside the Coliseum, it seemed like everyone we saw pointed at my pants, laughed, or sarcastically said something like, "Stylin.'" I couldn't wait to find my seat, for the lights to dim, and for the music to start so that everyone would be focused on the stage and not on my pants. When the lights did dim, the guy on my right lit up a joint, looked at me and my pants, then passed the joint down the row away from me. I wouldn't have smoked it anyway, but, dang, at least he could have offered it to me!

When the concert was over, everyone was talking about the show, so no one paid any attention to my pants. Although I didn't become as big a fan of Led Zepplin as I did of fishing, it was a great concert, and I was really glad we went. Over the next few years, I listened to a lot of Zeppelin and developed a top-five list of my favorite tunes by Zep. They are, in this order: "Nobody's Fault But Mine"; "Kashmir"; "Immigrant Song"; "Black Dog"; and "Rock and Roll." I have thanked my friend, Birdy, many times for getting me started listening to Led Zepplin and other bands with a harder edge to their music. During the summer, we took in a Jethro Tull concert, also at the Denver Coliseum. I wore beat up old jeans and a Led Zepplin T-shirt to that concert and fit right in with that crowd. The Tull concert was one of the tightest musical performances by a rock band that I ever saw.

Most of our Springtime-in-the-Rockies events were just Lenny and me because both Marco and Q needed to pick up work wherever they could to make some money. At first, I wanted the other guys to be there, but, after a while, I realized that our times together were drawing Lenny and me closer and closer together as friends. He opened up a lot about his mom and grandma and what it is like to be an orphan. I don't think that would have happened as easily with the other guys there. We talked about anything and everything, and he even asked me my thoughts about God.

19

Faith

As close as the Boys were to each other, we were kind of all-over-the-map when it came to issues of faith. Lenny's aunt and uncle never attended church and never talked about God unless they were recovering from a hangover and were mockingly hollering, "Help me, Jesus," as they were getting ready to go to work. His mom and grandma weren't spiritual women, so Lenny never had any input from his family concerning faith over his entire eighteen years on earth. He always said no when invited to some church activity by Q or Marco. They kept inviting and he kept saying no. Once Lenny told me that he just hadn't been able to develop a satisfactory theodicy. I had no idea what he was talking about, so he explained that theodicy was basically an understanding of how a good God could allow evil to exist in the world. From what he admitted was his limited understanding at the time, either God wasn't good because he allowed evil, or God wasn't powerful since so many evil things happen in the world. He talked about the Holocaust, innocent people dying in times of war, horrible diseases such as spina bifida, and tragedies like a vulnerable little boy first losing his mom and then his grandma to completely unnecessary deaths. Peeps thought more deeply about things than the rest of us, but he also never criticized or critiqued the Boys about what we believed. Peeps would talk about faith if we brought it up and asked his opinion, but it wasn't a subject that received his best and most serious thought.

The one religious activity that I knew about Peeps attending was a Young Life Club for South students, and he only did that once. Young

Life met in the home of a South student every Tuesday night at 7:00pm and lasted for an hour. The meeting started off with a game or a skit, then group singing led by the Young Life Club leader, followed by a lesson from the Bible by that same leader, and finishing up with refreshments and social time until 8:15. I attended off and on and always enjoyed the meetings, but Lenny's experience at YL wasn't a good one. Every now and then our club leader, Wes Owen, would break out a stool with a motorcycle battery taped to the underside of the stool and a ground on the seat itself. Once on the chair, the student would be asked questions on a variety of subjects and, if they gave an incorrect answer, Wes would push a button on his hand-held controller and zap the fool out of the person on the hot seat. Wes asked for a volunteer, and everyone there that night volunteered Peeps to go for a ride on the electric chair. Lenny is such a good-natured guy that he agreed even though Q said, "Don't do it my friend. He will shock you 'til your ears glow; roasted Birdy is on his menu tonight."

Q attended YL almost every Tuesday and was really into the club. It was at his invitation that Lenny came that night. Lenny figured that he could outsmart Wes, and he did for over five minutes, answering every question thrown him. Finally, Wes asked Peeps, "What is my favorite color?" When Lenny fired back, "Fuchsia," he immediately had twelve volts of electricity surging through his well-rounded and well-conditioned buttocks. He jumped so high that he almost hit his head on the basement ceiling, hollered "WOW," smiled and laughed, rubbed his butt, and sat down. Q told me later that it was the most laughter he'd ever heard for any YL Club skit or game. Lenny was a great sport, but, after the meeting, he told Wes that he needed to retire the electric chair because someone sometime was going to wet their pants getting shocked like that. He then added, "It was a good meeting, and you gave a good talk, but I won't be back." The electric chair was no fun for him, and Peeps figured other games and skits done as openers to YL meetings were also most likely geared towards making someone look stupid, and he wanted no part of that. He made a point to thank the host family for their hospitality, hopped on his motorcycle, and sped off.

Marco never attended YL because, if he did, the club would have to meet in the school auditorium. Once word got out that he was attending, half of South and a bunch of kids from other schools would be there faithfully every Tuesday evening. Marco knew that was the case, but, when I asked him to attend with me one night, he just shook his head and offered the following. "If I attended Young Life, I would have to deal with the

Baptists and the Nazarenes trying to convert me because I am Catholic. I know there are a lot of lousy Catholics in this town, but I am not one of them. I take my faith seriously, but they think that the only Catholics who are Christian are the Baptists and Nazarenes who are former Catholics. Answering their questions and debating scripture with them on their turf would not be good. I respect them and their beliefs but am not sure they have much respect for my faith." Marco's explanation made sense to me, but it also made sense that there was not a house in Pueblo big enough to hold the crowds who would show up just to be with Marco in an informal social setting, even if it were religious in nature.

Since Frankie was a regular at YL, I made a point only to attend sporadically. As much as I enjoyed the meetings and the YL activities and the leader, Wes, it was clear that Q was his own person in that setting. He was Frank Luna and not just one of The Belmont Street Boys. That was also the case for the church he attended almost every Sunday—the Free Methodist Church in the NW section of Pueblo. There everyone called him Frankie since that is what his aunt, the woman responsible for getting him to church as a little kid, called him. Aunt Nell, his mom's younger sister, loved her nephew and doted on him his whole life. Nell never married, so Q was like a son to her. He loved her, too, but Q consistently tried her patience, as he did all of his Sunday school teachers, youth leaders, and every person in positions of authority in the church. They never asked him to stop attending, even after Frankie had a very short date with the pastor's sixteen-year-old daughter.

It was a Friday night in April when all of the Boys were supposed to meet up at Sam and Ray's Pizza with their dates at 7:30. The plan was to eat some pizza, have some laughs, then head out to Bowlero Lanes for a couple of lines of bowling to conclude our eight-person, mass date. When Q showed up at Sam and Ray's without his date, we all asked him about it, and he just shook his head and told us the story.

"Well, I got to the Bates's home determined to be on my best behavior, but that only lasted about two minutes. Pastor Bates greeted me at the door and informed me that his sixteen-year-old daughter, Mae, had never been on a date before and that it was a big step for him to allow me to take her out. I told him that it was an honor for me to date Mae and that it would be a group date with some really good friends of mine, who are great people, and that I would have her home by 10:30. Then their dog came up and tried to get me to pet him, but I kind of shooed him away since I am allergic to dogs. Mrs. Bates said, 'Wimpy is part of our family.'

I put my hands on my knees, turned my head sideways to make sure I got a good look at the dog's belly, then stood back up and looked Mr. Bates in the eyes and said, 'I am glad I didn't grow up in your family. You just might have cut my balls off too.' And that didn't go over so well."

It was a good thing we hadn't ordered yet or there would have been Pepsi and pizza spewed all over the place. The Boys and their dates just lost it. No one else in the restaurant could hear anything over the noise of our laughter. Once we settled down, Sheila asked, "What happened next?" Q hadn't cracked a smile in telling us the story, because he wasn't trying to be funny with the Bates family or with us. He was simply telling it like it was from his perspective. That was one of the many reasons why we loved that guy so much.

"Well, Mae and I went to the car, and I politely opened her door, went around to the driver's seat, and backed the car out of the driveway. Before we were five houses down the street, she burst out crying and told me to take her home. So, as I whipped a U-turn, I said, 'I guess that means no goodnight kiss.' Then the crying went up a notch, and she bolted out of the car as soon as I pulled to a stop. I watched her run into the house, then shook my head a little and said out loud, 'I guess she really loves her dog.' That's the only thing I can figure out. But she should have been mad at her parents for cutting his balls off and not mad at me for point-ing out the fact!" At that, the laughter erupted again. Later on, we were able to convince him that it probably had more to do with him saying something that was completely out of the norm for that family, and just maybe she had some first-date nerves. Sunday afternoon, he told us that, to his credit, Pastor Bates greeted him with a hug at church that morning and said he was glad to see Frankie, but Mae and her mom avoided him before and after the service. Once again, our friend Q rolled with the punches, kept attending that little church, and continued to say whatever popped into that unique brain of his.

Word soon spread about the world's shortest date, and, in the next few days when his Aunt Nell heard about it, she took him out for ice cream and told him that she was proud of him for speaking his mind. She always told him that he was a smart and talented boy with a bright future and that he was "one-of-a-kind." She often called him Son and Q loved that, knowing he would be proud to have a mom like her. His response was always the same. "Aunt Nellie, you are the best." Q called her his Banie, which was code for Best Aunt Nellie. All his relatives thought it was just a childhood nickname, but it was Q's way of secretly letting her know what she meant to him. Every time she heard her nephew refer to her as Banie, Aunt Nell responded with a wink and a smile. They always sat together in church, and she did her best to encourage her nephew concerning all things of a spiritual nature. Also, I am sure she knew that if he were sitting next to her, she stood a better chance of minimizing his disruptive behavior during the morning church service.

Along with sporadically attending Young Life meetings and events, my family became members at Pueblo's First Presbyterian Church. Mom sang in the choir, and she soon became the assistant organist, so she was in church most Sundays, but we usually attended as a family only once or twice each month. Dad sometimes played golf or had outings with friends, and I was in the mountains or on an adventure with Peeps fairly often. The church had a decent youth program, and I plugged into those meetings and events on a semi-regular basis. All in all, we were the definition of a family of nominal Presbyterians. One time in Illinois, I was forced to attend a banquet, where Dad was one of several people being honored for their work in education, when I heard one of the speakers that evening quote some author with a line that went something like this: *It was noon on Sunday when the Presbyterian church on the corner let out her dead.* That is a bit of an overstatement for our church, but I never remember leaving a Sunday morning service especially inspired or passionate about what I'd heard or experienced. If someone had asked me if I were a Christian, I would most likely have shrugged, said yes, and not given it any more thought. I could recite the Apostle's Creed and some Bible verses that I learned in vacation Bible school in order to win some candy, but I didn't spend a lot of time thinking about my beliefs. Faith was important to me, but not more important than my family and the value they put on education, and certainly not more important than The Belmont Street Boys. That was not the case with Marco.

Marco Tattalinni was the young man that every Catholic priest hoped their ministry would produce. Marco was an altar boy and a helper for the Saturday morning catechism classes, and he met with his priest twice a month on Thursday evenings to learn more about his faith and whatever his priest wanted to teach him. He hardly ever missed Sunday morning mass and he went to confession every week to confess only-God-knows-what. In the minds of the Boys, Marco was the last person in Pueblo who needed to confess his sins. He was honest yet kind with his words, tough-minded and tender-hearted, vulnerable but never gullible, and giving but never enabling. The guy was dad-gum nearly perfect in every way that I ever witnessed. And when asked about his positive outlook on life and all the good he did for others and his ability to resist the temptations which come naturally to every teen-aged boy that I know, Marco always attributed it to his faith. Marco was a great friend, a great example to others, and a poster child for the Catholic Church.

Unlike me and Q, Marco was under no pressure to attend church or to be involved in religious activities to please someone else. He did what he did because he wanted to and because it seemed very natural to him. When he read the biography of William Wilberforce, it was his natural inclination to try to do something similar to what Willy Will did within the sphere of his influence, which was his school and neighborhood. Unlike me and Q, Marco actually listened to what was being taught in church and tried to put it into practice somehow. We listened some to what was being taught and tried a little to live out our faith, but Marco consistently put his faith into practice. Just before graduation we would discover how seriously Marco took his faith.

20

Prom

It was decided. The six of us would meet up at The Minnequa Club and share a table for the meal offered by the South High Prom Committee that night. The price was right, and the company would be outstanding, so we were all in. Well, mostly all in. Peeps would be doing his own thing at a nice restaurant with his date. He'd met a college girl named Tonya from Manitou Springs when the two of them were the paid dance instructors for a ritzy wedding at The Broadmoor Country Club. Their job at the wedding reception was to teach the wedding guests how to swing dance and to class-up the reception by being on the floor for every dance, including dancing with some of the older guests. According to Peeps, it was a great gig since it paid well, and, besides Tonya, he'd met several young ladies at the reception who he thought were prime dating prospects for the future. Peeps drove to Manitou, picked her up, and then, after their dinner at the Top of the Town restaurant, they joined up with us for the dance itself. He had told her that it was a formal dance and that she should come dressed appropriately, but Tonya didn't know that it was a high school prom until they walked in the front door of the Minnequa Club. Prom was different from homecoming in that you almost exclusively danced with your date. Maybe that was why Birdy asked Tonya to be his date that night. She would be able to keep up with him on the dance floor, so he knew he would have a fun night of dancing. At first, Tonya was mad at Birdy for not being totally honest with her and for making her feel out of place by being a twenty-year-old at an event filled with sixteen- to eighteen-year-old high school kids. That indignation lasted until she got on the floor with Birdy, and, after a few dances, it was obvious that she was smitten with him—not nearly as smitten as Sheila was with Marco, but way more emotionally involved than the dates Q and I had asked to prom.

My date was a girl named Laurel, who I knew from Concert Choir and Carolaires. She had a very nice soprano voice and was a lot of fun, but it was clear that she was mostly interested in simply having a date to prom and that I was the first guy to ask her. I was the utilitarian date—a phrase Peeps taught me—but that was okay in this instance. It was just another date with another girl to help me see the kind of woman who could grab my attention and hold it for a long period of time. We danced a lot, laughed often, and did some kissing later that night, but we never dated again.

Frankie brought a girl he knew from church. Her name was Kim, and she was a junior at Centennial. When he left to get the two of them a Pepsi, we started asking her questions. We'd heard from Q that she attended his church, so Sheila took the opportunity to ask her if she knew about Q's date with the pastor's daughter.

"Of course, I know about it," she quickly offered. "Mae and I are really good friends. She is a sweet girl, but she is also pretty naïve and socially inexperienced. When I asked her about the date, she couldn't bring herself to tell me what Frankie had said that got her so upset, so I asked him about it as soon as church dismissed the Sunday right after their date. When he told me what happened, I laughed out loud and told him that was both hilarious and thought-provoking. I have been around this guy for the past three years since my family started attending his church, and I think of Frankie as a great guy and a good friend. He is funny, smart, and kind of cute, too, but not boyfriend material for me anyway. Since I have two older brothers who say and do all kinds of things, I know how to stand up for myself if some guy says or does something out of line. I know how to slug, kick, and be sassy, but poor Mae is a pampered and protected only-child who had no idea of how to respond to what Frankie said, so she just lost it." With those thoughts, we all liked Kim immediately. When we saw her on the dance floor with Q, we liked her even more.

We all danced a lot that night, but Peeps and Tonya were on the floor for probably 90% of the dances. Q did his usual thing of being goofy, and Kim was uninhibited enough to go along with him. Once on a slow dance, Q and Kim did the Twist, and on the funky "Don't You Worry 'Bout a

Thing," by Stevie Wonder, they did a classic slow dance with their heads on each other's shoulders. When the DJ played "Stuck in the Middle With You," by Steelers Wheel, Frankie jumped up from our table and told Kim to follow his lead. That was all we needed to hear for me, Marco, and our dates to decide to sit this one out and watch the entertainment from a distance. The two of them danced behind Peeps and Tonya and tried to imitate every move they were making. When Peeps noticed what they were doing, he began doing more and more difficult moves with Tonya, which made the whole thing even funnier. After that dance and their two earlier goofy dances, they came back to our table with their infectious laughter, and we all fed off of their animation in a way that made the next few moments absolutely joy-filled. It was a hoot. A girl from my church had asked me to be her date for prom at Central the weekend before ours, and no one at that dance had nearly as much fun as we were having that night. Even Tonya had forgotten about the age difference and was as relaxed as could be with us. Others at the dance came to our table and stood around, trying to get in on the fun or maybe hoping the good times would rub off on them. As usual, Marco welcomed everyone, but they didn't stay for long since the table only sat eight and all the tables were close to each other in order to make the dance floor as big as possible. But Marco and the Boys had set the tone for the evening, and, from my perspective, everyone seemed to be having a really good time. Even a friend of mine named Jim, a bass in our choir and in Carolaires, who was as nervous as could be with his date, was able to loosen up and have a good time after coming by our table for a few minutes with his date. And that's the way it seemed to go all night long with the South High crowd.

Marco was his usual positive and fun-loving self that evening, but something was going on with him that wasn't entirely normal. At first, I attributed it to being the fact that our senior year was almost over and that everything was about to change for all of us. Marco danced every slow dance with Sheila, which was a little unusual, told the Boys "I love you guys" several times, and reminded us all that this was our last prom together. Q lightened the mood by saying, "This might be your last prom, but it's my first!" When the girls all went to the restroom together (I have never understood why they do that), Marco told us again that he loved us. He told me how happy he was that my family moved onto our block; he carried on for one or two minutes telling Lenny what a tremendous blessing he was to his aunt and uncle and how fortunate Q and him were to have Lenny as their longtime friend; and he told Q, calling him Frank

as he did when he was being serious, how proud he was that Frank had
matured so much over the past few years. Marco reminded him how he
used to say, "smell this" or "touch this," and it was always something disgusting or painful or intended to make others look bad. "Now you can
be trusted," Marco proclaimed. He then reminded Frank of how he used
to chew up a carrot and then spew all the tiny pieces, covering the face of
whichever neighbor kid was in front of him at the time.

"That was really funny, and you know it," Q said with a shake of his
finger.

Marco smiled and said, "Yes, it was. Pretty disgusting too, and you
know that." Q nodded.

This went on until the girls got back from the restroom, with Marco
pouring on the praise and appreciation to the Boys and then telling the
girls how lucky they were to be on a date with such great guys. As Laurel
and I got up to dance, I asked Peeps what he thought was going on with
our friend, Marco. He said, "I am not sure. Maybe he is feeling a little
melancholy over the unknowns of our future." After he explained to me
what the word "melancholy" meant, I agreed with him. We would soon
find out that we were both on the wrong track and headed in the completely wrong direction in our perceptions of what was going on in the
mind and spirit of our good friend. Just before the next-to-last dance,
Marco said we needed to have a meeting with The Belmont Street Boys
on Tuesday evening at 8:00pm. That was the night before graduation, but
we all nodded in agreement that we would be there.

We danced our last dances, said our goodbyes for the night to the
other couples, then later Q and I kissed our girls as much as they were
comfortable with, and Laurel was comfortable with a lot of smooching!
Lenny told us later that his college girl was ready to do more than he was
prepared for, so he had to find a way to politely shut down her advances.
Marco and Sheila never made out, so they did their usual thing of holding hands, enjoying each other's company, and finishing their date by
going to Sheila's house and sitting on her porch talking. Prom was a great
way to end our school year. We were done with tests and papers, so all we
had to do was show up for the two school days leading up to graduation.

As we were leaving prom, Marco reminded us about our meeting,
something he hadn't done before. We would never forget a meeting of
the Boys! We all nodded in agreement again, and my mind went back to
wondering what was going on with Marco. He never said what the meeting was about, and we didn't ask. Both Lenny and I hoped that the meeting

would offer some sort of conclusion to our question of what was going on with Marco. Q was oblivious to the change in Marco since he was completely focused on the very real possibility of getting to kiss Kim later on. An answer to my question was about to come, and, when it did, it would hit me and the Boys like a bomb had been detonated on Belmont Street.

21

The Bombshell

WHEN OUR FAMILY GOT home from church on the Sunday before graduation, I saw three cars parked in front of The Tatts's house. Catholics got out of church before Presbyterians, so Marco always beat me home from church on the one or two Sundays that I attended each month. Our church was doing something to honor the graduates that day, so the Bradford family chose the third Sunday in May for the whole family to sit together in our usual spot—the second row from the back on the left side of the First Presbyterian Church. The service was uneventful. I was given some book about being a man that I stuck on a shelf and never looked at again. After shelving that thoughtful but useless book, I saw five guys come out of Marco's backyard, get into three cars, and drive off. One of the guys was called Pig, short for his last name, Piganelli, and another was Z, short for Zanatelli. The other three looked kind of familiar to me so I figured they were from South, but none of them were seniors or in choir so I didn't know them. After Sunday dinner, I wandered over to his house to get the low down from The Tatts.

As I walked into his backyard, raised a finger quizzically, and waved it around, Marco started talking. "Those five guys are the toughest dudes in the junior and sophomore classes. I wanted to spend a little time with them and plant a vision in their brains about what they wanted to see South look like in the next few years. Once I am gone, everything could change but it doesn't have to. I told them what school was like when I first got to South and then asked them to compare that with what school was like this year. It was pretty cool to hear what they had to say. After they got done talking, I laid out a challenge for them to step up-to-the-plate and do some good during their remaining time at South." He smiled the great little smile that everyone who knew The Tatts loved to see, and then continued as if he was talking to the five tough guys.

"All of you agree that this was a fun year. If someone ran into you in the hall, for the most part they apologized, and you both moved on. There weren't very many fights, kids didn't feel threatened, they weren't worried about getting beat up over stupid things, and even the weird kids felt pretty free just to be themselves. You have heard about the problems at the other high schools in town and you know that nothing like that goes on at South. Am I right so far?" Marco broke from his talk to let me know that the guys were nodding in agreement with him as they devoured the cinnamon rolls that Mrs. T had set out on the picnic table. He then returned to the speech he had laid on the tough-guy underclassmen.

"What I really want you guys to understand is that you have it in your power to make sure that the tradition I was able to begin at South continues long after I am gone. It might be a real challenge for any one of you to pull it off by yourself, but together you can make sure that an atmosphere of intimidation and bullying and fear doesn't creep back into your school. When some thug starts to pick on a kid who is weak or not too bright or a kid who doesn't have any friends, you guys can step in and let him know that we don't do things that way at South. You can even learn the name of the kid who got picked on and call him or her by name when you see them in the halls. If you are able to continue the safe and friendly atmosphere that we now have at school, you will discover that fun times and positive things just start happening on a daily basis all year long." Marco paused for a few seconds, like he did with the guys in his back-yard, and then asked a question which I thought was a brilliant way to demonstrate what he was talking about and a good way to wrap up their time together.

"How many annuals do you guys think you will sign Monday at school?" Between the five of them they figured about 150, or somewhere around thirty apiece. "Last year I signed 637 annuals, and this year it will likely be over eight hundred. The reason for that is not because I am so good looking, such an athletic stud, and have the body of an Adonis and the best-looking girlfriend this side of Hollywood." At that Marco busted out laughing and said, "I cracked up before I could get that whole line out when I was talking with that group. When I say stuff like that, I know that Q has rubbed off on me over the years, but he would have delivered that line with a straight face and seemingly believed every word of it. The guys started laughing with me and laughed even harder when I told them about Q's influence on me over the years. They'd all seen him do his thing from time to time." Marco calmed down, after we both laughed for a few seconds, and told me how he finished the little confab he had with the underclassmen.

"I am not popular for any of the reasons that most high school kids get their popularity. My popularity is as simple as this. Kids feel safe around me. They know that I won't reject them; they know that I won't try to make them look stupid; they know that I won't bully them or take advantage of them in some way. And, if you guys will continue that when I am gone, almost everyone in school will want you to sign their annuals, too. Let me tell you guys, if you can pull it off, I think you will experience the same kind of satisfaction I feel right now about my time at South. At that I shook their hands and silently prayed that they would accept the challenge."

"How do you think it went? Did they buy in to what amounted to your Willy Will approach to life in high school?" I asked.

"I'm not sure. The three juniors had two years at South, and I always made it a point to be friendly with them. Pig and Z were on the football team, so I would talk to them during practice and games and in the locker room in hopes that they would really pay attention to how I operated on and off the field. I think they are on board, but only time will tell. The sophomore named Joey is a lot like Carl the Bull. He seemed to be reflecting on what I was saying as I was talking to the guys, but it is hard to know if he was evaluating what I was saying or just thinking about eating another cinnamon roll. The other sophomore I don't know at all. He came because Pig invited him. But, if the three juniors and Pig's friend are all in, I imagine they will have enough will-power and physical force to keep Joey on the team, even if he doesn't fully understand why he is playing by their rules. Time will tell, and I won't be around to do anything about it. As my alcoholic Uncle Vinny would say, you just have to let go and let God."

The whole thing shouldn't have surprised me, but it did. My friend, Marco; the leader of The Belmont Street Boys; the eighteen-year-old kid who was mature beyond his years; my teenaged neighbor who understood the power of love better than most adults I would ever know in my life had once again hit it out of the park. I ambled back home and ate the dessert Mom had saved for me after dinner. We talked as I ate one piece of cake and then another. As I told her a little about Marco's talk with the

South High tough guys, she listened carefully, gave me a big hug, and quietly said, "You are a fortunate young man to have a friend like Marco." As usual Mom was right.

Monday was the day for signing the *Remuda*, a name someone, somewhere along the line gave to South High School's annual album of class pictures, events, clubs, and such. A remuda is a group of saddles that cowboys choose from for their day's work, so I suppose the name has some sort of a loose connection to the South High Colts. But everyone at South just called it "the annual." Seniors handed in their books, signed annuals, talked, and goofed around, and that was about it. In choir, we rehearsed a song we would sing at graduation, but that was the only real schoolwork I did that day. The real work was figuring out what to write in the annuals of the kids that I didn't know very well. Q had it figured out though. When he got into the Nomad that morning, he was carrying a small briefcase, which was easily the strangest thing I had seen that entire year.

As he shook his head, Birdy asked, "Okay Poindexter, what's with the briefcase?"

"It's simple, Professor. Since I am an incredibly popular guy and a very eligible bachelor, I know that there will be a great demand for me to sign hundreds of annuals today. A family in our church owns a printing business, and I asked Aunt Nell if she thought they would be willing to make me a rubber stamp, so I didn't have to think of something to say and sign my name over and over again today. She thought that was a great idea and that was all the encouragement I needed. But the more I thought about it, I realized that I could do better than that, so I had them make up three rubber stamps for me. It cost me a few bucks, but it is worth it. Aunt Nellie must have given the owners a few bucks, too, because those three rubber stamps should have cost me more than four bucks. Anyway, one is for the ladies,and it says YOU'RE CUTE; one is for the guys, and it says STAY COOL; and one is for you guys that says GROW UP!" Once again, our Belmont Street bubby had us laughing. He continued.

"The stamp I use for the girls says 'Frankie' under the message, and the other two have 'Q' so that the lucky recipient of my stamp doesn't forget who stamped their book. But it's not like there is anyone else at South as creative as I am."

"Or as lazy as you are," Birdy interrupted. Frankie continued.

"But, just in case they did forget where the stamp came from, I thought it would be a good idea to put my name on it to remind them that I am the cool daddio who stamped their annual. But wait, it gets better." We all waited for about two seconds before Q took off again with his story. He was the worst at suspenseful pauses. They never lasted more than three seconds.

"When I got to the print shop, they had about twenty old rubber stamps that had worn out letters, misprints, and stamps that people had paid for but never picked up. I asked the owner if I could have a couple, and he gave me eight of them. One is a Benfatti Furniture stamp where the first 't' looks more like an 'r,' so they had to make another one. Benfarti Furniture is going to get stamped into no fewer than thirty annuals today. One stamp says, 'Accounts Payable,' so I will write in $2.00 on that stamp and see if I can make some money for my autograph today. There are stamps from CF&I, IBEW Local 12, Zoelsman's Bakery, Bowlero Lanes, and a couple of others. I am going to have some fun today stamping up a storm with no concern about getting writer's cramp. But then, writer's cramp isn't something that my less-popular Belmont Street Boys will have to be concerned about." We all smiled and wished him luck as we exited the Nomad for our last day at South. Q would stamp the annuals of his friends and randomly open others to put his stamp in them. Some kids thought it was funny and asked for a stamp, while others gripped their annuals tightly when they saw him coming. Marco thoughtfully signed 817 annuals that day, including a love letter to Sheila, which took up almost a full page in the back of her annual. (Under Marco's love letter, Q wrote *ditto times 2*). Sheila was hanging on Marco's arm the rest of the day after reading what Marco wrote. What a stud that guy is! I tried to write something nice in everyone's annual, and, by fourth period, I kind of wished I had thought of Q's idea. But even with a serious case of writer's cramp and writer's block, it was a really good day.

Tuesday morning was graduation rehearsal. Marco had somewhere he needed to be before the rehearsal, and Peeps had something to do right afterwards, so I gave Q a ride, and we were in our seats at 10:00am, right on time. It was kind of cool how the girls would be in white robes and the guys in black robes so that the view from the District 60 football stands

would be of a giant horseshoe, the emblem for the South High Colts. The
gold-cord seniors were seated in order of their class rank, and the rest
of the class was mostly seated by their class rank, except where changes
needed to be made to keep the horseshoe in form. It may have been a
little embarrassing for those at the end of the line to take their seats, but
they seemed to laugh it off as their friends said stuff like, "I'm glad you
made it; better to walk with us this year than to be in the class of '74; no
wonder you always asked to copy my homework," and stuff like that. Our
principal made it clear that he would not tolerate any nonsense during
the ceremony, and we believed him. Then we did a quick trial run on
the processional, ran through the order of things, and were done in just
under an hour. The Boys met up for a few minutes when we were dismissed, then went our separate ways until our meeting at Marco's house
at 8:00 that night. Q wanted to walk to his aunt's house to have lunch and
spend time with her that afternoon. She had taken the day off from her
job at the CF&I Credit Union to do something special with her favorite
nephew, so Q was looking forward to whatever she had planned. Nellie lived a few blocks from the stadium, and he preferred to walk to her
house, which was fine with me. I drove to the District 60 offices so Dad
and I could have lunch together. He let me choose the place, so I said, "La
Tronica's, here we come," and off we went.

The Boys were scattered in different directions all that afternoon and
early evening, but we all came together right on time at 8:00 at Marco's
house. When Mrs. T answered the door, she wasn't her usual cheery self.
Mr. T was sitting in front of the TV and waved at us rather than getting
up and giving us a hard time about whatever was on his mind. Mrs. T
then hugged each of us, which was unusual, and sent us through the garage door into the backyard where Marco was waiting for us. Something
was up and we all knew it. When we saw The Tatts sitting on the picnic
table bench with his head down, the three of us looked at each other and
braced ourselves for what we were about to hear. None of us had any idea
what it would be, but we knew there would be no celebrating on our last
night of high school together. We sat down without saying a word and
waited for Marco to tell us what was going on. The silence lasted about
one minute. One very long minute, then our friend and leader spoke.

"Guys, this is really good news, but it will be hard to hear. I have decided to become a priest. Over the past two years, I have spent a lot of time with Father John talking about this, and I am sure that this is the path I will be on for the rest of my life. And that path will begin tomorrow night." The three of us looked at Marco with blank stares, completely surprised by what we'd just heard, but none of us said a word. He continued to fill us in after a few seconds of silence, allowing his words time to sink in.

"Right after graduation tomorrow night, I will catch a bus to Enid, Oklahoma, where I will connect with some custom wheat cutters, like we talked about last month. The crew will travel through north Texas, Oklahoma, then Kansas and Nebraska, and into South and North Dakota and Minnesota in September and early October. It doesn't pay much but I will be working twelve- to sixteen-hour days with only a few days off for the next four and a half months. From there I will go to Washington for the October and early November apple harvest, then head to California for the November almond, grape, and walnut harvest. In mid-December, I will catch a bus to New Iberia, Louisiana, where I have a job waiting for me working on an oil rig in the Gulf of Mexico. I will be in the Gulf for three weeks at a time with one week off, and that job will last for one year. From there I will go to Newport News, Virginia, and work in the shipyards until the fall semester of 1975 and then begin my formal training in the priesthood. The two years of life outside of Pueblo with lots of different kinds of people should help prepare me with plenty of real-life experience that I think, and Father John agrees, will help me better understand a wide variety of people once I become a priest."

"Father John has lined up the jobs and places for me to live with parishioners in parishes where he knows the local priests. Almost all of the money I make over the next two years will go into an investment account that I can tap into later in life to fund some ministry I decide to start at that point in my life. The way I figure it, with all of the hours I will be working and the good pay on the oil rig and in the shipyards, I should be able to sock away around $40,000. With compound interest over the years, that should be a good chunk of change for me to use in some positive way later in life."

"I told Mom and Dad all of this over supper tonight. They tried to be happy for me, but it came out of left field and was really hard for them to hear. Italians love kids and grandkids, so my plans have really impacted their hopes for the future and their understanding of family. They said a lot of encouraging words to me, but it was obvious that their hearts weren't in it. I have no doubt that they will come around though. At 7:00, I went to Sheila's to tell her and her parents the news. Hearing what I had to say was especially hard on them because I think they all suspected that I was coming to their house to ask permission to marry Sheila. It was the night before graduation, and I had made an appointment to meet with the whole family; I should have seen that coming." He paused for a minute, shaking his head a little, and then continued.

"When I was done telling them everything, Mr. Grassley walked me to the door and shook my hand and told me that he was proud of me, but he had a tear in his eye because I had just broken his little girl's heart. Sheila was very brave, but, as I got into my car, I could hear Sheila and her mom crying. Man, that was hard to take. I really love that girl and her family." Once again, there were several moments of silence before Marco wrapped up the last official meeting of The Belmont Street Boys.

"Guys, I know I don't have to say this, but please look after my folks and Sheila. They will be hurting for quite a while, and I am pretty much cutting off contact with everyone for the foreseeable future. This will be hard on me, too, because of the 180-degree-change I am making in how I do life. I really need to immerse myself into this new life, so I think it is best if I release all of my ties to Pueblo and family for now. At the right time, I will grab hold of it all again, but, for now, I think this is the best approach. I hope you guys understand. You know how much I love you and how important you are to me. This time of separation will not change that in any way, shape, or form." We all nodded. Then without any words being spoken other than each of us saying, "I love you, Marco," we went our separate ways. The bomb had exploded, and we were all stunned.

I walked around the neighborhood until 9:30 thinking about everything and thinking about nothing. About thirty minutes into my wanderings, I remembered more clearly the talk where we shared what we wanted to do with our lives in the future, and it began to make some sense. Marco had told us all the things he wanted to do with his life, and, along with that, I thought about all the time that he had been spending with Father John the past few months. My head was still spinning as I walked in the front door of our house and went to my room and straight to bed. Somehow, I was able to fall asleep right away and wake up ten hours later. I guess the news had put me into some kind of a walking coma.

The next morning at breakfast, I told my mom the news. She was initially a little dazed by the unexpected report. Like the Boys, she had in some way imagined my life moving forward with Marco being an important part of our lives. After sipping on her hot tea, she offered, "Of course you know that you will need to support him however possible." I did know that but hadn't given it much thought. Mom's words helped me to regain my focus on how I could best support my friend. As I pondered that idea, I looked out the kitchen and saw Q drive past. He came back around noon, showed up at my front door, and said, "I just enlisted in the Air Force. I leave for boot camp one week from today." Q then walked over to Birdy's house and made the same announcement. It was more fallout from the bomb blast and one more challenge of how I would need to figure out how to best support another friend.

Early in the afternoon, Peeps and I went to Sheila's house to see how she was doing. Her mom said that Sheila was in no shape to speak with us, but she did fill us in on Sheila's immediate plans. Since Sheila was both our Valedictorian and a Boettcher Foundation scholar, she could attend any college in Colorado and have enough money to pay for all four years of education. Sheila and her parents would be leaving as soon as she got her diploma and begin a trip to Durango where she would enroll at Ft. Lewis College. Durango was as far from Pueblo and its memories as she could get and still attend college in Colorado. There wouldn't be too many kids from Pueblo at Ft. Lewis and no one from South that she knew of, so Sheila wouldn't have to deal with people who knew her story. Sheila would enroll and begin summer classes immediately. She needed to busy herself with classes and part-time work in order to try to free her mind from whom she was sure she would have become right after college graduation—Mrs. Marco Tattalinni. We walked away knowing that the fallout would probably continue.

Graduation couldn't have arrived soon enough. The Boys were reeling, and the graduation ceremony gave us a chance to focus on something other than the bomb blast we'd just gone through. We were still processing what we were feeling, but the band playing "Pomp and Circumstance," and the general excitement of the moment, allowed us to celebrate with all of our other friends.

Sheila managed to get through her valedictory address just fine, but just hearing her name and her words made the Boys feel the blast all over again. When each of the Boys' names were called, we were able to enter back into the experience of the moment and be happy with our class-mates. That was, until we heard "Marco Joseph Tattalinni" called, and, instantly, we were in Marco's backyard hearing the news all over again. When my dad, in his role as Superintendent, accepted the class as official graduates of South High School and we were dismissed, Sheila made a beeline to her parents' car, which was waiting at the field-level exit gate, and the Grassleys sped off into the night. Marco smiled and slapped high fives as he walked off the field, into the stands, into his parents' car, and off to the bus depot. No one tried to slow him down to talk, respecting his need to get away from everyone as soon as possible. Word had quickly spread about his decision to become a priest, so kids kept his exit simple and just said things like, "Good luck" and "See you later, Father." Within three minutes of my dad's pronouncement, he was gone. The Boys just stood together and watched him go. Once again, the bomb blast rever-berated in our souls.

The three of us went to four after-graduation parties, and the main topic of conversation at every party was Marco and Sheila. There was lots of storytelling and laughing, but the Boys mostly listened and let others do the talking. Birdy and I had never seen Q be so quiet. He took the news the hardest of the Boys. Several times that night, I thought he was going to cry as people talked about his lifelong friend. When we went to the party at Lana's house, I did tell the homecoming dance story about us being surrounded by the hoods from East. Hearing how cool and calm Marco was in a situation that scared the fool out of the girls and me made Q smile. Everyone at the party wanted me to tell them more, but, every time I spoke his name, it hurt. I had never experienced what it was like to have someone that I love die, but I was convinced that this is how it must feel. The Boys headed home around 2:00am, and I, for one, collapsed into bed from mental and emotional exhaustion.

We slogged our way through the next few days doing whatever we could to busy our minds. The Boys went to a movie one night and out for Mexican food another. I went to church with Q on his last Sunday in town and watched the people there give him a good send off. Mae even kissed him on the cheek. Frankie seemed to enjoy all of the attention, but he still wasn't himself. On the Monday following graduation, I started my job with the State of Colorado preparing the State Fair Grounds for the annual Colorado State Fair in August. That kept me busy until Wednesday when Q left for boot camp and the fallout rained down on us again and lasted for several days. Marco was a friend and leader who could not be replaced. Somehow, we would have to figure out what a new normal would look like for us. For Q, the United States Air Force would tell him what normal would be. For Birdy and me, we would have to figure it out in our own way. But at least we had each other.

22

Off to College

Two days after Frankie left for the Air Force, Birdy came to my house when I got home from the fair grounds and hit me with an idea I loved immediately. "I think we need to form a little duo and see if we can get some gigs for this summer. Here is a list of seventeen songs we can learn and easily put together in a sixty-minute set to do for receptions, maybe a restaurant, or even on the stage at the State Fair since you have an in with the people in charge there. You can come to my place four nights a week, when I'm not teaching dance, and we could rehearse. You can learn some basic chords on your piano, which will make your mom happy, so that you can back me up when I am on guitar, and we can take turns singing lead depending on the song and which one of us is best suited for the song. We will do a few blendy songs with nice harmonies by CS&N, America, and Three Dog Night, and a good selection of Beatles and other pop songs. What do you think?" With no hesitation I said, "Count me in." We started rehearsing that night.

Working for eight hours and rehearsing for four was a good routine for me the first couple of weeks after graduation. Being around kids from high school was no fun because all they wanted to talk about was Marco. By the end of June, that talk had quieted down, and I was ready to go on some dates, play a little tennis, and just goof off with whoever was available. By the Fourth of July we got our first gig. A husband and wife, for whom Birdy taught dance lessons, owned a little wholesale business and were having a party for their seven employees, family members, and

152

a few friends in their back yard, about twenty-five people total. When they invited Birdy to attend, he talked the couple into letting us be the entertainment for the party. They even agreed to pay us $30 for two hours of music. When I went all bug-eyed on him, Birdy said, "Don't worry about it. We will do thirty minutes and take a five-minute break, then do thirty more minutes and take a ten-minute break. Then I will do a thirty-minute set by myself with a five-minute break, and we will finish up by repeating the three or four songs we think sound the best. I have all the sound gear we will need, and Mr. Peats, the party host, will have a little stage set up for us. This will be a piece of cake." The prospect of a money-paying-gig helped me buckle down even harder to learn the music and fine-tune my performance skills. The gig went so well, that we got two offers to sing at weddings later in the summer, which was really easy money. We would show up, sing two songs, get paid ten bucks each, and then go to a reception afterwards to eat food and talk with pretty girls. After the first wedding I thought, "Way to go Birdy! Keep those great ideas coming!"

Birdy and I squeezed in a few fishing trips after work to places like De-Weese Reservoir, Rosemont Reservoir, an all-night camping and fishing adventure to Eleven Mile Reservoir, and two early, Saturday morning trips to Twin Lakes. Then there was the Jethro Tull concert in Denver, one waterskiing trip to Lake Meredith with the family of one of Birdy's girlfriends, several movies, and a trip to watch the AAA Denver Bears, which at that time was a minor league team for the Houston Astros. With work at the Fairgrounds, learning and rehearsing music, and a dedicated focus on having as much fun as possible, I was discovering that life without Marco could be meaningful and lively.

In late July, we got our first gig at a restaurant, Shakey's Pizza, which went so well that the manager of a local hang out, St. John's and the Dragon, gave us one night on their stage. It was a Tuesday night, which was usually pretty slow for them, but when all of our friends and family showed up, they knew it was a good business decision for the restaurant/bar. They offered us two more nights in August, but by then we were running out of time before leaving for college and had to turn them down. We were really focused on our ninety-minute show on a stage at the State Fair and wanted to nail that opportunity. My boss at the Fair was in charge of booking all the acts at the picnic grounds amphitheater, and I kept bugging him to let us play. When he asked me what our name was, I said, "He is Lenny and I am Nick, but we go by Manny and Bobo—he's Manny and I'm Bobo." My boss thought that was funny, and, when he heard us perform at Shakey's, he put us on the bill. Our show would be sandwiched between square dancers from the Prowers County FFA and readings by The Pueblo County Historical Society. "Thanks a lot, Ted. It's not as good as being on the same bill as Poco and Spirit, but we'll take it." He agreed to let us put a guitar case at the front of the stage for donations, so we would no doubt make a few bucks.

We were both excited for the opportunity and added the five new songs we would need to fill a ninety-minute show. Birdy taught me the basic chord progressions for his set of songs, and, hallelujah, his keyboard had a transpose feature, so I could play all of the new songs I was learning in the key of C. That made the learning process so much easier. We started talking our gig up to everyone we knew, and all of our friends and family did the same until we had a guaranteed audience of around seventy people and probably even more. With that kind of a decent crowd already on board, we figured we would attract people who would be walking by the amphitheater and would stop to check out what was going on. Even the Tattalinni and Luna families said they would come to the Fair that night just to hear us. If their extended families showed up, too, the picnic grounds could be packed.

When the night came, with the help of my dad and two friends from school, we had our gear set up and the sound check done ten minutes after the Square Dancers left the stage. There was a program for the night's events, and it listed Manny and Bobo in the 6:30—8:00 time slot. When Peeps began speaking, it was 6:30 on the dot and his natural stage presence made me feel totally relaxed. "Thanks for showing up to watch us try not to amuse you by making fools out of ourselves. You can tell us later if we succeeded. The program lists us as Manny and Bobo, but I just decided to rename our band Priest in honor of our loser friend, Marco, who abandoned us all to become one." That line got good laughs, even from Mr. and Mrs. Grassley who had slipped in and sat next to the Tattalinnis while we were setting up. He then tore into "Larry Norman's 71st Nightmare," a supercool song only a few people knew but everyone seemed to enjoy. We followed that up with "Penny Lane" and "American Pie" before we slowed the tempo down a little. People were already starting to come up and put some coins and bills in the guitar case, and some passersby stuck around to listen for a while before moving on to another part of the fair. We were one hour into the show and clicking on all cylinders when, all of a sudden, Birdy announced, "Now we are going to take some requests." I panicked and thought, what in the world are you doing, my friend? I quickly figured it out.

People would yell out some request and Birdy would point to some random person and say, "'Our House' it is," and we would do that song because it was the next on our list. After he had done the same thing three times in a row, some people figured out what was happening and started playing along. Mrs. Yankovich yelled out "Toccata and Fugue in D Minor," and Birdy pointed at her and said, "I love 'Don't Mess Around With Jim,' so here goes." Birdy's uncle, who, along with his wife had slipped into the crowd without me noticing, stood up and hollered, "I want to hear 'The William Tell Overture.'" Birdy pointed right at him and said, "Thank you, Uncle Will, for requesting one of my favorite songs," and we cranked out "Roll Over Beethoven." Birdy had people laughing and digging the music right up to our final song when he announced "I would like our friend, Laurel, and Nick's mom, Lucille, to come up on stage for our final song. Everyone is welcomed to sing along if you know it." Peeps had worked it all out ahead of time with everyone but me, and I was fine with that. (Laurel sang soprano in the Carolaires and was my date to prom). It ended up being a great surprise. Mom gave us our starting notes, even though I didn't know what we would be singing, but I quickly began singing the bass line of "The Lord Bless You and Keep You" on the fourth word of the song, thinking what a cool way to end our little concert. The four of us on stage had all four parts covered and it sounded pretty good for an unrehearsed song. As soon as we'd sung the Amen, Birdy said, "Thanks for coming out," and we were done. Our helpers came on stage quickly and worked fast to get all of our gear packed up and get us off the stage in time for the Historical Society to begin right in their designated time slot. Mom and Mrs. Grassley had the money counted and in a bank bag to give us as we headed to our cars to stow all the gear.

I looked back to see that only about twenty people hung around for the next act and felt a little bad for them until Mrs. Grassley said, "Congratulations, boys. There was $113.37 in your guitar case. You guys were a big hit."

"That is our best payday of the summer and easily the most fun we had at a gig," I said excitedly. Birdy nodded in agreement as we carried our gear to Dad's pick up. We were just coming into our own as a musical duo, but our time as a band was over. Birdy was headed to CU, and I would be at Mines, so the days of Manny and Bobo or Priest were numbered. It was a blast while it lasted, and a much more pleasant blast than the one Marco set off that night in May.

The morning after our big gig, Birdy showed up at my house and asked, "Now what are we going to do with our final three days before heading off to college?" That was easy.

With no pause at all, I rattled off, "One all-night fishing trip to Eleven-Mile, get dates and head out to The Great Sand Dunes, and a final night of a movie followed by Sam and Ray's Pizza with just the two of us." With a quick, "Let's do it," from Peeps, we were set.

Birdy said, "Back in June, I met this really cute girl from East at a record shop. She was looking at Top 40 music while I was checking out some obscure Rock and Roll albums that can be hard to find. I was also checking her out, and, when she noticed me doing that, we started talking. She gave me her number, and we've dated a few times, so I am guessing she will be on board for a fun day at The Dunes. Her name is Bobbie Jo. Cool name, don't you think?" I nodded and thought, if Q were here, he would have started singing the theme song from "Petticoat Junction." Man, I miss that guy.

Later that afternoon, I got my fishing gear together, made a few phone calls until I found a date for The Dunes trip the next day with the lovely Sheryl Kelly, and let Mom in on my plans.

Mom smiled and said, "It sounds like fun, but don't forget to make a list of everything you will be taking to college so that I can see if you have everything you need for dorm life." I sat down right then and made the list. The next morning, I saw that she had added about a dozen things that hadn't crossed my mind. Way to go, Mom!

Our all-night fishing trip ended at around midnight when the weather turned cold. We were miserable, so we called it quits. With seven fish weighing a total of around sixteen pounds, it was a successful trip. I was warm and in my bed by 2:30am, which meant Birdy and I would have plenty of rest to play hard at The Dunes. The girls packed picnic lunches for us, and we provided the car, gas, Pepsi, cardboard, and a ton of energy for an afternoon of climbing, rolling and sliding down The Dunes, and playing in the artesian stream that flows in front of The Dunes. We picked the girls up and were on the road by 11:45 that morning. Birdy's cassette player was blasting good tunes, and the girls were pretty and talkative, so the day was off to a great start. We ate our lunch as soon as we got to The Dunes and then headed off to make it to the highest peak. Halfway up, we left our cardboard partially buried so that it wouldn't blow away.

At the summit of the tallest dune, we rested for a few minutes, when Birdy said, "I know a guy who actually brought a camel up here." Following a bunch of comments like, "Really?" "That's hard to believe!" "Where did he get a camel?" "That's pretty cool," Birdy confidently shook his head and said, "It's true. As a matter of fact, he brought a whole pack of Camels up here." We all laughed, and Bobbie Jo, the girl from East I'd never met before that day, leaned over and kissed Birdy when she'd stopped laughing.

I looked at Sheryl as if to say, "Where is my kiss," and she looked me in the eyes and said, "You'll have to catch me first," and she took off down the dune. I did catch her just before the place where we'd left the cardboard, and she gave me a quick kiss and said, "Let's see if this cardboard works. I hear you are supposed to be able to slide on the sand with this stuff, but I will believe it when I see it." The cardboard didn't work great, but it was better than only rolling or doing somersaults in the sand. Whatever method we used to get down the dunes, every time I looked behind me, there was Birdy walking for a while, stopping and kissing Bobbie Jo for a while, and having another type of fun than what Sheryl and I were having. She saw it, too, but it didn't interfere with what we were doing. We laughed a lot, teased a lot, and thoroughly enjoyed our time together.

When the four of us got to the stream that often runs at the base of The Dunes, we cleaned the sand off as best we could, played in the water for a while, and then headed back to the car. Just before crawling into the back seat, Peeps grabbed my shoulder and said, "Nick, why don't you drive us back to Pueblo?"

Sheryl hollered, "Absolutely not! I am not going to sit in the front seat and listen to whatever it is the two of you decide to be doing all the way home while in the back seat. That is not going to happen." She said it with a laugh in her voice and a smile on her face, so it went over well, but as soon as we hit the highway, she started kissing me and making a lot of noise. Then she cracked up as Lenny and Bobbie Jo looked at us, and Sheryl let out with, "That is what I was talking about." There was a lot of nervous laughter for a few seconds, but then everything went back to normal as we listened to the tunes and talked about college plans.

On the way to The Dunes, the girls must have said ten times, "Who is this?" as they listened to Birdy's eclectic mix of songs. The third time one of them asked the question on the return trip, I shook my head and said, "Top 40, girls," and Sheryl slugged me in the arm when she realized I had just dealt her a mild put down.

Birdy took it from there and informed our dates, "I will tell you the artist, but I refuse to explain who that artist is since you won't know them anyway." Bobbie Jo slugged him but then quickly kissed the slug away. It was a good day with one more to go.

Mom woke me up at 8:00am with her cheery greeting, "Sunshine, it is time to get up and at 'em." After a quick breakfast of French toast, we went over my packing list one more time and began filling two suitcases and three boxes with all the stuff on the list. Mom set out all the things I would need but had forgotten to put on my list—stuff like bedding, curtains, towels, fingernail clippers, emergency sewing kit, band aids, and an emergency first-aid kit. Clothes, tennis racket, fishing gear, and stereo equipment were my priorities. We finished most of the packing by 10:15 when Mom announced that the Bradford family would be having lunch together at the Top of the Town restaurant. Dad would be ready outside the administration building at 11:15, and we would pick him up and head out from there. That was a nice surprise. Before leaving for lunch, I asked Mom to give me a final piano lesson, which was also pretty much my first piano lesson since I had always been a very uncooperative student up until that day.

"I would be delighted to finally give you a real piano lesson," Mom said. She took great joy in teaching me a few techniques to practice and also slapping my knuckles with a ruler when my finger placement was wrong. I laughed and hugged her real hard when the lesson was over.

Lunch was good, and Dad was relaxed, even though it was an especially busy week for him. He always did a great job of making family a priority while still making it clear that, even though we were the most important part of his life, there were other things which were also important, and he could not overlook those responsibilities. Dad was a great father, a great school superintendent, a great friend, and, according to Mom, he was a top-notch husband. All of that was communicated in one way or another over lunch that day, but, at 12:30, Dad said he needed to hurry back to work and most likely would work an hour or so late tonight. That was no problem for me since Peeps and I would be catching the 6:00pm showing of "American Graffiti" that night.

The movie was cool, and the Sam and Ray's Pizza was as good as usual. When the manager heard that the two of us were heading off to college, he had the kitchen make us a little pastry in thanks for all the times we'd been in his restaurant. He brought us the pastry and announced, "No charge for the dessert, but I am charging you double for the pizza." After laughing at his own joke, he said, "Enjoy the pastry, boys. I only wish that I could have done the same for your two buddies before they left town." We smiled and thanked him, while at the same time feeling sad that we couldn't have shared the past three days with Q and The Tatts.

Peeps jumped to his feet and said, "Let's go out to the car. I have a going-away present for you." We paid the bill, thanked the manager again for the good pizza and the free pastry, and headed out to the parking lot. Peeps must have hidden the present in his trunk. I couldn't wait to see what my generous friend had for me.

"This present comes with a condition. If you sell it, you have to give me half of the money you get for it unless you use that money to buy a better one. Agreed?" I shook my head yes even though I wasn't sure what he was talking about, and then Birdy opened the trunk. It was his acoustic Epiphone guitar. "I have a Guild D-50 acoustic, a nylon stringed Yamaha G Series, and a Gibson Les Paul electric, so I can give you the same guitar I started out on. This Mel Bay book shows you chords, finger-picking patterns, and a little bit of music theory which should keep you from having to spend too much time with the engineering wierdos up at Mines." I didn't know what to say. What a cool gift. What a cool friend. What a cool night with the guy who had become my closest friend.

"I love you, Lenny Peeples," was all I could say.

It would have been a quiet ride back home, but Birdy changed all that. In light of the movie that we'd seen earlier, we drove around Pueblo for an hour blasting loud music and talking to girls we saw driving around in their cars. When we finally made our way back to Belmont, the two of us reaffirmed our love for each other and the commitment to our friendship. The Belmont Street Boys had been cut in half, but there was no way on earth that our little gang would ever dissolve. Birdy and Scotty would make sure of that.

The next morning, I managed to fit my Epiphone in the car with all the other stuff and headed off to Golden, Colorado. Dad agreed to let me take my car to college as long as I agreed to keep the mileage down to no more than a thousand miles a month. Since it was 130 miles one way to Mines, I knew frequent trips home could not happen with that mileage limit. So, I would need to budget my miles wisely as I began the great adventure of being a college engineering student and preparing for the rest of my life.

23

Staying Connected

GOLDEN WAS AN INTERESTING town situated right up against the front range of the Rockies. While not being surrounded by mountains like Leadville or Westcliff, it is still considered to be a mountain town. Staying focused on studies would be a challenge for me with distractions like hiking up Lookout Mountain, fishing in Clear Creek, and at least six ski areas being less than an hour's drive away. Plus, Lenny was only twenty miles away at CU, so the temptation to meet up with him would be constant. All of that was running through my head until the first week of classes was behind me and the math and science courses started to kick my butt.

My roommate was a guy from Lakewood named Larry Brown, just like the ABA player and coach, who was about to become the new head coach of the Denver Rockets. This Larry Brown, though, probably didn't know that Denver had a pro basketball franchise, and, if he did, he couldn't tell you if they were the Rockets or the Broncos. His lack of interest in sports worked fine with me since he always seemed to have time to tutor me and get me up to speed in calculus and Intro to Materials Engineering. He definitely was the engineering wierdo-type Birdy knew I would run into at Mines, but he was a nice enough guy and a decent roommate. He did have one peculiar ability that I let him know was not acceptable to practice in our room. Larry knew a few other Mines students from his days as a member of a Denver-wide science club he was part of during his junior and senior years of high school. Often when those friends saw him, they would say, "Larry, fart," and he would. My roommate had the ability to fart on demand. Unbelievable! We came to an agreement that he would save his gas until I was out of our room and for a time when he could use his engineering skills to harness that energy for some useful purpose. He smiled at that thought, then said, "So it's okay for me to be your tutor but not your tooter," and started laughing hysterically.

I grinned and said, "Good one," but that mildly amusing pun was by far the funniest thing I heard Larry say the entire time I knew him.

Two weeks into school, I couldn't take it any longer and headed off to Boulder. I had to find out how Peeps was doing at CU and figure out some way to stay in better contact with him. Since I didn't have any Friday afternoon classes, I drove to CU and stood in front of the Alferd Packer Grill, named after Colorado's infamous cannibal, hoping that my buddy just might be eating at the university's main dining facility that day. After around thirty minutes, I asked someone where the freshman men's dorms were and took off in that direction. Once there, I asked almost everyone I saw if they knew him and got a lot of shrugs until a group of girls walked by and one of them said, "Is he tall and handsome and forming a band?"

"That's the guy," I said, and she pointed me to a music building where she thought he and the band were practicing.

About ten minutes later, I walked in on The Spinsters—Lenny and three other guys working on developing their first set of songs. He looked up, finished the song they were practicing, said, "That's enough for today, guys," and then introduced me to the band. From what little I heard of the band, it sounded like Peeps had found three decent musicians to work with.

We spent the afternoon hanging out, eating at the Packer Grill, filling each other in on our classes and social life (his was great and mine pathetic), and exchanging our dorm floor phone numbers so that we could make plans to get together again soon. He invited me to sit with him in the student section for the CU/Baylor football game in a few weeks. I took him up on the invitation, and it was a lot of fun to sit in Folsom Field with the Flatiron Mountains in the background for a major college football game and watch the Buffs beat up on the Bears. It was amazing to me how many people at CU knew Birdy by then and how many girls were interested in me just because I was hanging out with him. I thought about transferring to CU for an hour or so, and then came back to reality. Mines was the place for me, and I knew it.

One of us called the other once a week until fall break came and we were back on Belmont Street. Our first day back, we went to Frankie's house to find out how to get in touch with our buddy, followed by a trip to the Grassley home to get an update on Sheila. While at the Grassleys, it dawned on me that I had pretty much ignored my folks and Chrissie for the past month and a half, so I decided that the next two days would be reserved for them. That was a good move, which Mom and Dad really seemed to appreciate. Birdy went back to school early to catch another football game and to rehearse with his band, so that gave me a few days more to relax at the house. My brain needed the rest from academics, and my mom especially needed time with her son.

Thursday afternoon that week, I wandered over to the Tattalinni home to say hi and received a warm, Italian greeting from Marco's folks. Mrs. T pulled out some pastries, opened up a bottle of Pepsi, and started rattling off a dozen or more questions about how I was doing, what college life was like for me, did I miss home, was I dating anyone, and so on.

Mr. T interrupted her with, "Let the boy talk," before he threw about twenty postcards on the table from Marco for me to check out. "My boy has been doing a lot of traveling and making a lot of money," Mr. T proudly announced as he took over and started pummeling me with questions. The two of them went on for ten minutes or so as I read the postcards sent by Marco from Texas to N. Dakota and all states in between. It was obvious to me how badly they missed their son and how important it would be for me to spend time with them whenever I could. Over the next few years, our relationship would deepen to the point that I viewed them as almost being a second set of parents to me.

That relationship solidified when, during Christmas break of my senior year in college, Mrs. T said with tears in her eyes, "Nick, you have become a son to me."

When I responded with, "Thanks for saying that, Mom," she grabbed me, hugged me tight until she'd finished crying, then she kissed me on the forehead and pushed me away as she hollered, "Now get out of here, kid, before I put you to work!" What a moment that was.

When I asked if they'd heard from Q, they talked over each other to tell me that he called them twice a month and that military life has been real good for him. It was great to hear their excitement over their much-loved neighbor boy and to find out how well Frankie had adjusted to the radically different way of life he had chosen. Really, it wasn't surprising, because Q seemed to be able to adapt to whatever life presented him and consistently stay a positive and happy dude. I asked Mr. and Mrs. T to be sure to tell Frankie to call me at home over the four-day Thanksgiving weekend, and they, of course, agreed to do that. Man, I missed my old buddy and couldn't wait to hear from him again.

Since Marco had made me promise to check up on Sheila, I made a return trip to the Grassleys by myself on Saturday morning to see if they were ready to share something more than just her general well-being at that time. The whole Grassley family had been so devastated by Marco's decision. In light of that, I knew it was important for me to be really careful with them, since my questions about Sheila and my friendship with Marco could have easily dug up all the emotions that were likely buried just below the surface of that three-person family. But, if my visit caused their pain to reignite, they sure didn't flame up during my short visit. Mr. and Mrs. Grassley seemed very happy to see me and to catch up on any news I had about the other Belmont Street Boys. They let me know that Sheila was unbelievably busy, carrying twenty hours of classes and working a weekend job at the Durango Diner. She didn't need to work, they told me, but she really didn't want to have free time on her hands during her freshman year. Her goal was to finish college during the summer of 1976 and to enroll in law school as soon as she graduated. "Well, if anyone can do it, I know Shelia can. So, she will be in law school while the rest of us are beginning our senior years."

Her dad smiled and nodded as he said, "That's our Sheila." We talked for a few minutes more, and they agreed to make sure that Sheila contacted me when she was home over Christmas break. The Grassleys would be going to Durango for Thanksgiving to spend a few days skiing with Sheila, but Sheila would definitely be in Pueblo for five or six days over the Christmas break. It would be great to see her then.

As Mrs. Grassley walked me to my car, she held onto my arm and said, "I kind of hoped that maybe you and Sheila might start dating at some time."

I paused for a few moments and then said, "I have given that idea careful consideration. Sheila is beautiful and smart and everything I would want in a woman, but the two of us would spend too much of our time thinking and talking about Marco. I'm not sure I would ever be able not to measure myself against him, and that would leave me feeling perpetually inadequate. That's not who I want to be and not what Sheila needs in a man. Sheila needs to meet some guy who never knew Marco and date that guy. He won't measure up to Marco, but, at least, he also won't be aware of that fact."

Mrs. Grassley smiled and said, "I suppose you are right."

I hugged her and said, "But I will be taking her out on a date over Christmas break. Sheila, Lenny, and I will be taking in a movie, eating some pizza, and laughing until one of us cries." That made her chuckle, and she waved as I drove off.

It seemed like only a few days rather than four weeks had passed when I found myself back in Pueblo. The fourth Thursday in November was the day to play in the Belmont Street Annual T-Giving football game and to enjoy the Bradford Family Thanksgiving Feast. As Mom and Chrissie were cleaning up and Dad was filling Tupperware containers with what was left of our fifteen-pound turkey, the phone rang, so I answered it. As soon as I said hello, an unmistakable voice shouted out, "Surprise, surprise, surprise. Scotty is that you?" It was so good to hear Q's voice after almost six months of no contact with him.

"Yes, it is. Is that you, Gomer?" We both laughed for a few seconds before I started in again.

"Are you a sergeant yet? If so, I'll bet you are the best dang sergeant in the whole dang Air Force." I knew he would love the quote from "No Time for Sergeants."

"Give me a few years, and I will be," he said. From there he went on for five minutes about how much he loved the Air Force, how many friends he had there at Robins Air Force Base, and how much he was enjoying Georgia. My good friend hardly took a breath. But when he started talking about his girlfriend, Rhonda, the intensity in his voice went to a new level.

"She is so pretty and smart and funny and talented. I need to send you a picture. She's the kind of girl Birdy would date, if that gives you an idea. She is going to finish up her associates degree next year, which means she will be a registered nurse just three years out of high school." He went on like that until he finally slowed down enough for me to say something.

I very calmly said, "She sounds great, Frankie. But does she know that she's your girlfriend?"

"Man, you stink! There is nothing about you that doesn't stink! I'm glad I got a thousand miles away from Pueblo, so I don't have to smell your stinking stinkiness anymore!" That's all it took. I was laughing in the way only Q could make me laugh.

"Frankie, you are the best! If Rhonda is a real person, hopefully she will love you as faithfully as the Boys do. So, when you finally introduce yourself to her, go ahead and ask her out. Once you go on an actual date, please have someone take a picture of the two of you together so I can show the picture to Birdy and then to Sheila when we see her in December. And don't forget what Marco said to you about not falling for the first girl who lets you kiss her."

"Nick, it might be too late for that. I care about her a whole lot. I don't know what love is, but it sure seems like I am traveling a road with her that is headed in that direction. We met at a pie social hosted by a little church close to base. You know how I love pies, so when I saw a flyer for it in the commons area, I decided to attend. There was a really good-looking, coconut cream pie on the table, and I had the high bid on it. That meant that, not only did I get to take the pie back to the barracks with me, but I also got to eat a slice of that pie with the girl who made it. When Rhonda brought the pie to me, I told her that I couldn't believe such a pretty girl could make a great-looking pie. And when the pie tasted great, too, that's all I needed to keep a good conversation going for the next hour or so. She told me about her plans, and I told her about Pueblo and the lousy friends I left behind there."

"Q, as The Eagles would say, 'Take it Easy.' Go slowly, my friend. If it is love, it won't need to be rushed. Let it be a slow burn. Good things are worth waiting for." I didn't really know what to say. I was happy for Frank. He is such a great guy and has a kind spirit and tender heart, but he is also susceptible to the kind of woman who could get him hooked on her and then misuse him.

"Sounds like you are preparing for a career in writing bumper stickers and T-shirt slogans," Q said to ease the tension which was building. "Don't worry. We aren't going to elope or anything. I still have to win over her family, since they are a little leery of flyboys, who are here for a few years and then move on. Plus, I'm not sure they'd ever met a Mexican before me. But thanks for your concern and your love. I know I always have those two things . . . and your never funny remarks about some aspect of my appearance, brains, and personality."

"That's a given," I said.

And he responded with, "Of course."

I gave him my school address and told him that, if he wrote me, I would always respond. We started regular correspondence after his first letter. Q sent me a picture of Rhonda, a cute brunette, in one of his letters and informed me that he would be staying in Georgia when he was on leave and over holiday breaks in order to be with her. Plus, he thought that, while he was stationed in the South, he ought to use that opportunity to travel around and see the South. That made sense to me, so I encouraged him to do just that. So, it didn't seem that we would be seeing Frankie anytime soon.

The word "schizophrenia" popped into my mind when I thought about not spending time with Q. I was happy for him but very sad about not being able to hang out with such a close friend. It was very similar to the schizophrenic reaction I had when Marco shared his news with the Boys. Maybe The Belmont Street Boys were becoming The Schizophrenic Boys. Only time would tell.

It was great to get away from Golden, engineering classes, and dining hall food for three weeks. Birdy and I got in two days of skiing, and he introduced me to ice fishing in the days leading up to Christmas. Mom's meals tasted terrific, Dad's jokes and conversation were interesting, and I had rediscovered what a sweet girl Chrissie was. She'd turned thirteen while I was at Mines, and she was becoming a very pretty and interesting young lady. Mom and Dad were excited about my grades. "All As in engineering," Dad proudly announced, and Mom repeated. They wanted me to relax and enjoy myself over Christmas break after all my hard work that first semester, so I relaxed with all my strength! Besides the skiing and fishing, there was lots of lounging around the house, eating Mom's Christmas cookies and fudge, and lining up a few dates with old girlfriends. Life was relaxingly good!

Christmas Day was lots of fun with the family. After opening presents and then eating a nice brunch, we headed for Rye with two inner tubes and spent several hours sliding down a hill that ended up on the ice of Lake Isabel. It was surprising to me to realize how much fun I was having just watching my parents and sister laughing and playing together. Mom had said often how much enjoyment she got out of watching me have fun, and, for the first time in my life, I felt like I understood what she meant by that. What a great family I have!

As soon as we got home, I called Sheila to make sure she was going to be available for our evening together on the 26th. We spoke briefly, but she made it clear that she was looking forward to being with me and Lenny.

As soon as we hung up, I called my friend, Richard Terlap, who worked at the Chief Theater and made arrangements with him to get three tickets to the second showing of "The Sting" on the 26th. Lines would be long, so I would come by his house the next morning, pay him for three tickets, and then show up at the alley emergency exit as soon as the previous showing was letting out. That meant that we would be the first ones in the theater for the late afternoon showing. It ended up being a great idea since lines outside the Chief stretched all the way down the block.

Birdy's uncle had a 1969 Pontiac Firebird with a bench seat, so he drove that evening and the three of us sat together in the front seat. I jumped out of the car to get Sheila, and she was waiting for us, coming out the front door before I had time to ring the doorbell. She gave me a hug, waved to her folks, jumped in the car, and said, "Let's go have some fun, boys. It's been a while since I have had a blast!"

"Well, you have come to the right place, little lady," Peeps offered as he put his arm around her and gave her a hug. It seemed like old times.

Sheila filled us in on college life at Ft. Lewis, and then Birdy and I did the same about CU and Mines. We were having very different experiences at our colleges, but the thing we all had in common was that we enjoyed the challenges of school and the wide range of professors and students that we saw on a daily basis. To wrap it all up, I said as we were getting out of the Firebird, "It sounds like the three of us are flourishing."

Shelia paused as she scooted out of the car then offered, "In many ways that is true." I figured that subject might come up again after the movie.

Richard let us in the alley door with our tickets already torn, then we found the prime seats three-fourths of the way back in the auditorium, right in the center of the screen, and I filled them in on the latest from Q until the movie previews began. The Chief was cram packed by the time the lights dimmed.

"What a great movie; I loved the ragtime music; did not see that ending coming; I could see that again." Comments like that continued all the way from our seats at the Chief to our seats at Sam and Ray's. When Sheila said, "That Robert Redford is one good-looking hunk of homo-sapien meat," Birdy and I looked at each other and simultaneously responded, "I didn't notice." That made Sheila laugh, and we were on to subjects other than the movie and handsome movie stars.

After a few minutes of bouncing from one subject to another, Birdy looked at Sheila and asked, "So beautiful, are you dating anyone these days?"

With no hesitation, Sheila tore into a rant beginning with, "No!! My first week at Ft. Lewis, and I am not exaggerating, I got asked out every single day! The pace slowed down a little until all of the fall semester students showed up, and then the pace picked up dramatically. In between classes, during class, guys coming to my dorm and asking for me, sitting next to me in the library and dining hall, coming by work and leaving me big tips followed by 'how about a date, good looking;' it was non-stop throughout the day and unbelievably annoying. After two weeks of that, I asked myself a question which surprised me when it first popped into my brain. And here is the question. 'How would Frankie respond to all this unwanted attention?' It took me about five minutes to process through all the possibilities, but this was my conclusion. I went to a grocery store, bought a fly swatter, and whenever a guy even spoke to me, I would swat him with it."

"You did not do that; sweet Sheila, treating guys like they were annoying pests; that is hard to believe; it does sound like something Q would do." Birdy and I could not believe what we were hearing. With stunned expressions on our faces and repeated questions to be sure she was telling the truth, I leaned back in my chair, laughed a little nervously, and said, "Tell us more." And she did.

"After two weeks of getting swatted, the guys at Ft. Lewis got the message and left me alone. Some of the most persistent guys that I swatted the hardest even avoided me for a while. All except this one guy. He was a junior and fancied himself to be quite the ladies' man. One day he walked up to me in the hall and said, "I don't care how many times you swat me I am not going to take no for an answer. Will you go on a date with me?" I hit him so many times and so hard that I broke my fly swatter on that goofy guy. He took off running, and, that afternoon, I went to the grocery store and bought two more guy swatters in case he came back." Lenny and I were laughing so hard that Sheila couldn't hold it in any longer, and she laughed until she cried. "You should have seen the look on his face when he couldn't take it anymore and took off running." The intensity of her laughing doubled for the next few minutes.

When we finally calmed down, one of us would start laughing again, and off we went for another round. I said, "Guy swatters" and we lost it again.

Sam Dazzio, the owner, came to our table and said, "It is great to have you kids back in my pizzeria. No one laughs as much as you guys when you're here eating my pizza." We nodded appreciation. His little visit gave us time to gather ourselves and move on to something else.

"Sheila, you are a beautiful girl, but, when you laugh, your beauty intensifies. It does! It is hard to take my eyes off you when you laugh. Unless I laugh until I cry, then I can't see a thing." Lenny's words were a true compliment; an observable fact and not some weak come-on by the kind of guys she ran into in college. She knew that was the case and responded by saying, "Shocking." We had no idea what she meant, and she knew it, so Sheila slowly and somewhat reluctantly explained herself.

"Marco regularly told me how attractive I was and that was always nice to hear. But one day after our whole crowd had been together and laughed a lot like we often did, when he took me home, Marco looked at me and said, 'Shocking.' When I asked him what he meant he said, 'You are gorgeous, but when you laugh you are shockingly gorgeous.' After that he would occasionally say that to me in public, and no one knew what he meant. Frankie would say it from time to time just because he'd heard Marco say it, but he didn't know the meaning behind the word. It was kind of our little secret word." Birdy and I remembered hearing Marco say that a few times, but he never let us know what he meant by it. Now it made sense.

Sheila paused for about ten seconds with a lowered head, and, when she looked up, her eyes were filled with tears. "That is the first time in seven months that I have said his name." As soon as the words left her mouth, Sheila began to sob. I moved next to her, and we held our good friend until she got it all out. We were in a corner booth, so Sheila was sandwiched in between Lenny and me, giving us as much privacy as could be had in that setting. It took several minutes and four or five napkins before she could say, "Thanks, guys." Once Sheila had regained her composure, I moved back to the bench across from her.

"Back to answering your question, Lenny, no, I haven't dated anyone. There is this one guy, who was in my Western Civilization course, that I might consider dating. He is a nice- looking athlete who seems to be a good guy. We sat next to each other in class, and one day he leaned over and asked me, 'Why do you hit guys with a fly swatter?' Without saying a word, I grabbed my swatter and smacked his arm. Just as I did that the professor looked up and hollered, 'Miss Grassley, there will be none of that in my classroom!' I nodded but Rick the Stud, as he is known on campus, said, 'It's okay Professor Johnson, there was a fly on my arm.' He must be kind of cool and possibly someone I could go out with based on that . . . and his looks . . . and his studliness." Peeps and I encouraged her to do so, and then she continued talking.

"As I said earlier, a certain former boyfriend used to tell me often how attractive I am, but physical beauty wasn't something my family emphasized. His compliment always made me smile, and it was good to hear his words, but I always moved on to other things which seemed to me to be more important. My parents talked a lot about virtue, hard work, and wisdom while I was growing up, so I just had never given my physical beauty a lot of attention. Once when I was ten years old, I asked them if I was pretty, and Mom and Dad sat me down, looked me in the eyes, and told me that I was the most beautiful girl in the world. In my little ten-year-old mind, I figured that I didn't need to be concerned about beauty anymore, so I focused more on the three qualities they regularly talked about. Now, once again, back to your question!"

"One day, the week before Thanksgiving, I'd just taken a shower after playing in an intramural volleyball game, and, as I was getting dressed, I looked in the full-length mirror in my dorm room and saw myself standing there in my bra and panties and stared for a few seconds. I turned sideways and saw my profile, then did the Betty Grable look over my shoulder to see my backside and said out loud, I am gorgeous! Thanks, Mom and Dad. My roommate, LaTonya, whose dad pastors an AME church in Denver, added, 'Don't forget to thank God.' I pointed at her and nodded in agreement. Then it made sense to me how much attention I had been receiving from the guys on campus and other guys in Durango."

Birdy shook his head and said, "Thank you, Sheila, for being vulnerable enough to tell Nick and me that story. I only wish I could have been there to share that moment with you."

"Ahhh," she shrieked. "Mr. Dazzio, do you have a fly swatter?" We laughed, finished our pizza and Pepsi, and promised to do this again twice a year for the remainder of our college years. We kept that promise!

24

The Routine of College Life

ONCE THE FIRST SEMESTER of college was behind me, I was able to establish a routine. It was a great routine of daily, weekly, monthly, and yearly activities. A daily routine of classes, study, and some recreation; a weekly routine of calling my folks, calling Birdy, social events on the weekend, and writing to Q; and a monthly routine of going to Boulder to hang out with Birdy, going home to see my family, hitting the slopes once or twice, and working on major class projects due at the end of the semester. When summer break arrived, it was my yearly routine to head back to Pueblo to work the job I had the previous summer for the State Fair, practice music with Birdy so that we could get a few gigs, go on some dates, do some fishing, and enjoy the newly finished Pueblo Reservoir. Dad bought a boat so that we could do some water skiing and a little fishing. We could have our boat in the water twenty minutes after jumping in the 1971 Chevy Cheyenne pickup Dad bought just before he found a boat in his price range. The three rental houses Dad owned in Illinois had finally sold. Rather than moving the Bradford family to a nicer part of town, he decided to buy a rental in Pueblo, one in Golden which I would use while in college, and then drop some cash on the boat and pickup. When he told me what he'd done with his money, I slapped him a high five and said, "Good move, Dad. I will teach you everything Birdy taught me about fishing." Fishing would be new to him and boat ownership and water skiing new to both of us, but we would figure it out. That's what smart guys do.

Birdy was spending at least half of the summer in Boulder because his band, renamed Canudigit, was staying pretty busy. They were mostly a cover band, but they did a lot of songs that weren't on Top 40 radio, so it sounded like original stuff to the kids attending their shows. They did an entire set of Larry Norman songs, which included "Readers Digest," "Pardon Me," "Larry Norman's Nightmare #71," and "Ha Ha World." They also did some blues, a few Hendrix songs, songs by Mountain, John Mayall, Spirit, and even the Bill Chase classic, "Got to Get it On." Lenny did the trumpet solo on his keyboard, and it sounded really good for synthesized horns. When the Average White Band released "Cut the Cake," the band learned it and, as a result, had more wedding-reception gigs than any band in the area. Everyone wanted that song just before the bride and groom cut their cake. Birdy's ability on guitar and keys was really improving, so, when we did our gigs together, he did all the heavy lifting musically while I just added some background fill and sang harmonies. But that was good enough for me. It was just fun to be on stage with him, even if it was just a cramped corner spot in a local restaurant. We got our big show at the State Fair again with similar results—a good crowd with lots of cash in the guitar case.

When Sheila, Birdy, and I met in June for our semi-annual movie and pizza outing, we saw "The Conversation." We enjoyed it but decided that after seeing "The Sting" and "The Conversation," that the next movie we saw together couldn't start with "The." When we got to Sam and Rays, I took charge of the conversation. "Last month Q called me when I was home and told me a story that you have to hear. He said there is a guy in his barracks who spends most of his free time sitting on his bunk reading, and the guy just happens to smell terrible. Coming from our friend who grew up in a home with lots of bad body odor, when he said the guy smelled bad, I figured it had to be way beyond normal smelly. So, one day, Q stopped at the guy's bunk and asked him what he was reading, and the guy told Q it was *The Power of Positive Thinking* by Norman Vincent Peale. To which Q shot back, 'Are you sure it's not *The Power of Positive Stinking* by Norman Vincent Unappealing because you positively stink, and it is powerful and unappealing.'"

"Classic Frankie; that sounds about right; if it pops into his mind, it almost always comes right out; that was a quick response," and other comments like that from the three of us. Then I continued. "The cool part of the story was that, the next day, the guy came up to Frankie and told him, 'Thanks for telling me. I had no idea.' And since then, they have been hanging out and are developing a good friendship."

Sheila loudly announced, "That is a great story! Frankie doesn't have a mean bone in his body. He says crass things and is often blunt, but he doesn't want to hurt people, and he will befriend anyone!"

Birdy nodded in agreement before offering, "Well said." After an hour of catching up with each other, we parted until our next pizza and movie outing over Christmas break 1974.

The next few years breezed by. The routine that I had established helped me round out recreation and exercise with study and family time. My tendency would have been to spend way too much time studying and then binge on the fun stuff. With the routine I'd established, all facets of my college life pretty much stayed in balance. Sheila let us know, during one of our semi-annual outings, that she dated Rick the Stud, but nothing came of it. Q kept me informed on his life in Georgia, and I passed that on to family and friends. Judging by what I was hearing from Birdy, he was quickly becoming a Big Man on Campus at CU.

Birdy had decided to be a business major, but he would take a PE course in the Fall in order to get in shape for ski season. In 1974, he took a course that featured two weeks in seven separate athletic disciplines. Coaches from the CU athletics department taught part of the class related to their sport so that the students could learn strategy and techniques for one week and then play the sport the next. When the two-week Track and Field segment came up, Birdy high jumped 6'9", pole vaulted 13'2", and ran the 440 in just under sixty seconds. The head track coach offered him a full scholarship on the spot, telling Birdy that with a little coaching he could high jump 7' and possibly become a very good decathlete. Later, following the basketball segment of the class, none other than Sox Walseth, the head basketball coach at CU and a Colorado legend, told Birdy that he could be a walk-on for his team and probably be on the traveling squad. Since Birdy had grown to 6'5" and had long arms, Walseth liked his game and saw him as an interesting prospect for the basketball team. Birdy was flattered by the offers but told me: "I am an orphan, which entitles me to get certain government grants and a couple of private scholarships, so I don't need the financial help. Being on a team at a major university team would take up all my free time. Because of that,

I told both coaches that I was honored by their offers but would remain a regular old student."

On our first visit to the slopes in early December 1974, Birdy told me about his decision to major in business. "I have gotten to know a lot of people at CU from a wide variety of backgrounds. Being the front man in our band means that a lot of people know me from the dozen or more events we have done on campus and a bunch more gigs in the community. When I took the basketball class, there were two guys from CU's team who helped out in the skills part of class, and I hit it off with them when I dunked on one of them during a little scrimmage we had. Then I ran into one of the rich kids from school when we were skiing Arapahoe Basin the same day, and he recognized me from one of my gigs, so we skied the rest of the day together—plus, the fact that I have dated lots of pretty girls seems to get me noticed. So, since I know athletes, wealthy kids, and a whole lot of other people, I just figure that I will have a career in business, focusing on putting people together."

To which I said, "Keep talking."

"Okay, this is what I am thinking. CU has quite a few athletes who are going to need agents when they turn pro, which includes the track and field athletes who will technically still be amateurs. Why not me? I know a bunch of them and occasionally hang out with the jocks, so I already have my foot in that door. About a month ago, this kid, who was in my dorm last year, came up to me and, for some unknown reason, he just started telling me about this property his family had in the NE part of Denver that they wanted to sell. Since I knew about the growth in that part of Denver, I put him and the wealthy kid from A-Basin together. Well, their fathers met and are working out a deal, and it looks like I am going to get a $1,500 commission check just before Christmas. So, basically, this is my idea. I don't want to start a business. I want to be a business. I will just continue being me and connect people to opportunities and to other people who need what they have to offer. A business degree is the best way for me to achieve that goal."

"Sounds good to me," I said as I nodded approval. It seemed like Birdy was developing his own routine, which would outlast his time in college. A little over a year later when I went to a CU basketball game with him, he told me about his routine with the ladies.

The CU basketball team wasn't very good that year, but I had never been to a major college basketball game before, so Birdy got two tickets, and we made a day of it. CU beat Oklahoma 71 to 69, so my first Big 8 game was a good one. After the game, we found a restaurant on the Pearl Street Mall that wasn't too busy and found a table. Peeps must have said hi to thirty people who called him by name as we walked around the mall looking for a place to eat that served Pepsi. Once at our table, a pretty girl came up from behind him, squeezed on to his lap, gave him a big kiss, and said, "Call me again," winked at me and walked off. I looked at him inquisitively, and my friend Lenny Peeples smirked and said, "Yes I had sex with Carol, along with probably seventeen other girls over the past three years." I was really surprised by what I'd just heard Birdy say, so I looked away from him and just stared at my menu until the waiter showed up. We ordered, and then sat in nervous silence until Birdy finally started talking.

"I lost my virginity a week or so after Marco left us to become a priest. Remember Bobbie Jo, the girl I took to the Sand Dunes? After meeting her at the record store and going out on a date, I stopped in a few times to the motorcycle shop that her dad owns and where she works. I would look at parts for my bike, pour on the charm with Bobbie Jo, and after our second date it was clear to me that she was ready for whatever I was interested in doing with her. So, for our third date, we took in a movie, and then I took her to my place, knowing that my aunt and uncle would be passed out drunk by then, and we had sex. A few nights later, it was with the college girl that I brought to our New Year's Eve party, and, before the summer was over, I'd had sex with four different girls, who I knew were willing just by the way they'd talked to me in the past. I'm not sure how many times I had sex with those four girls that summer, but it was a bunch. Once I got up here to Boulder, there was no shortage of pretty, young, and willing girls, so I didn't practice much self-control. Marco had always been my conscience, so, once he was out of the picture, I just did my thing. Some guys keep track of how many girls they've had, but that seems to me to be degrading to the girls, so I have never done that, but the seventeen number is pretty accurate. Somewhere along the line, though, I became aware of what Marco used to talk about." He ate a few bites of his fish sandwich, drank some Pepsi, and then continued.

"Marco used to talk about the power of sex and how it isn't just a physical act. He quoted the Bible verse that states, "the two shall become one flesh." I never got that until I'd had sex with all those girls, some of whom lost their virginity with me. For five of those girls, and I distinctly remember each one, when we were done having sex, they would hug me tightly, bury their face in my chest, and tenderly kiss me. By the time it happened the fifth time, I knew what Marco meant. For me, I love the female body and all the physical contact and really, every aspect of sex. But when it's done, I'm done. That wasn't the case with those five girls. For them, we had become one flesh. Sex was a powerful expression of intimacy, and, for them, what we'd experienced together opened the door to love. So, when I didn't follow up on our sexual experience with some sort of emotional commitment, I basically walked out and slammed the door that I'd just opened, and that feels pretty lousy to me." Again, Birdy ate some food, gathered his thoughts, and continued.

"It would be hard for me to say that I am now committed to celibacy until I marry, but I think that is where I would like to be. The thought of me breaking girls' hearts or using them for pleasure and then tossing them aside is not who I want to be or what I want to do. But, dang, my friend, it is going to be very hard to completely turn off that part of my life. The other night with Carol, the girl who just sat on my lap, was my first time for sex in over six weeks, so I am definitely working at changing the hard wiring in my brain when it comes to women."

"What I think I have come to understand about myself is this. Not only did my conscience follow Marco out of town, but so did my impulse control. Twice, in the first three weeks after Marco left, I got mad at some guy for some stupid reason, and just punched him in the face. I'd never flown off the handle and done that before, but, can you believe it, I did that twice, and it could have easily been four or five times! My size, strength, and the intensity of my anger allowed me to get away with it, but beating those guys was not at all satisfying, and I have no desire to do that again. On the other hand, having sex with a pretty girl feels intimate and very satisfying, but there is more to sex than just how it makes me feel. The way I see it now, when I slammed the door of intimacy in the face of those five girls, I most likely hurt them worse than I did the two guys I punched in the face." After a brief pause, Lenny finished his little confessional to me.

"With all of the alcoholism and drug abuse in my family, I know that impulse control is a major flaw that I need to be aware of and try hard to master. Just because I want to do something to satisfy a need or desire, and I can do it and get away with it, doesn't mean I should do it. So, I am telling all of this to you, because I want my conscience back, and I need to remind myself on a regular basis that I am still a Belmont Street Boy and should conduct myself accordingly!"

My head was spinning. Peeps was living the dream life of almost every guy I knew who wasn't named Marco Tattalinni, but the depth of his character wouldn't allow him to continue his shallow approach to personal gratification. Lenny Peeples never knew his dad. His mom died of a drug overdose. His grandmother basically drank herself to death. He was raised by two alcoholics, who loved him and cared for him but who also drank until they passed out drunk virtually every night that he lived with them. He no doubt seriously lacked healthy touch for his entire adolescent life. He must have craved the love that he missed out on as a kid, but here he was recognizing the pain he was inflicting on young girls while in the very act of intimate pleasure. As those thoughts and more ran through my mind, I looked at my buddy, smiled, and said, "I am proud of you, Lenny. You are a deep thinker and a good man. Now if you need me to take any of those lovely ladies off your hands, just let me know." We both laughed, finished our meals, and I headed back to Golden. It looked like Lenny was in the process of developing a new routine when it came to dating the pretty, and all too willing girls, in the college town of Boulder.

25

Meeting the One

WITHOUT SO MUCH AS a "Hi, how are you doing, What's up, or How's it going, the voice on the other end of the phone said, "I know you are going to be really mad at me, but I got married last weekend." Well, Q was right! I was so angry I could hardly speak. Angry, hurt, disappointed, betrayed, and stunned. After about twenty seconds of silence, I started yelling. "A Belmont Street Boy delivers life-changing news to me over the phone; a Belmont Street Boy doesn't invite me to his wedding, much less ask me to stand up with him; a Belmont Street Boy leaves me out of an event that is meant to be shared with those closest to him. So, yah, I'm angry. I am beyond angry. I want to beat the crap out of you right now and then take you to one of those buffets where you can stuff your face so that in a couple of hours there will be more crap to beat out of you. How could you do this? I feel like I just got punched in the gut! This is unbelievable! And wait until Birdy hears about this. You are not long for this life, my former friend." The rant lasted another minute or two. Once I ran out of steam, Q quietly and calmly tried to explain.

"Please listen to me, Nick. Rhonda is an incredible girl, and I am so lucky to have her. You are going to love her too, I guarantee it. But I knew that if you and Birdy showed up for the wedding, most of my attention would have been focused on you guys and stories about Marco. You know how I can get. I would have gone on and on trying to impress Rhonda and her family with stories about the best friends a guy could ever hope to have. We would have been laughing and talking about old times, and Rhonda deserved better than that on her wedding day. So, I made a decision. Besides me, the only person from Pueblo at the wedding was Aunt Nell."

He took a breath, and then continued. "After our phone call, I am going to call my parents and tell them that Rhonda and I eloped and that I will bring her to Pueblo the first chance we get so that they can meet her. Right now, I figure the first chance we will get is sometime in 1993, because I am crazy about Rhonda and not so crazy about my goofball parents. Please forgive me, Nick, please. It broke my heart to have two guys from my unit and a guy from church standing up with me instead of the two of you, but it just had to happen that way. Rhonda deserved the day to be about her, and I knew Aunt Nell could help me keep my focus on Rhonda, so that's why I wanted her to be there. Nellie has always been the mom I never had, so she had to be with me on that day. Please forgive me, Nick. Beat the crap out of me if you have to, but please forgive me."

It took a few moments for me to gather my thoughts. "You did the right thing, my friend. I never thought these words would come out of my mouth, but, Frankie, you made a very mature decision." We both laughed a little at that. "Q, you have my blessing, my best wishes, and Rhonda definitely has my prayers. I will call Birdy and then Sheila to let them know the news and explain your reasons for leaving us out of the loop. Just be sure to let us know if you and Rhonda are anywhere in Colorado, so we can meet Rhonda and then beat you up." We hung up, affirming our love for each other, but not before one more apology from Q and one more effort on my part to convince him that he was forgiven by me and would be forgiven by Birdy and Sheila. When I called to let them in on the news, both Birdy and Sheila were understandably surprised and hurt by the news, and in total agreement that Q had made a difficult and mature decision. We were all proud of him.

It was October 1976 when Q let me in on his big news, early in my senior year at Mines. Birdy was on track to graduate from CU with his business/marketing degree in the spring of 1977, and Sheila was already enrolled at The University of Denver's College of Law, having graduated from Ft. Lewis earlier that year. Before Thanksgiving weekend would arrive, a short six weeks later, more life changing news would sweep over The Belmont Street Boys.

"Hey, Nick. I am glad I found you at your place. Hope you are doing well. Uncle Will just called to let me know that Aunt Martha died last night in her sleep. He told me that, when he woke up this morning, his bed was wet and she was cold, and that's about all he had to say besides asking me to come home for a few days. Man, this is weird. I am sure it will be a really small funeral since they didn't have many friends and no relatives that they ever kept in touch with. They just never talked about family. Probably a few people from work. Maybe you and I could sing something at the funeral." Birdy spoke in short sentences with loosely connected thoughts for several minutes. He was obviously hurting, a little disoriented, and deeply concerned about his uncle's well-being. They were two alcoholics, who had only had each other once Birdy left for college. I assured Birdy that I would head home in a couple of days and stay until after the funeral to support him and Uncle Will however I could.

The funeral went as well as could be expected with around twenty-five people in attendance. Birdy and I sang "Peace in the Valley," a pastor none of us knew said a few words, and then Uncle Will treated everyone in attendance to dinner at Furr's Cafeteria. He seemed pleased with the way everything went that day, Saturday, November 13, 1976, and told me how much he liked the song that Lenny and I sang. A short eight days later on his way back from a drive he loved to take to Westcliffe, Uncle Will drove his car off a steep drop-off which runs alongside the Hardscrabble Road, rolled it three times, and was killed. Birdy thought he was most likely drunk at the time of the accident, but no tests were done, so he didn't know for sure. This time there was no funeral, just a private graveside burial with only Birdy, Sheila, and me at the burial site. It was an incredibly sad day. Birdy agreed to stay in town and have Thanksgiving with us, and, for the first time in over fifteen years, there was no Thanksgiving Day Belmont Grandiose Bowl. Tragedy had visited our neighborhood that holiday season, but we celebrated Thanksgiving as best we could.

When Birdy, Sheila, and I got together over Christmas break 1976, it definitely had a different feel to it. Sheila was a law-school student, seriously wrapped up in her studies. I was about to finish up my senior year and begin looking for a job, Lenny informed us that he was now a rich young man. "Uncle William had a $200,000 life insurance policy, Aunt Martha had one for $150,000, they had another $250,000 in investments and a retirement account, and a little over $3,500 in their checking and savings accounts, along with their house and cars and the touring motorcycle, which were all paid off. I was named the executor and sole beneficiary of their estate, so, as of last week, I am loaded. One of the business professors from CU met with me to talk about what I should do with the money, so I think I have a good handle on it for now. He advised me to buy a home in Boulder, since the housing market in a college town will always be strong; a couple of houses in Colorado Springs, because of the military bases there; $30,000 worth of gold, one car wash in Denver, and put $20,000 into a high yield mutual fund for my retirement. So, I did all that and still have around $70,000 sitting in the bank." It was crazy to sit there and listen to our friend talk about all that money as if he were discussing what he'd had for lunch the previous week. He was as calm and as matter of fact as could be.

"Well, I guess that means you are buying the pizza and Pepsi this time" I said. He smiled and nodded.

Sheila patted him on the shoulder and said, "I am so sorry for the circumstances that brought you all this money but am so glad that your aunt and uncle loved and trusted you enough to take such good care of you. If you need legal help with any of that, I would be happy to find someone at school to help you out."

"Kind, as always," Birdy responded.

It was great to be together with my pals and to know that Birdy would come through this tragedy in good shape. Earlier, he and I had discussed his family history of alcoholism, and he reassured me that he would not fall into that potentially lethal addiction. The destruction that he had seen addiction bring to his family was going to stop with him! Even though he attended one of the most notorious party universities in the country, Birdy assured me on several occasions that he had never been drunk or high in his more than three years in Boulder. "I'm good," he said, and I believed him. The next time I saw Birdy turned out to be another life-changing event.

Plowing through the final four months of college proved to be extremely hard for me. It was time to graduate and get on with life, but, before that could happen, there were classes to attend, exams to take, papers to write, and competency tests in my field of engineering. The only thing that helped me survive the slog was some weekend ski trips, a few dates, hiking in the foothills, and three all-expenses paid, out-of-state, job interviews. I took the trips to New Mexico, Arizona, and Washington just to break up the monotony of my final semester, and to give me some leverage for upcoming interviews within the state. There was no way I was moving out of Colorado, but my potential employers didn't need to know that.

On one of my trips back home, Dad told me that he was planning a big Spring Break trip for the Bradford family; probably the last vacation we would be able to do together. I told him that it sounded great, and our family vacation ended up being just that. When I got home for break and Dad got off work the final Friday of school, we jumped in the car and drove straight through to Los Angeles. Dad and I took turns driving, until we pulled into the parking lot of the Ambassador Hotel in Santa Monica. Our first night there, we walked on the Santa Monica Pier, ate fresh seafood, and then slept long and hard until the next morning. The next few days, we swam and tried our hands at surfing on Venice Beach, walked around Hollywood, and went to Disneyland and the Le Brea Tar Pits. We finished our California vacation by spending one more day on the beach, this time on Muscle Beach. Dad really broke the bank on our final vacation as a family. We took three days to drive back to Pueblo with stops at Grand Canyon and El Morro National Monument on the way. The sights and experiences were great, but it was even greater to see what a fine young lady Chrissie had become (I had to chase off several admirers of my very attractive, sixteen-year-old sister when she walked on the beach). And seeing how much in love my parents were after twenty-four years of marriage was a fantastic experience. When we pulled into the driveway on Belmont eight days after we left, I high fived my dad and said, "This vacation was everything I'd hoped it would be. Way to go, Dad!" My words of appreciation to Dad were followed by Chrissie whooping and hollering in agreement and hugs all the way around. A look of satisfaction and a, "Glad you enjoyed it, Son," was his typical understated response. Boy, did I admire my father.

"I have a wedding gig in Wheat Ridge next Saturday. Why don't you come to the reception, sing back up with the band on the songs you and I used to do, and meet some pretty girls?" It was an offer that I couldn't refuse. Every part of that invitation sounded great to me. It had been more than three months since I'd seen Birdy, and I badly needed to get away from Mines, so on April 30, 1977, I made the trip to the Richards-Hart Estate in Wheat Ridge for an enjoyable evening, which ended up changing my life.

I was seated at a table near the stage with five people I didn't know when my time came to go on stage and do some backup vocals. The band had already done three songs before I joined them, and we did two more before taking a short break. When I went back to the table, the people there suddenly became more friendly, but that stopped abruptly when the band took the stage and a pretty bridesmaid came up to me and said, "Why aren't you on stage, band boy?" When I explained to her that I wasn't really part of the band and the whole thing about Birdy and I doing a few sets together in Pueblo, she sat down and said, "Tell me more, kind of band boy." So, I did. For the next fifteen minutes, I told her about moving to Pueblo, The Belmont Street Boys, Mines, and just a little about Marco and Q.

Someone in the wedding party hollered "Julie, we need you for some pictures; it is time to cut the cake!"

She got up and said, "That's me. I am Julie and you are . . ."

"Nick."

The exchange of names was followed by Julie saying, "Don't go anywhere, Nick. We need to talk some more." At that Julie rejoined the wedding party and Canyoudigit tore into "Cut the Cake." I definitely didn't go anywhere, because I wanted to talk more to that attractive young lady. She came back with a couple of pieces of cake and said, "Tell me more," so I did.

For the next twenty minutes or so, we talked, danced a couple of dances as I talked, and she kept asking me to tell her more about the Boys. She must have said, "That's so cool," ten times. When the band took a break, she asked me if I liked Leon Russel, and when I said, "Who doesn't?" she grabbed my hand, marched us up on stage, sat at the keyboards, told me, "Let's see what you got," and then announced to the crowd, "The band might stop but the music never does," and started playing "Tight Rope." I gave it the best imitation of Leon I could muster, which happened to be pretty good. Julie looked at me, smiled, and said, "Not bad, but let's see if you can hang in there, Little Leon." I already liked her because she'd given me two nicknames in a short period of time. I'd no sooner said, "Give me your best shot, Chickie," than she tore into "Shootout on the Plantation," followed by "Delta Lady" and "A Song for You," and I never missed a beat. (I knew that we would see each other again after our little on-stage performance, and she knew we would marry).

The wedding party was going crazy by this time seeing their friend tear it up on the keyboards and her new friend extemporaneously singing along. We were feeding off the crowd and having a blast, when Lenny and the band took the stage for the final sendoff song for the newlyweds. As Julie and I were walking off stage, she turned to me and asked, "Are you a Christian?" The question surprised me, but when I said, "I suppose so," she grabbed a pen off a nearby table, pulled my shirt sleeve up, wrote her phone number on my arm, looked at me sternly, and said, "Call me." Her expression changed when I looked at her and said, "Definitely." Six months later, she told me that she went to her fellow bridesmaids and announced, "I am going to have that man's babies!"

The next afternoon I called Julie, and we met that night for a date. Instead of me doing all the talking, this time I got to learn about Julie Smith, the girl from Center, Colorado. We ate some Mexican food, walked around Sloan's Lake, and I got to hear about life as the daughter of a potato farmer in the San Luis Valley where priorities of the Friends Church, family, hard work, music, fishing, and hunting were well established. Julie was in her second year working as a CPA in a mid-sized accounting firm after graduating from Regis College in Denver. We shared a lot of interests in the outdoors, music, and thinking deeply about things. Neither one of us had experienced a serious relationship with the opposite sex, so there was nothing we had to work through in that regard. I invited her to come to my graduation from Mines on May 14, and she agreed, knowing that she would meet my parents then. We had two more dates before that, including attending Birdy's graduation, and I called my parents to tell them about Julie three days before they came to Golden. Mom, of course, was beside herself asking questions. I was going as slowly as I could, but, when we held hands and kissed on our first date, it seemed as natural as could be to do that. Talking to Marco about her was something I desperately wanted to do, but that was not an option. So, after a four-year break from any real spiritual activity, I started praying again, visited a Friends Church in Denver a few times and one in Pueblo when I was home, and looked forward to meeting her family.

There was a two-week break between graduation and when I started work for the State of Colorado as a Civil Engineer, so I used that time be with Julie, take her to Pueblo, hang out with Birdy, and take a trip to

Center to meet the Smith family. Julie had a sister, two years younger, and twin brothers, who were fifteen. Since Julie promised me a fishing trip to Smith Reservoir ("Not named after my family," she said), I packed for two nights and told Birdy he had to come, too, in order to take advantage of some of the best trout fishing in the state. When we got to her home, it was obvious that Carla, Julie's sister, was smitten with Birdy. He paid her lots of attention but did not lead her on. There wasn't room for her in the boat, so she missed out on the time with my buddy that she desperately wanted.

It was a great trip. I really liked her family, fishing at Smith was outstanding, and even Birdy seemed to enjoy the simple church service with all twenty-seven attendees at the Center Friends Church. As we were leaving the Smith home, I overheard Julie's mom say, "He's a keeper." Julie hugged each of her family members, and we hit the road with a short stop at my folk's house.

When we dropped Julie off at her place in Denver, I told Birdy, "I think she just might be the one."

"She's a keeper," he said, and we both started laughing. "That was the worst whisper I have ever heard in my life," he said, and I shook my head in agreement as I laughed. A little over a year later on June 17, Julie and I were married.

Birdy was my best man, Q made the trip from Georgia to be my first groomsman, and Julie's brothers, Paul and Tony, were also groomsmen. Julie and Sheila had become fast friends, so, along with Carla and two friends from college, the wedding party was set. It was a great weekend of Julie meeting Q and all of us meeting Rhonda, of trying to find entertainment for our bachelor party in Center, and of just being with people that I loved. The honeymoon in Santa Fe, New Mexico was outstanding, and life in Denver was developing an enjoyable rhythm. Dad sold the home in Golden, so we had to find a place to live, and we chose a decent home with a nice-sized yard in North Denver and began attending the Denver Friends Church. Birdy came by every few weeks or we met him and whoever he was dating at the time (usually long-legged blonds) at a restaurant or at some gig he had. Married life was great. We decided to start having kids before Julie turned twenty-seven, and it was easy to believe that we had it all figured out. Life was going smoothly and was fairly predictable until a phone call from out of the blue stunned our sensibilities.

26

The Phone Call

"Whatever plans you have for Saturday, July 28, change them. You need to stand up with me at my wedding. Call Peeps and Frankie and tell them the same." It was the unmistakable voice of Marco, but what he was saying was so unexpected, that it took me some time to get oriented to what I was hearing. "The rehearsal will be Friday at 5:00 at Sheila's church, followed by a meal with the wedding party at LaTronica's, and then what better be a great bachelor party. You are in charge of the party, so do it right. I know you are a little stunned right now, but I will come by your place tomorrow, and the four of us will go out for some good Mexican food. You choose the place," and he hung up.

When I told Julie, she started squealing like a little girl. She was so animated with excitement for Sheila that she hollered out, "I am so wired right now that I think we ought to go make a baby, but it might be a little late for that." My wife really is something. It ended up that she was, in fact, six weeks pregnant at the time. Wow! So much for the predictable life I thought we had.

When Marco and Sheila showed up at our place, I shoved him as hard as I could (which had little effect on him because the guy was way stronger than I remembered) and yelled, "Where's your collar, Father Marco?"

He just laughed and said, "I am going to be doing way too much talking tonight, but that's the way it has to be. And it is very nice to meet you, Julie Bradford." All three of us nodded in approval, but Julie took it one step further.

She gave Marco a big hug, then a kiss on the lips and said, "It is so nice to meet a best friend I've never seen before. And I don't just mean Nick's best friend." We were all surprised by what we just saw and heard, but, for the second time that day, I thought, *My wife really is something.* Then we jumped into the Nomad and headed out to Sam's No. 3 for a Colorado Buffalo Burrito and whatever the others wanted to order. On the way there, I filled The Tatts and the future Mrs. Tatts in on The Boys.

"Birdy had to cancel two gigs to be at both the wedding and rehearsal but insisted that you let the Boys sing a few songs at the reception, which I figured you would want us to do anyway." Marco and Sheila nodded and said, "No doubt," with no questions asked. Julie told me later how much she admired the complete trust the two of them had in the Boys.

"Q's story is a little more interesting. When he went to his commanding officer to ask for leave, he was immediately told that his request was denied because of insufficient time to make proper arrangements. When given permission to speak again, he said something along these lines."

"Sir, you know it is my intention to be a career soldier and to attain the highest rank possible for an enlisted man. And you are also aware that I am a hardworking, loyal, Staff Sergeant who is really good at his job. But sir, if I am not allowed to attend this wedding, I will not reup when the opportunity comes in twenty-three months and six days. It would mean the world to me, Sir, if you would grant me permission to attend my best friend's wedding."

"Q said the officer sat there for a few seconds before saying, 'Permission granted.' Q followed up with a quick, 'Thank you for your kindness, Sir,' and sprinted to a phone to call Rhonda and then me to pass on the good news. They will be coming in on the Tuesday before the wedding in order to have plenty of time with all of us. Aunt Nell has plenty of room for them all."

"All," Marco asked?

"Well," said Sheila, "there is Frankie, Rhonda, and their two-year-old son, Marco." It got quiet for a few seconds before Marco said, "I am surprised he didn't name him The Tatts." The Nomad was filled with laughter. Marco was almost as good at deadpan humor as our friend, Frankie. As we pulled up to Sam's No. 3 and were getting out of the car, Marco let us know that Q would be his best man.

"I would have been surprised if he wasn't," I said. "If Frank Luna won the Congressional Medal of Honor, he would be prouder of being the best man at your wedding than of the President hanging that medal around his neck." Marco smiled and said, "Thank you for understanding." We went into the restaurant, ordered, and Marco gave Julie and me the details we had been dying to hear.

"This is going to take some time, so interrupt me if it becomes too much." We never did. We were never tempted to.

"The twenty-seven months that I spent working across the country in a wide variety of settings in four different jobs was a great experience. I learned so much about people and cultures, parish and family dynamics, and the pressures that ordinary people face at work and with their finances. Basically, I really grew up during that time. Plus, I made a whole lot of money working fourteen-hour days, six days a week, and even more than that when I was out in the Gulf of Mexico on an oil rig. We were supposed to be two weeks on and two weeks off, but I was out there for six weeks at a time when I covered a two-week shift for one of the roughnecks who needed some time off. Then, in the shipyards, I took all the overtime that they would give me, so I always had forty hours at $6.50 an hour and then twelve hours at time-and-a-half and usually eight to twelve more hours at double time. My dad accused me of robbing banks all across the country when I would send him thousands of dollars at a time. Dad was good to invest the money for me in the accounts I'd set up before leaving Pueblo. What free time I did have, I usually spent volunteering at the Catholic Parish where Father John had set me up with host families." The Buffalo Burritos showed up. Both couples were splitting an order and eating from their shared plates. It was funny to me that we were doing the same thing. Two burritos smothered in green chili and four Pepsis—it was a thing of beauty. Marco took a few bites and continued with his story.

"I attended Saint Vincent De Paul Catholic Church while in Newport News and hit it off with the parish priest, Father Pete. He got a kick out of me saying Father Pete the Parish Priest every time I saw him. Father Pete recommended me for entry into the philosophy program at Marymount University in preparation for becoming a priest, and I was accepted. Between Catholic Church scholarships and some work-study programs, it was a free education. Along with philosophy, I took all of the Spanish classes I could get. When it came time for the church to place me in a ministry setting, my Spanish-speaking ability would open up more fields of ministry where I could do some good. My time at Marymount was challenging and rewarding, and I really loved it. Once every quarter, I called my folks to check up on them. Mom connected with Mrs. Grassley once a month and very slyly asked if Sheila had any guy she was seeing, how she was doing, what her plans were, and that sort of thing. She passed the info on to me because I still loved Sheila even though I was really enjoying every aspect of preparation for the priesthood. Every day I prayed: Lord, bring a good man who loves you into her life, a man she can love, a man who will love and admire her. It was the same prayer every day. It saddened me when that prayer wasn't being answered." Marco took a few bites, squeezed Sheila's hand, took a long drink of Pepsi, and continued.

"After three-and-a-half years of study, candidates in our program are offered a semester practicum to complete their degree, but I asked for a special allowance to extend my practicum for eighteen months before entering seminary. It was my intention to serve as a postulant with a Franciscan Order in Honduras, and I'd hoped to be there long enough to really connect with the locals. The diocese granted me permission, and off to Central America I went. Just like everything else I'd done for the previous five plus years, it was a total blast. There were plenty of challenges and difficulties for sure, but none of them interfered with the joy I was experiencing in serving God and his church. There were several teenaged girls who asked me to counsel them concerning the impure dreams they were having about a Catholic priest, the postulant who basically told me the same thing, the local tough guys who regularly tried to test my self-control and physical strength, and the lonely women in the parish who wanted more from me than I could offer. I can truthfully say that it was all joy. The priests that I worked with were good men with great wisdom and skills they'd developed over years of genuinely valuing the Fruit of the Spirit. But there was one priest, who I suspected was a homosexual, maybe even with some pederast tendencies, who hadn't done a great job of controlling his desires. One day my suspicions were confirmed."

"When a teenaged boy fell during one of our games, I watched the priest as he washed the boy's back before tending to the nasty wound on the boy's shoulder blade. The priest enjoyed washing the boy's back way too much, so I took him aside after the event was over, smiled, and said: 'Father, if I ever see you touching another boy or a postulant for any reason, I will report you to the Diocese after hurting you badly. Do not pretend that you don't know what I am saying.' He walked away without acknowledging what I said, but he made a point to avoid all physical contact with men and boys after that. Even that event, I would say, was pure joy." Marco

ate what was left on the plate, I picked up the bill, and we found a bench a
block or so away where we could finish hearing Marco's story.

"Toward the end of my time in Honduras, the Franciscans sent me
on a three-night and four-day silence and solitude retreat in a mountain
cave, bringing a Bible and a blanket as my only companions. There was
a wooden bench and a cot waiting for me in the cave, and, every morning while I was sleeping, someone would drop off the bread and water
I needed for the day. It was a great experience until the evening of the
third day. I'd been assigned to read and meditate on the parables of Jesus,
and it was going great until I got to Matthew 18 and the parable of the
lost sheep. As I meditated on that parable, these words came to me and
shook me: Sheila is the lost sheep. I walked around the cave, meditated
on a cross I'd drawn on the cave floor, read other parables, and tried to
think about something else, but I couldn't shake those words. Every time
I dozed off that night, those words woke me over and over again. Sheila
is the lost sheep. Sheila is the lost sheep. Sheila is the lost sheep. And the
idea that Sheila was somehow lost was more than I could stand."

"As I continued to meditate with those words ringing in my head,
it never crossed my mind that Sheila was spiritually lost in any way. But
what did cross my mind was the scary thought that she was terribly alone
and might even be vulnerable to some predator with the skills to exploit
that isolation. Since she'd been abandoned by me, I couldn't completely
rule out the idea that it might fall on me to provide for her rescue. As
hard as it was for me to consider that idea, I had to ask myself if I might
be the one called to leave the flock of people that I loved serving in order
to pursue her."

"When I returned from the retreat, I called my mom to ask her about
Sheila. Mom said that she had met with Mrs. Grassley two days earlier
and that Sheila was doing great at the law firm and seemed to be enjoying
life. Well, that was a relief, but the words, *Sheila is the lost sheep*, regularly
came back to me on a daily basis. The Franciscans gave me permission to
stay a few more months with them, and I began to seek spiritual direction
from a priest in Tegucigalpa whom I knew and respected. After he understood that I wasn't having a crisis of faith or trouble controlling my sexual
desires, we began an intensive discernment process of trying to hear if
God's voice was in the words that I heard in the cave. We met weekly
for three months and both came to the same conclusion. If the shepherd
would gladly leave the ninety-nine to find the one, then I should be willing to do the same. That was our theoretical conclusion. The next step was

to decide if putting the theoretical into practice was something that I had to do. I asked for a nine-month extension of service with my Franciscan brothers and was granted that extension. When the nine months were up, it was crystal clear to me that I was to step away from the priesthood. Three days after leaving Honduras, I showed up unannounced at Sheila's office, and I will let her take it from there."

Sheila was beaming as she told us what happened next. "Yesterday, at 10:30, my secretary buzzed me and said, 'Miss Grassley, there is a gentleman here who wishes to see you. He does not have an appointment and says his name is Marco. Are you available to meet with him?' I told her to give me two minutes and then send him in, knowing that it would take me that long to compose myself and to put on my professional face. When he walked into my office, I stood, put out my hand, and said, 'Marco, it is so nice to see you. To what do I owe this pleasure?' He on the other hand, very unprofessionally brushed my hand aside and gave me a long hug. Then he grabbed my shoulders, looked me in the eyes, and said, 'I wondered if you didn't have plans for lunch, maybe we could get married.' I slapped him in the face as I screamed WHAT so loud that my secretary came running into the office to see if everything was okay. Angrily, I yelled at her not to let anyone else in my office for any reason. 'Now get out,' I screamed as I pointed at the door."

Marco added, "That was really cool. I'd never seen her that angry before." Shelia continued.

"'Marry you today! I'm not going to marry you today,' I yelled as I slapped him in the face again. I suppose that the trauma of his words caused me to instinctively protect myself by slapping him. 'I'm not going to marry you tomorrow or the next day or the day after that or the week after that,' I hollered as I alternately shoved him in the shoulders and turned my fists sideways to beat on his chest. 'Marry you? Marry you? Marry you?' I yelled as I punched him in the stomach as hard as I could. Then I paused for what seemed to be an hour, threw my arms around him, and said, 'You have to give me a month.' Marco tenderly kissed me on my forehead and said, 'You have three weeks.' At that I just lost it and started to cry uncontrollably." Sheila paused for a moment, hugged Marco's arm as she kissed his cheek, then resumed her story.

"When I was finally able to talk again, I realized that there were feelings bottled up inside of me that I hadn't allowed myself to feel for eight years. But the bottle opened up as we stood there holding each other. I told Marco that he'd ruined me to every other guy I had ever dated. Whenever a guy I was dating tried to make out with me or get all feely with his hands, my first thought was always that Marco would never try that with me. So, I would dump that guy as quick as I could holler, "Take me home," while thinking, you long, runny egg. My roommate in college and I used to say about guys, he's a good egg in the long run, but who wants long runny eggs? Besides the long runny eggs who were easy to dump, I tried to fall in love with good, handsome, talented, successful men, but I just couldn't do it. Marco had stolen my heart when I was sixteen years old, and he wasn't able to return it to me before leaving to become a priest. Well, he brought my heart back with him when he walked into my office yesterday, and I will spend the rest of my life thanking him for that wonderful gift. I am no longer ruined. I was, in a very real sense, the lost sheep, isolated and in some ways vulnerable, like Marco said. Now I am free to love, unbroken, content, and I am going to be doing a lot of this for the next few weeks," she said as the tears flowed and as the beating on Marco's chest resumed. By then we were all crying and laughing at the same time. It was a mess. A glorious, joy-filled mess, which would continue in one form or another for the next three weeks.

27

The Big Talk

JULIE SPENT ALMOST EVERY evening with Sheila for the next two weeks helping her with wedding arrangements and planning. Mrs. Grassley spent the first week at Sheila's apartment in Denver working on wedding details and sending out invitations. Since Sheila, Mrs. Grassley, and Julie all have good administrative skills, they had all the bases covered to make sure that this would be the best-ever wedding planned in three short weeks. Sheila was so impressed with all of Julie's great work that she asked Julie to be her wedding coordinator, which made my wife very happy. On Wednesday of the first week of wedding preparation, Julie started having morning sickness, and, just like clockwork, she would eat, throw up, eat a little more, and then be good to go for the rest of the day. I would hold her long hair as she puked, put a wet washcloth on her neck for a minute or so, and then we would go on with our day after that. The third day that happened she said, "You are the doctor who gives me what I need." I smiled and said, "We make quite a team. I am Doc Holliday, and you are Wyatt Earp."

Julie smiled, said, "You are funny," and gave me a quick and stinky-puke-breathed kiss, which I received with no complaint. The thought crossed my mind that love is smiling as your wife gives you a nasty smelling kiss. After all, I got her pregnant, so I guess puke breath is part of the package.

Friday night after work, Julie and I headed for Pueblo to work on the wedding there. Sheila and her mom got to Pueblo a couple of hours

194

earlier, and Birdy showed up Saturday morning to help out any way he could. Marco was spending most of his time in Pueblo, arranging the rehearsal dinner, the catering for the wedding reception, picking out a wedding cake, and doing all of the odds and ends Sheila and her team had instructed him to take care of. With all of his Italian cousins in the food business and Sheila's calm approach to things, Marco had the easiest job of all. Since Sheila wasn't a Catholic, the wedding would have to be at her church, and Marco was okay with that. Julie would convert to Catholicism after they were married, and the two of them would go through the necessary rituals so that their marriage would be recognized by the Catholic Church. Marco and his family were surprisingly laid back about everything, so they did not add any stress to the rush of getting prepared for a big wedding in a short amount of time. When Julie and I headed back to Denver that Sunday afternoon, Marco and Sheila were hard at work on their wedding vows and ceremony. Their ceremony would end up being a blend of traditional wedding services, along with Catholic and Presbyterian influences. Since they were a spiritually sensitive, mature, and very intelligent young couple, there were also a few surprises which gave the ceremony a unique feel.

The second week of wedding prep was much the same as the first, and, by the time we rolled into Pueblo one week before the wedding rehearsal, everyone involved felt like the Tattalinni/Grassley wedding would go off without a hitch even though there was only one more week to prepare. My mom was helping Mrs. Tattalinni with her responsibilities, and even Aunt Nell had shown up the first week to address wedding invitations. Marco asked Q and Rhonda if they thought Little Marco would be able to handle ring bearer responsibilities, and they both said he would do great. Apparently, the little guy was like his old man and loved to perform in front of a crowd. Sheila had stayed close to her college roommate, LaTonya, and her three-year- old daughter would be the flower girl. Birdy took the week of the wedding off so he could be with Marco to help with whatever, and Frankie and family showed up on Wednesday evening. Sheila had the week of the wedding off, and Julie and I showed up Wednesday to tie up any loose ends and to spend time with Q and Rhonda. Even if something went wrong, and nothing did, we had plenty of talent, manpower, and time to take care of any problem that might arise. It was so cool to work with such a great group of talented and loving people. And to top it off, we had plenty of time to catch up with Q and to learn more about Rhonda. She was a great girl. Frankie was lucky to have her, and he knew it.

When Frankie and Rhonda walked into the Tattalinni home, we were all there. After lots of hugging and introductions, Peeps broke the ice when he looked at Rhonda and said, "You are in my prayers, and I am not a praying man!"

Without missing a beat, Q shot back, "I warned her that your jealousy of me would show up in some very ugly ways."

After a minute of back and forth teasing between the Boys, Marco gave Rhonda another hug and told her, "I am sure that you have gotten to know me pretty well with all the stories your husband has told," and she nodded.

He then looked at Frankie and said, "Tell me something about this fine lady of yours." With no break whatsoever, Q started talking.

"One night, about three months into our marriage, we were having supper, and I let out a big fart, looked across the kitchen and out the window, squinted, and said 'geese.' My dad used to do that all the time. Well Rhonda calmly picked up her plate and without saying a word, she went out onto the front porch and continued eating. After about five minutes, I realized she wasn't coming back to the table, so I opened the screen door and saw that she'd finished eating. Well, I went back to the kitchen and cut us both a piece of the cake her mom had given us the day before and sat next to her. Rhonda said, 'Thank you,' took a bite of cake, and then calmly let me know that if geese ever flew over our house again during mealtime that she would be eating all of her meals out on the front porch. So, one thing I can tell you is that Rhonda is a southern girl who demands and gets respect. But the story doesn't end there."

"Not too long after that, we were at her parents' house for Christmas dinner. I had to report for duty that day on the base, so the family waited until evening to have their big meal. When we walked in the front door, the house smelled great, and I hollered, 'What's for supper, Mrs. B?' She was so excited to tell me that Rhonda's dad and brothers had been successful on their hunt the day before so we wouldn't just be having a Christmas goose, but that we would be having Christmas geese! Rhonda looked at me, and I looked at Mrs. B and said, 'I guess I will be joining Rhonda on the front porch then.'"

"Rhonda started laughing and couldn't stop. Mrs. B just shook her head, figured it was some kind of an inside joke, and went back to the kitchen. Mr. B, who was in the living room and heard the whole thing, walked into the kitchen, looked at me, and said, 'Son, you are an odd duck.' The rest of the evening, whenever someone asked for more goose, I would lift my cheek slightly, and Rhonda would start laughing again. There was a lot of, 'I don't get it; what are you laughing about; what is going on here?' for the rest of the meal. With a straight face, I shrugged my shoulders as if I didn't know what was going on and just pointed at Rhonda. That night, when we were in bed, Rhonda hugged me and asked if her dad had hurt my feelings when he called me an odd duck, and, if he had, then she would set him straight. I kissed her forehead and said, 'Rhonda, you heard your dad call me an odd duck, but I heard him call me son.' At that she kissed me real good, told me she was proud of me, and I knew then that my wife was protective of her man. So let this be a warning to the Boys: You guys had better treat me with more respect than usual, or this southern belle just might just say, 'Darlin, what did y'all just say to my husband?' and then go all apey on your face."

"We will treat you with all the respect you deserve," and different variations of that statement went on until Birdy hit "play" on the Tattalinni stereo cassette player, and "The Boys Are Back," by Thin Lizzy, rang out until Mrs. T hit the stop button and announced, "The Belmont Street Boys might be back in town, but this party is over!" No one ever argued with Mrs. T, so Julie and I went across the street to my folk's house, and Q and Rhonda drove back across town to stay with Aunt Nell, who'd helped them put Little Marco to bed earlier. Birdy spent the night with Marco, and they stayed up until the wee hours of the morning talking but kept it quiet in order to avoid the rage of that beautiful and good-hearted, no-nonsense, Italian matriarch. My time with Marco would come early Saturday morning.

Thursday morning was full of the guys getting fitted for our tuxedos, the girls doing girly things, and everyone meeting at Sam and Ray's for a final Belmont Street Boys and their gang pizza lunch. The restaurant was filled with the wonderful smells of Italian food, lots of laughter, and one story after another being told and embellished just like old times. When things quieted down a little, Peeps asked Rhonda how she felt about how the Boys always picked on her husband. With very little hesitation she gave us her/his perspective with her endearing accent.

"Frank explained to me that things aren't what they appear to be with y'all. Usually, when you see someone being picked on, it is because they are being initiated into a group or they are the low man on the totem pole, or they are just plain afraid of having their behind whupped. Things like that. Mean-hearted people do mean-hearted things, and sometimes good-hearted people mess up and say mean things to those they love, and that's just the way it is. But Frank made it clear to me that y'all, the Boys, might say things that sound mean to an outsider, but they really aren't. The Boys love him and respect him, and the reason he gets picked on is because he has this uniquely happy personality that is able to shed the teasing and see the genuine affection behind the attention he is getting. He knows that and y'all know that, so that's how the friendship has evolved with y'all." (That girl sure said y'all a lot).

Peeps immediately stood up and, with a bottle in his hand, announced, "A Pepsi toast for the Best Man at Marco and Sheila's wedding." The staff and everyone in the restaurant joined in as we toasted our buddy, Q. All of the girls and Little Marco then took off to resume their wedding plans while the Boys hung around a little longer just to be with each other. I let Marco know that part of our bachelor party plans was to take my dad's boat to Pueblo Reservoir and do some waterskiing before it got too dark. Marco had never been to the reservoir, he had never waterskied, and he didn't know that Dad had a boat, so it all sounded like a new and great outing to him. As we walked out the door to hop into the Nomad, Birdy let us know that his girlfriend would be driving in for the wedding rehearsal on Friday night so she could be part of the bachelorette party and get to know everyone a little.

"She is only twenty-one years old, but she might be the one for me." We all paused for a minute, slapped him high fives, then busied ourselves with wedding prep before meeting everyone at Pueblo City Park for a big Tattalinni/Grassley-families-plus-the-wedding-party massive cookout. I had a room reserved at the Vail Hotel, where the Boys could crash on Friday night. Unless something else came up, I figured that I had fulfilled all of my responsibilities and was ready for the big day. Mostly, I had figured right.

Friday was a blur of activity as Mrs. T and Julie gave each of the Boys things to do that, apparently, we had overlooked. There was no time for lunch that day, but we made it to the wedding rehearsal at First Presbyterian at 4:00pm, on time. I hadn't seen Lana, Sheila's maid of honor, since her wedding, and she looked great, so I made a point to give Julie a big hug and kiss right after making small talk with Lana and her husband. Julie looked at Lana, and, knowing that I'd had a crush on Lana during my senior year, she said, "Dang she's pretty," and kissed me again. That woman never ceased to amaze me.

The rehearsal went really fast because of all the fine work done ahead of time, and Birdy's girlfriend, Shelly, walked into the church just as the wedding party was leaving for LaTronica's. Julie looked at Shelly and said, "Double dang," and kissed me again. Then she said, "There are going to be more attractive people at this wedding than at any event I have ever attended in my life."

Marco overheard her and said, "Wait until you see my dad's side of the family. They will bring the overall beauty average way down and the average weight way up." Julie and I looked at each other and smiled. No matter what they looked like, we couldn't wait to meet Marco's extended family.

The rehearsal included lots of good Italian food mixed with plenty of great stories. Those who wanted to, had an opportunity to stand up and tell stories about Sheila and Marco while everyone was eating. The stories were really fun to hear, but Marco put an end to it because he was a genuinely humble guy who was getting pretty uncomfortable listening to what a great guy he is and how proud his loved ones are of him. "Everyone, I want to thank you for all the thoughtful and mostly accurate stories. Sheila and I feel loved and appreciated by all of you, but these stories are cutting into the conversations you could be having with the loved ones seated next to you. So, with that in mind, along with the fact that I really want to get out to the reservoir and have plenty of time before it gets dark, I want to hear one more story from my best man, Frank Luna. But the story has to be about some experience you have had in the Air Force so that we can catch up with the other Belmont Street Boy who has been gone for so long. Take it away, Q, but keep it kind of short." Frankie jumped up and was immediately ready to go.

"When I reached the rank of Sergeant, it became my job to give the new soldiers, fresh out of boot camp, the low down on their roles in our platoon. I go over all the basic information of what they need to know, while the rest of the platoon stands at attention and patiently listens to stuff they've heard several times before. When I am done, I always ask if there are any questions. If there is a pause, I always say the same

thing. 'Men, there is no such thing as a dumb question.' Invariably, some
new recruit will ask a question, and then I start laughing uncontrollably,
bending over at the hip until I can control myself, stand up straight, point
at the recruit, and yell, 'That is the dumbest question I have ever heard
in my life,' and start laughing again. The soldiers who have been with me
awhile know that it is coming and also know that they are not allowed to
laugh with me, but, boy, do they get a kick out of it. When I go home and
tell Rhonda that we had a new recruit briefing, she immediately starts
laughing. Word spreads throughout the whole company, and I get an 'at-
taboy' from airmen and officers alike for a week or more." As usual, my
buddy, Q, had everyone laughing at one of his stories. We beat it out of
LaTronica's a few minutes later and headed for the reservoir.

Dad had the boat hooked up and ready to go when we got to the
house. As we exited the Nomad, Dad told me not to worry about cleaning it up when we got back later on. "I will take care of it in the morning.
Go have some fun, boys, I mean, men, and be careful not to ski too late.
There will probably be a few drunks out on the water so watch out for
them." All of the Boys showed their appreciation to Dad as we loaded up
and headed to our destination. Birdy and I were in the cab while Marco
and Q sat in the bed of the pickup. Thirty minutes later, the boat was in
the water, the trailer parked, and Birdy was giving Marco the low-down
on how to water ski. With Marco's strength and balance and Birdy's clear
instruction, Marco got up on his first try and skied for about two minutes
before he cut too sharp and bit it. We gave him one more run before the
rest of us took turns. Birdy was really good on a slalom ski, of course, and
I was adequate on one, so he skied while I drove the boat and vice versa.
Birdy never lost control, so he skied until he got tired, and I took two
turns then yielded to Q. Our buddy, the sergeant, had spent a little time
behind a boat in Alabama, and would have tried it on a slalom ski if we'd
had more time. He tired out after five more minutes behind the boat, so
we gave Marco another turn, and then back to Q as the sun was setting.

There was time for one more run, so that went to Marco. After he
crashed crossing the wake as fast as he could, he hollered out, "That's it
for me. That was fun, but I'm done."

As he swam close to the boat, I punched the motor and said, "Not
so fast, wedding boy. You have to ski naked for thirty seconds before
we let you in the boat." I made sure we were in the middle of the lake
so that he couldn't swim to shore. The Boys and I had talked about this
while Marco was on his next-to-last run. Marco knew we were serious,

so without an argument he took off his trunks, threw them into the boat as he said, "Wierdos." He skied for a little less than a minute and then let go of the rope. We laughed the entire time, and I think Marco did too. As we helped him into the boat he said, "Wierdos" again, put on his trunks, wrapped up in a towel and said, "Thanks again, Boys. Apart from the naked thing, this was a great time. If we don't do anything else, this has been a perfect bachelor party in my book." We knew he meant it, and that made each of us very satisfied.

The next couple of hours were enjoyable, but uneventful, as we took the boat back to my folk's house, climbed into the Nomad, and headed to Sambos on Abriendo for some ice cream. Marco loved ice cream and Sambos, so all of us knew we would end up there before it closed for the night. After some ice cream and a Sambos' orangeade, we just drove around in swimming trunks and T-shirts and reminisced about old times and old places. A little after midnight, we got to the Vail and cleaned up. The three of us had parked our cars there so we could leave whenever we needed to. That plan worked out really well for each of us as we all had to leave the hotel at different times. With all of our activity and the excitement of the day, we settled down pretty quickly, and the conversation turned thoughtful after just a few minutes.

Birdy told us why he was serious about Shelly and how she was helping him move in the direction of faith. He met Shelly through one of his band members. She was a close friend of his drummer's younger sister, and the two girls came to several gigs the band had around Boulder. Birdy asked her out and, on their second date, found out that Shelly was a virgin who took her faith very seriously. The two of them had very meaningful conversations about important things. As they spent more time together, Birdy said, "I saw that her inner beauty was every bit as attractive to me as her outer beauty, so I am pretty sure I am done with other women." They would need to have a conversation soon about all his other women, but he said, "I am pretty sure she has a good idea about that already." We asked questions and Birdy talked some more about Shelly and faith and it was good just to hear him talk about that stuff. The Boys all felt good about the direction our friend was headed.

When Frankie started talking, he opened up and told us some pretty heavy stuff. "You know when I told you the story about Rhonda's dad calling me "Son"? Well, that meant something to me because growing up I never heard my dad call me that. He called me dummy, stupid, little bastard, ugly, goofy, and other names. The man had lots of lousy nicknames

for me, but he never called me "Son." When Aunt Nell came to my wedding, we were talking about how mean my dad was to me, yelling and
cussing at me for no reason at all, and she told me why that was. He isn't
my real dad." We all sat up straight, wide-eyed, and not sure what was
coming next.

"I've never told anyone other than Rhonda about this, but it doesn't
really change anything, so I figured I would tell my best friends, too. According to Aunt Nell, my dad has always been an angry man. Dad would
yell and gripe about the least little thing, and Mom got tired of it, so she
got a job just to try to get away from him as much as possible. My oldest
brother and sister were in high school, and, when my brother, Harvey,
turned fourteen years old, Mom got a job working as a teller at Minnequa Bank. Dad did shift work at the Steel Mill, so Mom could be out
of the house when he was on afternoon shifts or sleeping during the day
following his evening shifts. According to Aunt Nell, the manager of a
local restaurant, a guy named Salvatore, would come into the bank three
or four times a week and would always go to her window and flirt with
her. He was a happy and funny guy, and Mom was enjoying the attention. After several months of that, Mom started going to his restaurant
whenever she could for lunch or after work for coffee until they finally
began an affair that lasted for several months, until Mom got pregnant.
Well, Salvatore didn't want anything to do with a baby, so he changed
banks and girlfriends, and Mom was stuck with Dad for eighteen more
years because of me. About six months after I was born, Dad figured out
that I didn't look like him or his other kids, so he pulled back his affection
from me, and my siblings all followed his lead and did the same. It had
to drive Dad crazy that I was a naturally happy kid and that none of his
abuse could make me share in his bitterness. For Mom, she was stuck in a
lousy marriage because of me, so she wasn't the kind of Mom a kid ought
to have."

"Thank God for Aunt Nell and the Tattalinni family," Birdy yelled out.

"You've got that right, brother. Every day of my life for the past fifteen years I have thanked God for those wonderful people. Otherwise,
life in that Luna house could have easily made me into someone other
than the friend all of you love and envy so much." Rather than abusing
and pounding on Q like we usually would have done, we hugged him,
told him how proud we were of him, and affirmed him as much as possible. There were even some tears shed over our buddy. Then Q looked at
his watch and said, "This has been great, but it is 2:00am, and I need to

beat it. I love you guys. You are the best friends a guy could ever hope to have," and he split for the evening. After he left, the three of us talked for a few minutes about how proud we were of our old friend. Frank Luna had grown up and become a good man. Q would always be a little goofy, but that was part of what had endeared him to us.

About thirty minutes later, Peeps said that he needed to go, too. He was staying with Marco's family and would try to sneak in quietly through the back door. Shelly was expecting him to pick her up at 9:00am from the Grassleys and show her Pueblo for a few hours before our scheduled 11:00am song rehearsal. Birdy told us how much he loved us, how happy he was that Marco and Sheila were getting married, and left, so it was just Marco and me. Right around 4:00am, my best friend opened up after I made a casual remark about how his parents seemed to be so happy with the wedding and with each other. "It wasn't always that way," he said, and he was off.

"My dad wasn't as bad as Frankie's dad, but there was a lot of unhappiness in our home. Dad would get drunk and hit me, yell a whole lot at everyone, and generally be an unpleasant person to be around. I am pretty sure that he hit Mom from time to time, but Mom hid it well. Dad would be ashamed of what he'd done, but, instead of apologizing, he would just sulk or double down with more yelling and intimidation. There were plenty of good times, too, but the bad times would last for a couple of weeks at a time and were pretty unpredictable. We all got used to it, but it took its toll on Mom."

"There was a couple in our parish, named Fred and Cindy, who my folks chummed around with, as they would say. Fred was a plumber, who did residential and commercial construction and owned his own business. Fred and Cindy would come to our house and play cards with Mom and Dad once a month, and I liked that because Dad was always in a good mood when they were around. But after a few years of spending all of that time together, I started to notice that Fred always seemed to volunteer to serve on the same fundraising committees for the parish that my mom was on and that his business truck would drive by our house several times a week. So, when I came up from the basement one Sunday afternoon and saw Mom and Fred hugging in the hallway next to our kitchen, I backed up and made some noise so that they could hear me. When I came around the corner, Fred was giving Mom some papers for their committee, then he smiled at me and went downstairs to see Dad. I was fifteen years old at the time and had no idea what I should do. So,

I went outside, sat in a lawn chair to pray and think, got on my bike, and rode to St. Mary's to talk with Father John. By the time I returned home, my plan was set."

"That evening I confronted my dad and told him the hitting was done and that he needed to back off of the yelling and intimidation. Of course, he went berserk and took a swing at me as he was letting me know what he thought of me. I grabbed him and wrestled him to the floor. I'd known for several months that I was already stronger than him, but he didn't know that. When I let him up, he took another swing at me, and I had to wrestle him to the floor again. As I held him down, I told him again that he could no longer hit me and Mom and that he needed to figure out another way to handle his frustrations instead of yelling at and intimidating his family. By then, Mom and Mary were in the room, and Mom was yelling at me, 'Marco, you let your father up. That is no way for a son to treat his father.' After letting him up, I handed Dad a book I'd gotten from Father John, *Why Am I Afraid to Tell You Who I Am*, and Dad threw it across the room. He was mad and humiliated. I felt terrible, but I knew I had to do something."

"Monday after school, I rode my bike across town to Fred's Plumbing and asked to see the owner. Fred greeted me with a smile, but that didn't last very long. When I told him that he would leave my mom alone, or I would punch him in the face every time I saw him, that got his attention. He tried to play dumb, but when I told him that I saw them hugging, he mush-mouthed some reason that I didn't pay any attention to. I let him know that he had to start attending another parish immediately and that if I ever saw him at mass or at any parish function that I would punch him in the face; if I saw his truck drive down Belmont, I would show up at his office the same day and punch him in the face; if I answered the phone and someone immediately hung up, I would ride to his office and punch him in the face. Well, that got him mad or scared or something, so he tried to intimidate me with tough-guy talk, but I let him know that, even if he could easily beat the snot out of me, he would have a lot of explaining to do about why that crazy Tattalinni kid keeps attacking him. I made it very clear to him that my pretty mom was not going to be wife number three for him and that he had better get his spiritual and marital house in order soon. He'd better get his eyes off my mom, get them back on his wife, and figure things out or I would be relentless in attacking him. Then I got on my bike and rode home."

"That night, I told Mom that I needed a ride to school to pick something up, but, once we were in the car, I asked her to drive to City Park so that we could talk alone for a while. When we got to the park, I spotted a secluded picnic bench, sat down, and told Mom everything. She was really embarrassed, but she didn't deny anything. After crying for a minute, Mom looked me in the eyes and said, 'All we ever did was hug. That's it! Marco, that's the God-honest truth!' I believed her, but I also knew that they could have gotten more involved if I hadn't done what I did at that point. Mom then understood the incident I'd had with Dad the night before and let me know that I needed to do something to help him become a man again. I let her know that Father John and I had talked about that, too. Dad had been sulking since then and refused to make eye contact with me, so I knew I needed to act right away to help Dad return to being the man of the house."

"For the next week, I made a point to ask Dad permission to do things, asked him his thoughts about sports and what I should do for a summer job, and told him what I was doing at school to see if he approved. Several times he got angry and said, 'You're a big man now, so why are you asking me?' I let him know over and over again that he was my dad and that I respected him and would always honor his decisions about things. After a while, he tested that by denying me permission to hang out with Frankie one Saturday, and I said, 'Yes, Sir,' and went to my room. It took some time, but he started acting like my dad again, but without the hitting and a lot less yelling. Several times, I even caught him reading the book Father John had given me and complimenting Mom about her cooking and appearance. Mom would come up behind him while he was watching TV and give him a neck massage, and Mom had coached Mary to ask her dad for help with her homework. All three of us were helping him learn how to be a different kind of husband and dad than he was before. The really cool thing was that he was willing to learn and change. Around four or five months later, Dad even told me thanks for the book. 'I'm learning some good stuff,' he said and patted me on the back. From there, things kept getting better in the Tattalinni home. So, yes! Mom and Dad are happy together. I have nothing but respect for both of them!"

We were silent for several minutes before I said, "Listening to Birdy and Q was just incredible . . . and then you. Wow! I am so honored that you would share that with me. With your permission, somewhere along the line, I will tell Julie about our conversation, but it will never go beyond the two of us." Marco nodded approval. He knew that he could trust me. Then I looked at my watch and couldn't believe that it was 5:30am.

"I've got to get to my folks' house and get a few hours of sleep so that I don't nod off on the platform. How about you?"

Marco just shook his head and said, "Mr. Grassley wants me and my dad to meet him at his favorite barber shop for a shave and haircut at 7:00am, so I will just pull an all-nighter. It's no big deal." I was exhausted from the day's activities, the waterskiing, and the big talk, so I had to get some sleep. But if anyone could do all of the same things as me and then get married and begin a honeymoon, I knew my buddy Marco could do it.

28

Shocking

"Nick, it is 10 o'clock! You have to get out of bed now," Julie yelled. I sat up and wondered why she had let me sleep so long when she said, "For two hours I have been trying to get you out of bed, but you sit up, look around, and then lay back down. Not this time, Buddy Boy. Get your feet on the floor and get yourself in the shower." I must have been really out of it, because I didn't remember any of that. The shower woke me up, and three of Mom's strawberry pancakes gave me some fuel, so I was ready to go. When Birdy and Q showed up at the house, we went over the three songs that Marco wanted us to sing at the reception, and we were all set to make the newlyweds proud.

Mom loved to hear us rehearsing and told us, "You boys sound every bit as good as The Casinos." We would be singing "Then You Can Tell Me Goodbye" for the bridal dance, and then "Pride and Joy," followed by "Just the Way You Are." Marco wanted us to be out mingling with family and friends instead of on the stage, but he also wanted, in his words, 'to show everyone how talented the Boys are.' It was a great honor for us to sing for Marco and Sheila, so we wanted to be at our best. We had managed to squeeze three decent rehearsals in prior to Saturday morning and felt pretty good about our sound. Mom's compliment gave us that little extra confidence as we wrapped up, grabbed some lunch, and then headed to the church to get dressed for the big event. Marco was waiting for us when we got there.

I'd told the Boys about Marco pulling an all-nighter, and they were amazed at how good he looked. Birdy playfully pushed Marco and said, "As my aunt would say, you look wide-eyed and bushy-tailed."

I pushed him and said, "My dad would say you are full of vim and vigor."

Q gave Marco a little shove and chimed in with, "As my dad would say, get out of my sight, you little bastard!" And there we were again, laughing at something Q said as he stood there with a matter-of-fact look on his face. Unlike in his younger years when he would laugh harder than anyone else at his own humor, now it was a rare thing to see Q laugh at anything he said. His humor was now straight-faced, deadpan, I am just telling you the way it is. His humor was sharp, and his style made it even funnier.

Marco looked at us and took charge. "Let's go get dressed and do this wedding thing! This has been, is now, and will be a great day." So, we headed to our dressing room where we went over all the details of the ceremony again and made sure that everyone was clear on what they were supposed to do during the ceremony and reception. For the third time that day, I thought, I/we are ready to go!

As we were dressing, Marco floated the idea that the Boys find one weekend a year to put on our calendars for a Boys-only retreat. We would each take a turn on a four-year rotation of planning where we would meet and what our agenda would be for our time together. After throwing out several options, we agreed that the second Friday in August would be the beginning of our weekend together, starting next year. After four years of our annual retreats, we would reevaluate the dates but not the event, at that time. We were all excited at the prospect of being together every year for a Belmont Street Boys retreat.

With the little bit of time left before the wedding ceremony was to begin, Marco gave us each a present that we had to wait until later to open, but each present came with a note from him. The notes were short but very personal, and Marco made us each read our message from him out loud. Each note was unique, but one by one, we read messages that were filled with words of love and appreciation. Marco made a point to communicate how much we had contributed to his life, helping him to become the man he is. There was no doubt that each of the Boys would put their note some place safe and save those words from Marco for the rest of our lives. As soon as I had finished reading my note, the pastor walked into our dressing room to pray with us and then lead us out onto the platform. The wedding service for Marco and Sheila had begun.

My mom was the organist for the service. The men entered when Mom was about two- thirds of the way through "Clair de Lune," Sheila's favorite song by Debussy, and our entrance was the sign for the ladies to come out of their dressing room. When Julie gave Mom the cue that the ladies were ready, Mom began playing Debussy, the men took their places on the platform at the appropriate time, and then Julie told the bridal party to line up and wait for the wedding march. Everything went perfectly. Even Little Marco and Carly, LaTonya's little girl, did a fine job in their roles. Some people were unsure of what to do when Sheila walked down the aisle to "Here Comes the Bride," but Sheila's mom didn't stand. It was a statement of simplicity and humility that Sheila and Marco wanted to communicate to those in attendance. Although it was their special day, they did not want to communicate that Sheila was to be honored more than God in the words or actions of their wedding service. Most of the people sitting in the pews didn't get it, but that didn't matter to Marco and Sheila. The two of them knew what they were doing, and that was what counted. But, when I saw how gorgeous Sheila was when she walked down the aisle, I thought that, from a practical standpoint it was a good idea that people weren't standing. That girl would have made knees buckle as she walked by the onlookers. She was simply radiant!

The vows were beautiful, the lighting of the unity candle while Mom played "The Lord's Prayer" was meaningful, and watching Marco and Sheila receiving communion from the pastor was a moving experience. And when the pastor announced, "I now pronounce you husband and wife," there was a spontaneous eruption of applause and a standing ovation by everyone present. It was awesome to be on the stage for that. When things finally calmed down, and the pastor said, "I am happy to present to you Marco and Sheila Tattalinni," the church erupted again. Mom really cranked up the volume for the wedding recessional, but it was still hard to hear her skilled playing over all the applause and cheers. As Q and Lana were making their exit, I saw Lana laughing so hard that she had to bury her face in Q's shoulder. Marco's little sister, Mary, was the bridesmaid I escorted, and, when we got to the lobby of the church, I asked Lana what was so funny.

"It wasn't really that funny when I think about it, but right at that moment it just ambushed me. Frank looked at me so sincerely that I thought he was going to say something meaningful and reflective about what we'd just experienced, but, instead, he said, 'Well, your dream has finally come true. You get to walk down the aisle at a wedding with me.' And I just lost it. He did nothing but annoy me in high school and now he cracks me up every time he opens his mouth." Q just stood there with a what-would-you-expect look on his face, then hugged his son and told him what a great job he'd done as Uncle Marco's ring bearer.

Picture taking went pretty quickly. Q announced that he'd tried without any luck to bribe the pastor with $20 to announce Marco and Sheila as The Tatts and the Misses instead of Marco and Sheila Tattalinni. Sheila smiled and said, "That would have been cool." She was so happy at that moment that I believe "That would have been cool" would have been how she responded to almost any thought offered by the wedding party.

We were able to get to the reception at 4:15, where we found the people snacking and mixing and having a good time. After a little bit, Marco and Sheila cut the wedding cake, posed for a few more pictures, and then it was time for the Boys to sing. Julie and I had been mingling during that time, and members of Marco's family would corner us and start telling us one story after another about Marco. As the Boys were walking up to sing, I went by the head table and said to Marco, "We will try to make you proud, Bugsy." That caught Marco off guard, and he almost spit on himself when he heard that nickname. According to his Uncle Fat Joe, when Marco was a little boy, he had a toy submachine gun that he walked around with all the time while wearing a little fedora. Marco enjoyed pretending that he was a gangster, the kind he'd seen on a Saturday morning cartoon show. All of his relatives loved it and said he looked like Bugsy Siegel, so they called him Bugsy for years after that. After the Bugsy remark, I asked Marco, "How many Uncle Joes do you have?" That made him laugh some more, and he told me that he'd have to give me the details later. The Boys then knocked it out of the park with our three songs.

It was incredible to watch Marco and Sheila dance as we sang "Then You Can Tell Me Goodbye." They were so much in love. Their dancing was fluid, and they stared into each other's eyes with such a pure gaze that, when we finished the song, the place erupted again in applause. Although the Boys did a great job on the song, it was clear that the applause was more for the couple than for us. Marco was really embarrassed by that, so he invited everyone else to join them on the floor for the next two dances as he grabbed his mother's hand and Sheila grabbed her father's. Our old friend, Wes Ankeney, was the emcee, and he kept things moving by playing records people could dance to and giving directions to the guests at the right time. When not dancing with the guests, Marco and Sheila went around to all the tables that were set up and thanked everyone for being there to help them celebrate their important day. As the two of them eased up to our table, Marco said, "I will keep this as short as possible," and then told me about his many Uncle Joes.

"The guy who told you about me being Bugsy is my Uncle Flat Joe. He loves to tell that story. Some people call him Fat Joe because they don't hear his nickname properly. His real name is Tony, but he loved Joe DiMaggio so much that everyone just started calling him Joe. Well, when he was fourteen years old, he and his sister Betsy got into a big argument when their folks were gone, and Joe stormed out of the house. Since it was his chore to take out the trash, he grabbed the kitchen trash as he threw open the back door, his sister yelling at him the whole time. When Aunt Betsy saw the lid from a green bean can on the floor, she picked it up, yelled, 'You forgot something,' and threw it at him. She was hoping it would fly by him and scare her younger brother, but instead it flew in front of his face and cut the very tip of his nose off! Walk by him and check out his profile and you'll see. It's a wild story, but everyone in the family swears it is true, and since then he has been Flat Joe. Aunt Betsy never apologized for what she'd done. If you ask her about it, she'll say that she wished it had been the lid from a gallon can of green beans so that it would have cut his head off."

"So, they can't stand each other," I said.

"No! They love each other to death," Marco informed me. "That's just the way they talk to each other. You never know what you are going to hear from my family. Earlier, I heard my dad and his cousin, Big Joe, who I call my uncle even though he is really my cousin, talking and doing their Italian thing. Big Joe told Dad that it looked like he was putting on some weight. Dad said, 'Yeah, my goal is to become fat and disgusting by the time I am fifty. I know how to get fat, but I am going to hang around you so that I can learn how to be disgusting.' Everyone laughed, especially Uncle Joe Willie. He is another of my cousins old enough to be an uncle. Joe Willie is a good-looking guy who thinks any humor about someone else's appearance is hilarious. His name is Bobby, but everyone says he looks like Joe Namath, so he is Joe Willie. My dad's Uncle Joe is the only family member whose real name is Joseph. So, the answer to your question is that I have one Uncle Joe, but three other relatives I call Uncle Joe. Now, one more thing before Sheila and I move on to the five other tables we haven't yet visited."

"Since there are lots of Italians here in Pueblo, there will be some guys who will come up to you with an envelope they want me to have. It would normally go to the best man, but since Frankie has to leave early tomorrow morning to get back to Georgia, I told Dad to direct the envelope guys to you. I used to protect some kids in junior high and high school from getting beat up, and those guys had relatives who are connected to the mob. So, my guess is that some guys in dark suits and sunglasses who didn't come to the wedding will show up and give you envelopes and say something about wanting to show their respects to the newlyweds. Just tell them thank you and ask them who you can say the gift is from. Then when they leave, write their name on the envelope, and we will connect in the next few days so I can get the loot." It sounded easy and a little exciting, so I told Marco it would be my honor to do that for him. Sheila pulled him away, and they continued being hosts to all their wedding guests.

The party continued until 7:30, when Wes got the crowds' attention and announced, "It is time for the bridal bouquet to get tossed and for this great couple to head up to The Broadmoor. So, Sheila, take your place, and all you interested young ladies find a spot behind her." As soon as Sheila tossed the bouquet, Marco came up from behind, swooped her off her feet, and carried her to the waiting car. No one had written anything on the Nomad. There was no rice thrown into the car or in their faces as they left. Instead, everyone had a single strip of paper with a word written on it that showered them as they left. Love, peace, joy, bounty, prosperity, children, kindness, and other such words of blessing were swept up as soon as Marco and Sheila drove off, and then put in a bowl for the couple to read at a later time. Everyone had so much respect for Marco that all they wanted to do was to show the new couple nothing but love and support.

When the newlyweds made their exit and we went back into the hall, it was just as Marco had told me it would be. Some guy approached me, said a few words, gave me an envelope, and then left. As we were wrapping things up, it happened eleven times, and the envelopes were fat. I was running out of pockets and room in Julie's purse to hold them all. Julie and I waited until the next morning to count the loot, but, unless they were all one-dollar bills, I knew that Marco and Sheila made quite a haul that night.

"There must be $3,000 in these envelopes. Wow! Those Italians are some seriously generous people. Either that or The Mob figures they owe Marco protection money from way back. Or maybe a little bit of both." Julie hadn't counted the money, but she opened the envelopes enough to see lots of 20-, 50-, and a few 100-dollar bills. We looked across the street and saw that Marco's folks had skipped mass that morning, so we walked to their house after breakfast to see what we should do with the loot. Mrs. Tattalinni tried to feed us something and we couldn't say no, so we drank some hot tea and split a cannolo. It was clear that they were all still on Cloud Nine from the wedding, so we let them talk for a while. Mary was giddy about being in the wedding party and getting to spend time with her big brother for the first time in years.

Once things calmed down a little, I asked Mr. Tattalinni what I should do with all of the money given to me the night before. "Well, it's yours until Marco tells you different. Don't spend it all in one place," he said with a belly laugh. Then he added, "They are staying at The Broadmoor, so why don't you call him now and find out. That's a lot of cash to be carrying around. You can go ahead and use our phone." So that's what I did. It felt a little awkward about calling someone on his honeymoon, but it felt even more awkward to be holding all that cash when it didn't belong to me. I found the hotel number, and, reluctantly, made the phone call.

After the sixth ring, I started to hang up when I heard a click and a sleepy voice say 'hello.' It was definitely Marco, so I said, "Man, I am so sorry to disturb you, but I don't know what to do with all this money." What followed was a brief, but once-in-a-lifetime conversation.

"What time is it?" Marco asked. I told him that it was 10:30, and he said, "Why don't you and Julie join us for an early supper here at The Broadmoor on your way back to Denver? Let's say 4:30." I agreed, and he continued. "Bring $800 with you, then give the rest of the money to my dad to put into my savings account." As Marco talked, he continued waking up and realizing some things. "Hey, thanks a lot for calling me Bugsy last night. Sheila refused to call me anything else all night. When we checked into the hotel, it was Bugsy this and Bugsy that. Even the clerk at the desk called me Bugsy." By then he was fully awake.

"Maybe that all-nighter wasn't such a good idea. I just realized that I am fully clothed, lying here in my tuxedo. I must have collapsed on the bed after we got into our room and didn't wake up until you called. That means I am still a virgin!" Right then, Sheila must have come around the corner of the honeymoon suite because he added, "But not for long; gotta go." And just before the phone hung up, I could hear Marco say, "Shocking."

29

The Boys in Real Life

It was unbelievable to see how quickly the Boys fell into a new routine. I never would have imagined it would work out this way. Birdy and Shelly would show up once a month to hang out with us, or we would meet up at one of his gigs in the area. We saw Marco and Sheila at least once a week, and Q called each of us every month leading up to the first-ever retreat for The Belmont Street Boys. Q planned our first retreat since he was sure to be stateside for the summer of 1982 and didn't want to miss his turn to be in charge. The three of us flew to Georgia where Q quickly took over and showed us a great time. We hit the links at Moody Quiet Pines Golf Course, ate lots southern cooking, stayed at a Hilton Hotel, and got to meet Rhonda's family. Q was so proud of being able to introduce us to his in-laws. They were his family now, and he wanted them to know his buddies. We kept our time with them short, so that the Boys could spend as much time together as possible. It was great to catch up with Q and see him in his now-comfortable, Georgia home and his soldier lifestyle, hear about what was going on in everyone's lives, talk about important things, and laugh a whole lot. The Boys listened as I told them about being a dad to my seven-month-old son, Jon, named after my dad. I suggested that we name him Jonathan and call him Jon, but Julie said, "If we're going to call him Jon, we're going to name him Jon" so that's what we did. They laughed when I told them, "And she's never called him Jon one time. She has about ten nicknames she uses for him."

Q, naturally, had to give his perspective on the subject and added, "Well, you should have named him Punkin or Goob or Bobo so Jon could be his nickname." It never ceased to amaze us how his mind worked.

While telling us about life in the military and in the south, it became clear to the Boys how much Frankie felt at home in Georgia. Without question, he loved it there. But he and Rhonda had decided that, when he retired from the Air Force, they would live in Colorado, close to the mountains and close to the Boys. Rhonda took me aside when we were meeting her family and told me that she loved who Frankie was when he talked about and spent time with his buddies. "He is a good man, a proud sergeant, a wonderful husband, and a great dad. But when he is with y'all, he shines a little brighter. Frank becomes better at what he is already good at when he is with the Boys. And I just love y'all and y'all's wives to death." I let her know how happy it made me to hear her say that. We talked for a few minutes, and I made it clear that all of us would look forward to the day when their move to Colorado actually happened.

Q was excited for the Boys to meet his fishing buddy, Mike Carlton. The two of them had met in church and had become fast friends. Mike was a groomsman in Q and Rhonda's wedding. Mike was an alcoholic with three years of sobriety under his belt and was quite a character. "He is the most unique person I have ever known," Q told us.

Birdy shot back, "That says something, coming from the most unique person we have ever known." Marco and I shook our heads in agreement.

"I have known you guys for all these years, and you still don't get it," Q stated with a look of amazement on his face. "I am the normal one in this gang. You three are wierdos, who I feel sorry for." He moved his hand in a circle and continued. "This is a pity friendship. If it wasn't for me, you losers would not have any friends." At that we piled on our friend and whaled on him until we were laughing so hard that our punches lost all their sting. When things calmed down, Q asked, "Are you guys ever going to stop hitting me? When will you finally outgrow this juvenile behavior?"

It was almost always Birdy who responded to Q's statements or questions, but after a lengthy pause I offered, "The way I see it, Frank, you'd better hope you outlive us, and, if not, you'd better have a closed-casket service at your funeral. Here's why. If you are lying there in an open casket, you will get slugged one last time by each of us as we cry and tell you how much we loved you!" At that we all hugged our buddy.

"Thanks, guys. Obviously, I am the only one of the Boys tough enough to take all of this physical abuse, but I am warning you right now. At my funeral, there will be thumbtacks just under the surface of my military uniform!" That sounded about right. One last practical joke from the most unique person we knew.

Marco and Birdy let us know what was new with them. Marco had a job he really enjoyed with Catholic Social Services in Denver. He talked about some of the interesting experiences he had there and then very casually informed us that Sheila was six-weeks pregnant. As we were high fiving him, Birdy let us know that the day before he left for our retreat, he proposed to Shelly, and she accepted. They would be married next summer, so there were more high fives and hugs all the way around.

Sunday morning, we got up real early and went fishing with Frankie's friend, Mike, before joining him and Rhonda's family for church. It was a great morning of fishing and fun. Mike asked us to tell him stories about Frank and what he was like in his younger years. Marco and Birdy told one story after another, and Mike would laugh and say, "Frank, I love you, but you are even more of a character than I thought." It seemed like every time when Mike was laughing the hardest, he would hook another bass and yell out, "Keep the stories comin' boys. They are good luck." During those more-than-three hours of fishing with Mike, he must have said six times "Frank, I love you." The Boys knew that we were leaving our buddy in good hands with Mike.

It was a great way to finish our first-ever, annual retreat of The Belmont Street Boys. We caught some bass and caught a nice worship service before catching our flight back to Denver. Unfortunately, Q had to miss the next two retreats, Birdy's wedding, and the ten-year, high school reunion of the South High class of 1973 because of a two-year deployment to South Korea. Fortunately for Q, Rhonda and Little Marco were able to make the overseas trip with him. There were lots of letters exchanged during that time and a few postcards from some interesting places in Asia, but we threw him a big party when he returned from South Korea to his new assignment at Peterson Air Force Base in Colorado Springs. Apart from a few shorter deployments, Frankie was able to finish his career there and retire as a Chief Master Sergeant in 2003.

Our annual retreats took us to South Florida for snorkeling, whitewater rafting on the Arkansas River, hiking 14,000-foot peaks in Colorado, fishing in Montana, Yankee Stadium in NYC, and lots of other interesting and fun places. Our families were growing, and our jobs and lives were changing, but the constant was always our friendship and faith. We laughed and cried together, sharing our most intimate thoughts and deepest concerns with each other. On every one of our retreats, at some point, we found ourselves praying together over those concerns and the dreams we had for the future. I wouldn't have thought it was possible, but we left each retreat feeling a closer bond to one another than we had prior to our time together. Love truly knows no bounds. Genuine love just continues to grow stronger, increasing in intensity and commitment, dissolving whatever is of inferior quality in the person and relationship, and bringing out the best in those who have vowed to live as brothers with one another. It was kind of like what Rhonda said about Frankie on our first retreat. We made each other better men, better husbands, better fathers, and better in every area of life. After our first four retreats, our wives were excited for us to go because they looked forward to how they would benefit from our time away. I am pretty sure they were somewhat envious of not having their own version of the Boys, but our wives were never anything but supportive of what we had together. And what we had together was transformational.

As our families grew larger and older, it was so cool to hear the children of the Boys excitedly call out to Uncle Nick and Aunt Julie. Every time I heard those words, it warmed my heart, and every time my three kids spoke of their three uncles and aunts, it made me proud. Over the years, we attended weddings and funerals, concerts and ball games, and even a few confirmation and baptism services. Almost every family visit to Pueblo became a trip down memory lane, as I told Julie and later our kids, about the significance of people and places there. And on many occasions, I hugged and kissed my parents and thanked them for moving from exciting and huge Chicago, Illinois, to dull, little, and unknown Pueblo, Colorado, one day before the start of my senior year.

www.ingramcontent.com/pod-product-compliance
Lightning Source LLC
Chambersburg PA
CBHW061504030726
47503CB00005B/1808